STANDING TALL

A NOVEL

DEBORA G. DE FARIAS

Debora De Farias

Debora G. De Farias
Jacksonville, Florida. USA
www.defariasbooksandarts.com

Publisher's Note: This is a work of historical fiction. Some names, characters, places, and incidents are a product of the author's imagination, while some are real and well researched. Locales and public names are sometimes used for atmospheric purposes, used fictitiously.

Book Cover Designer: Waldson G. De Farias
Book Layout © 2017 BookDesignTemplates.com

Standing Tall. Debora G. De Farias. -- 1st ed. 2020
ISBN 978-1-09834-266-1

This book is dedicated to those who are determined to overcome the barriers of prejudice, indifference and rejection—especially to those heroes and heroines who achieve greatness practically unnoticed.

“A strong woman is one who feels deeply and loves fiercely. Her tears flow as abundantly as her laughter. A strong woman is both soft and powerful, she is both practical and spiritual. A strong woman in her essence is a gift to the world.”

(Native American Saying)

PROLOGUE

Cecilia was born in November of 1859 in Buenos Aires, a city that by that time was not yet the capital of Argentina. Her mother, Jane, who was of Irish descent, had been convinced that her first child would be born near Christmas, or Navidad, as the people in the southern hemisphere of the New World would say. As a cultural tradition, the first son would be named after the paternal grandfather, while the first daughter would take the name of the maternal grandmother. For that reason, the child would be called Juan Guillermo or Ana Maria, if the names were translated into Spanish.

But sometimes in life things are destined to be. And the birth of Cecilia Grierson was one of those things. The baby decided to come into the world early. More than a month early, in fact, after one of the longest and most brutal winters ever experienced in Argentina. Jane did not have much of a chance to enjoy that spring, because by the end of November, she started to have unexpected labor pains and bleeding. Although she was nervous, she assured her Scottish husband, John Robertson Grierson, that everything would turn out all right. John, who had come into town from the family ranch on business that twenty-second day of November, rushed two midwives to her.

Jane had not been sure about moving temporarily to the city in the middle of her pregnancy, along with her main servant, Maria Eugenia, but once again, John's wishes had prevailed, and now she was thankful for his wise decision. It would be safer to have the baby in the city, where doctors and midwives were more accessible and available.

After an entire day in labor, the cry of a tiny healthy baby was finally heard throughout the house. It was a miracle that the fair-skinned baby girl, with brown hair and lively eyes as blue as the sky, not only survived, but thrived. One of the midwives broke the good news to *el Señor* Grierson, who was praying in front of the small altar of the Virgin Mary, in a corner of the large kitchen. When he was allowed to enter the large bedchamber where his wife and newborn daughter were resting, Jane's words sounded like the voice of an angel, singing praises to a new beginning. "My dear, the Heavens have heard our prayers. I introduce to you Cecilia Grierson."

"Cecilia Grierson," John repeated, holding his sleepy baby in his arms, his heart bursting with joy. As if she could read his mind, Jane immediately told him where that unexpected, eloquent name came from.

During her labor, her servant had remained by her side, holding her hands and praying words in a Spanish form she could not clearly understand. Instinctively, Jane knew the words meant no harm. So, when the baby was finally delivered, Jane asked Maria Eugenia what she had been saying. Maria Eugenia told her she was praying for St. Cecilia, the saint of that day, to bring forth a healthy baby, one full of life. A baby who would bring light and brighten the path of others, a baby who would bring happiness and a noble purpose to this family. A child who would bloom, just like the red ceibo flowers were blooming all over the country, in this time of the year.

Jane, her eyes wet with tears, brought Maria Eugenia's hands to her lips, giving them a soft kiss. With a smile, she whispered, "In your honor, Maria Eugenia, we shall name this girl Cecilia Grierson."

Chapter 1

"Some dreams tell us what we wish to believe.
Some dreams tell us what we fear.
Some dreams are of what we know, though we may not know yet.
The rarest dream is the dream that tell us what we have not known."
(Ursula K. Le Guin)

Buenos Aires, Summer, January 1902

Cecilia woke up soaked in sweat. She thought she'd managed to go to bed early the night before, but now she was feeling as if she did not sleep at all. She believed she could handle one restless night, as most people her age could. What she could not stand, though, was the fact that the same pathetic dream had returned. The dream that made her feel emotionally drained.

She remained in bed for a few minutes, staring at the ceiling, trying to understand her feelings and get her mood under control. She could not afford to let a stupid dream set the tone for the day that had barely started. She knew she deserved a decent day. But she felt a dull, throbbing pain at the back of her head, and the only thing she could do was to ask herself, "Why?"

Why had the dream suddenly returned? The last time was maybe a month or more ago. She could not track the repetitions. She did not want to track or even think about them. She thought the less attention she gave to those dreams, the less important they would become. And usually this tactic worked well. After a few hours she would be free from whatever malevolent ghosts from the past the dream represented, and she would never think about it, until the next time, when it brutally, suddenly, hit her again.

The house was quiet, but she could hear the bursting of a city waking up outside. Since Dona Maria Eugenia had passed away, a summer ago, Cecilia had decided that the new housekeeper, a young girl named Clara, should not stay on the weekends. This way, both women would have their own freedom and moments of solitude preserved. It was also a trial, especially for Cecilia, since in the beginning, it was hard for her to share the house where she was born with any another person. In this life, some people come into your path to bring out the best of you, during your best moments, but mainly during your worst ones. For that reason, you know you will never be able to replace them. Dona Maria Eugenia was one of those people. Unreplaceable.

Cecilia thought about the morning strolls she used to do with Dona Maria Eugenia, their Saturday routine when they walked, arms locked, to the markets in the Calle Florida, the most elegant artery of the city, where they would pause to sip some coffee or tea after attending the ten o'clock mass at St. Ignacio de Loyola. Still lying on the bed, Cecilia looked at the double-bell alarm clock, showing it was almost nine-thirty. Dona Maria Eugenia would never let this happen on a Saturday morning, she thought. They would be halfway to the church by this time. But Cecilia hadn't stepped inside a church for a year now. Sometimes, she thought she would end up receiving a heavenly punishment for her rebellious act of not attending masses anymore.

Was it a rebellious act? Honestly, she didn't think so. After all, she was not a rebellious person. She was just a practical woman. A very practical one. In her lifetime, she had heard and read several sermons about how the human being is the temple of the divine spirit. After the passing of Dona Maria Eugenia, Cecilia concluded that such a statement sounded reasonably true. So, she decided to stay at home, praying and somehow being connected with the spiritual realm, on her own terms.

Despite the headache, Cecilia settled on a plan of action. Maybe she could retrace the routine of the past summers, this time just skipping the church and changing the sequence. She would stop first at El Molino, the Windmill Bakery. A strong coffee was not a remedy for all malice, she knew. It might not offer a cure for a bad dream, but it might alleviate the nonsense headache it had caused her.

In her spotless bathroom, she poured an ewer of cold water into a washbasin, splashing some water on her face. She reached for a small bottle of lavender eau de parfum, spraying a light mist on her neck, hoping the aroma would clear her mind and heart of any hidden sorrow from the past. As she saw her reflection in the mirror, she wondered if she could see herself beyond her appearance, beyond her career, beyond what she had accomplished. She no longer saw the young woman she once was, but she was still able to see the beauty on her mature face. "What have you become, Cecilia?" she asked herself. "Who are you deep inside? What is deep inside this mind of yours that has allowed those dreams to resurface, from time to time? Why do you feel so lonely now, so restless, so ... hopeless?" She wished she had an answer for half of those questions.

A tear rolled down her face, but she quickly tapped it dry with one hand. "Stop right there, Cecilia," she told herself with the same authority she had employed to teach her students. "You have no reason to resent the past. Your life is a blessing and you will not throw yourself into a pity party at this stage of the game." Going to her wardrobe, she chose a white cotton blouse with small black polka dots, matched by a gored black skirt, for a casual tailored outfit. She clasped her hair into a loose bun, forgetting, maybe on purpose, the formality of a hat. The turn of the century had not yet brought major and drastic changes to the citizens of Buenos Aires. But doing justice to the city's name, its inhabitants were looking forward to those fair winds that the new century for sure would bring, including some simplicity and practicability, without losing the sophistication that the Argentineans carried in their blood. That thought made Cecilia smile.

When she stepped outside into the busy streets, pedestrians, carriages and trams were moving at an electric frantic pace, something to be expected in any big metropolis. Buenos Aires was still not quite a metropolis, much less a big one, if compared to New York or Paris. But the city was evolving from a colonial port village into a chaotic cosmopolitan capital, where the optimism about an imminent bright future was seen on every corner.

One could almost sense that, with all the bold urban transformations that had occurred in the last twenty years, the city would soon become one of the wealthiest places in the world. And this was not just a collective, wishful thinking of the *porteños*. You could walk into any café, sit on a bench in one of the many plazas or parks, walk into a billiard parlor and all you would see were men and women reading the newspapers, discussing the avalanche of headlines that every day invaded the city. "Ted Roosevelt: The Youngest President of the USA"; "The End of an Era – The Death of Queen Victoria"; "From Italy, The First Transatlantic Radio Signal Reaches the Americas"; "Energy Does

Not Flow Evenly. The New Theory of Max Planck," and so on. The list of global transformations and achievements seemed endless. The world was spinning fast and Buenos Aires would not dare to lag behind.

By the time Cecilia reached El Molino, the sun was at its peak and the humidity was taking its toll. She was glad to find an empty table at the back corner. This small café specialized in sweet breads and the typical Spanish *galletitas*, the sugary cookies made with pounds of butter and flour. The café was once located across from one of the first windmills installed in the city, and since its opening, it had been a center for socializing, a refuge for the community, for those who were hungry and thirsty for a personal bond.

As Cecilia looked at the faded black-and-white picture of a windmill behind the counter, she thought of her mother telling stories about the ingenious gentleman Don Quixote of La Mancha. She remembered clearly the adventures of Alonso Quixano, the medieval noble who lost his sanity after reading too many chivalric romances. For a moment, Cecilia could almost trace a parallel between the Spanish tale and her own life, and she questioned her own mental status. Was she seeing things for what they were? Or was she becoming a female version of Quixote, unintentionally trying to save the world from God-knows-what, with an unreal idealism and pretended nobility that could cost her own life?

Could the black-and-white windmill on the wall be a representation of an imaginary enemy? Or was the enemy real, hidden somewhere? Was there a correlation between the recurrence of the dreams and a physical and mental exhaustion of her persona? Maybe she was reading too much, she thought. Maybe she was indeed lonely. Or maybe she was working and thinking too much. She missed Dona Maria Eugenia nearby, reminding her from time to time, "Hard work has never killed anyone, but cutting back some of your work obsession might add years to your life."

Absorbed by those thoughts, Cecilia did not notice the tall young gentleman approaching, and the soft tap on her shoulder startled her.

"Dr. Cecilia Grierson!"

"Professor Martin Francisco! What a delightful surprise," she exclaimed.

"Please, no need for formalities. Call me just Martin."

"Fair enough. As long as you call me just Cecilia." Both friends laughed, as if signaling an unconscious agreement for less ceremony between them.

"It's so good to see you. You have been missed by all the artists guild of the Casa LaValle," Martin said, while pulling a chair next to her.

"I am sure nobody can easily forget a lady who doesn't have any idea of what a color wheel is, and shows up to an oil painting class with no brushes nor oil on her hands," she replied.

She had started going to these private art meetings about six months ago, after Estella Gutierrez, one of her nurse friends from the Hospital de las Clinicas, had convinced her to attend the gathering for just one night. The eclectic small group was originally created by Martin Francisco, a self-taught artist, and Antonio Mancini, an Italian bohemian painter who lived in LaValle Street. Antonio had offered a spare room in his house that was quickly converted into a private art studio, where freelance artists frequently met.

Estella, invited by her friend Martin, had been part of the group for at least two years. She was amazed at how she found peace and serenity with the strokes of her brushes on the canvas, in addition to the company of other painters, a few poets, a musician and a potter. One day at the hospital lunch break, when she heard Cecilia complaining that the hallways' bare walls deserved some color, some life, "maybe even some art work, for God's sake," Estella took this opportunity to invite her *avant garde* friend to try the art group—and maybe find something new, possibly an exciting hobby outside the surroundings of the medical center.

"We were starting to get worried about you, but Estella assured us there was no need, that you are just very busy, involved in many other projects," Martin said.

"Yes, I am so sorry. There are no excuses for me to not stop by, to at least say hello to our group. I need to find time to go back to my paintings again. I am just overwhelmed lately with meetings, the children and the nurses in need. I was thinking the other day we should gather our best realistic and modern sketches, paintings and drawings, frame and hang them in the corridors of the Children's Hospital. Children are naturally inclined for art, and nothing would be better than having our own locally produced work to cheer up and color their souls and spirits."

Martin seemed to be mesmerized by her words, and that made her blush. "I am so sorry for talking too much and sometimes too fast. I didn't even ask how you are doing. How impolite I am," she said.

"Among all the qualities you have, rest assured that impolite did not make it into your list, *señorita*. I am doing very well, thanks for asking. And about the paintings at the hospital, I think that would be fantastic. I am sure we can talk about it with Antonio, as well. As influential as he is, maybe we could put on a charity exhibition to benefit the hospital. Perhaps your director will appreciate that; it is definitely an idea that could help everybody."

"It is a marvelous idea, indeed. Therefore, I must find time to return to our gracious and inspiring art soirees," she replied. "I am wrapped up with several obligations for the rest of this month, but I give you my word that I shall be there the first Saturday of next month, regardless of my agenda."

"It will be a pleasure, as always. By the way, Antonio and I are involved with the organization of a ball at the Victoria Theater, coming up in the next season. I should have more information about it next time I see you. We will be delighted to have you join us at the event."

"A ball at the Victoria?" Cecilia paused, not sure if she could commit to that invitation right away. "I will talk to Estella about it and we will see how my schedule is by that time."

"Then I will be praying your schedule is light, so we can steal you for just a few hours on a Saturday night." Martin laughed. "Miss Cecilia, I would love to spend the rest of this day in your company, assuming that you had nothing else more important to do than talk to a freethinker like me, but my sister is arriving from Montevideo this coming week, and I have a few errands to tackle before she is here."

"I understand, Martin. I will see you in few weeks. Is Estella still attending the meetings? I haven't seen her lately. She has been temporarily transferred to another hospital, to train some new staff."

"Yes, she should be there. She hardly misses any classes."

As they stood to leave, Cecilia offered her hand, expecting a friendly handshake. Instead, Martin planted a light kiss on her knuckles. She smiled, still keeping her composure, hoping he hadn't noticed the slight awkwardness in her face.

She would not feel awkward if it weren't for Estella, who one day had casually commented that she had an impression Martin might be developing some feelings towards Cecilia. Cecilia immediately dismissed that thought, saying such an idea was totally absurd. Estella insisted she did not see any absurdity, claiming that her friend was just too rational to analyze the possibility with different lenses.

"There are no lenses, my dear," Cecilia had replied. "I just see the world the way it is."

Martin Francisco was about ten years younger than Cecilia and a widower. His young wife had died during a cholera outbreak that wiped out thousands of the citizens of Buenos Aires in 1886. Cecilia remembered well that laborious year, when she was still an intern, left in the hospital with only three other doctors. Days had turned into weeks and weeks into months, as she took care of the sick and offered the little comfort she had available to those who faced death.

She wondered if she had treated Martin's wife at that time, if perhaps she'd been able to alleviate some of her physical pain, to give her some hope. Any hope. If in life one needs hope, how much more one needs it in death, Cecilia believed. She wondered how different Martin's life would be, if she could have done anything different during that time.

Deep inside, though, she knew she had done everything she could have. In fact, she did something that no one else had even achieved by then: being a medical student, as a woman, treating sick patients in a public hospital. That was in itself already a miracle. And she had not only survived that period, but also restored the lives of countless men, women and children who were affected by illness.

When Cecilia left El Molino Cafe, her earlier headache was already fading away. The encounter with Martin made her wonder if it would be prudent to make time in her busy schedule for the next art meeting. Although she was not usually inclined to work on the weekends, she decided to head to the College of Medicine, where she kept most of her papers and medical books. There, she should be able to get some work done, gaining some free hours as credit toward the beginning of the next month.

She'd returned a year ago from her first trip to Europe, where she immensely enhanced her studies in obstetrics, gynecology and microbiology, and since then she'd been writing reports on public health and education. Her observations in Paris, London and Edinburgh had awakened in her a determination to improve and better organize the practice of medicine in her hometown. So far, she was thankful the government not only was interested in her work, but also had the funds to support her.

The College of Medicine occupied a large three-story building in front of the Hospital de las Clinicas, in the northern part of Corrientes Avenue. This was the second medical center built by the University of Buenos Aires, a more expanded setting than the first School of Medicine in San Telmo. Cecilia had studied and worked in those two establishments for years, and although she missed the eclectic and multicultural neighborhood of San Telmo, an area where thousands of European immigrants lived, she truly enjoyed the convenient location of the new school. The area was lively, even on the weekends, with students strolling at leisure, walking to the library or riding bicycles to a laboratory.

Cecilia always felt tremendously proud of being part of such a great institution, the school she had carried in her heart since she was a teenager. She held onto an Irish saying that her mother used to repeat to all the children on their ranch: "What we want is to see the child in pursuit of knowledge, and not the knowledge in pursuit of the child." As Cecilia approached the entrance of the medical center, she smiled, realizing that those men (and the very few women) she could see around had all been children at one point. Just like her, they'd probably played as doctors and professors, scientists and researchers, artists and engineers, in a world of make-believe, where everything was possible.

Now, despite being grown-ups, despite knowing that not everything is always possible, they were still keeping the game of life going, they were still learning, still looking for knowledge, searching for the truth. A truth that could be measured, proven, and duplicated by science—because that was the way their society and the civilized world would progress and evolve. That was the thought of this new era. The bronze busts of the three doctors who founded the first School of Medicine in the country sat behind the main iron gate. Ironically, the first bust was of an Irish physician.

Cecilia rang the bell at the main entry and had to wait a few minutes before the familiar face of Señor Gonzalez, the security guard, showed up. He unlocked the heavy door, letting her in. The school was closed on the weekends, but a few professors and the chairmen of the departments had a privilege pass to use its facilities. As the founder and director of the School of Nurses, Cecilia had a small office inside the College of Medicine, where she could perform some of her research during those quiet weekend moments, when the students were kept out.

"Good morning, Doctor Grierson. Working on a new book?" The elderly man with gray hair, thick glasses and a bending back from years of scoliosis held out the pen for her to sign the registration book.

"It's almost noon, Señor Gonzalez, so it will be good afternoon. I don't think I have too much time left today to work on any book, but I hope I can move on with some of my reports. There aren't a lot of people here today, as I can see by the signatures."

"No, indeed. It's summer. I believe most of the professors are still on vacation, cooling themselves in Mar Del Plata or up north by the rivers. It is just too hot and too noisy to stay in the city all year long. Plus, not everybody is so compassionate and involved in their work like you are, Doctor Cecilia."

Cecilia smiled and tapped his shoulder. "Like us both, I shall then correct. You are the only person who never leaves this work, rain or shine." She could see the sense of pride rising in the elderly man. She left him with those words, climbing the stairs to the third floor.

The long hallway that led to her office was dark and quiet, except for the sounds of her footsteps on the wooden floor, and the light shining from an open door on the right corner. As she got closer, a series of loud, sharp crashes of objects falling onto the ground suddenly filled the corridor, followed by the mumbled words, "Stupid bookends." When she reached the door, she could see a sign with bold letters: "Dr. Giuseppe Moretti. Assistant Professor."

Cecilia knocked at the open door, peeking inside. "Hello—do you need help with anything over there?"

A young gentleman with a handlebar moustache rose from behind a desk filled with a pile of papers, books and newspapers that could have been there for ages, considering their ochre tint. Behind him, an empty shelf might be the one to blame for all that mess. The small room had a stale odor, and Cecilia wondered if the windows in the back could be opened, although any influx of air current might transform the office into a war zone in a blink of an eye.

"I am doing all right, thanks for asking. Not sure about half of these books here. I wasn't expecting anybody in this building today. I am Doctor Giuseppe Moretti. And you?" There was a subtle emphasis on the word "doctor," which Cecilia found interesting, coming from such a young man.

"I am Cecilia Grierson. I had no idea I would come to the school today, but plans changed early this morning, and here I am, maybe to save a doctor from flying books and stupid bookends."

Giuseppe Moretti gave a small laugh, the kind hinting at a little sarcasm that only perceptive ears, such as Cecilia's, could catch. "I am glad at least I didn't use any worse cursing word," he said, picking up the rest of the books from the floor.

"May I help with something? I would suggest we start by compiling those loose papers first. Then we should immediately open those back windows, assuming they are not rusted and locked in. It seems this room has been closed for centuries, and the last thing you need, Doctor, is to have your airways narrowed and swollen, with extra mucus triggering an episode of coughing, wheezing and, worst of all, shortness of breath. That could easily lead to a true medical emergency and we don't need that."

"I confess I am very impressed with your knowledge, Señora Cecilia. You must work at the Pulmonology Department, but I quite honestly don't remember seeing any female staff in that area," Giuseppe said, looking a little perplexed about the woman standing in front of him.

"It's simply because that department doesn't have one. I am a doctor in the Obstetrics Department, and I spend most of my hours between the Women and Children division of the Hospital de las Clinicas. I also direct and teach at the School of Nurses."

"Oh, my goodness, I am so sorry for my clumsiness and not offering you a proper greeting." He sounded slightly embarrassed. "I have just accepted this position as an assistant professor in the Department of Neurology. And, of course, I have heard wonders about the female doctor at the University of Buenos Aires, but I didn't put two and two together. It is a pleasure to meet you, Doctor Cecilia Grierson."

"Please, just Cecilia among us," she said with a smile. "And no need to apologize. So, where do you come from? I don't remember seeing you around here. I am assuming you didn't graduate from this school."

"You are correct, I was born and raised in Italy, and I was lucky to attend the University of Naples, one of the oldest public nonsectarian universities in the world. We are very proud of that school, because Saint Thomas Aquinas studied there."

"Now that is impressive. We must say we are lucky to have you here, then. I believe we are in need of young leaders and professors that can catapult us, especially the public, to a raised level of consciousness and commitment to science that is anchored in the principles of equality, morality and ethics." Cecilia spoke enthusiastically, while walking to the back window, verifying it could be opened. "You should find some weights to hold down those papers at the desk, because I am opening this."

As soon as the young man obediently placed the loose papers in an empty drawer, a rush of fresh air entered the room. "Much better," Cecilia said, turning back and getting ready to leave. Then her eyes were caught by a thick, brown leather book on top of a chair. As she read the golden letters on the cover— "The Interpretation of Dreams," by Prof. Sigmund Freud—she froze for a few seconds in front of it.

"Straight from the oven," Giuseppe said, picking up the book and handing it to Cecilia. "Have you heard about it?"

"Well, I have heard about Dr. Freud and I have read some of his articles, but I didn't know he was particularly interested in studying dreams. I was fortunate enough to be in Vienna a few years ago, and although I did not have a chance to meet Dr. Freud personally, I have heard his theories are opening new paths to uncharted segments of the human mind. I have met a few doctors who are starting to take his propositions into consideration," Cecilia explained. "Although my career is centered on woman's health and social medicine, I find each day the importance of seeing the human being as a whole. Therefore, trying to understand how the human brain works is fundamental in the process of treating our patients, bringing them to health." She opened the book, still perplexed by its title.

"You have a brilliant mind and you seemed to be interested in the book. I have glanced through it on my journey here and although some chapters look complex at first, I am sure that will not be a problem for you. Would you like to keep it for a week? I will be too busy settling this room and finishing the thesis I am overdue for publishing."

Cecilia scrolled through the contents index. The third chapter seemed to scream at her— the dream is the fulfilment of a wish. She could feel a slightly rapid heartbeat and she tried to disguise the rhythm of her breaths. "That is so kind of you, Giuseppe. If you don't mind, I will keep your copy safe and I will start reading it tonight."

"Absolutely. Just be careful with it. According to my friend, who gave the book to me last year, it seems there are only six hundred copies in circulation at that moment, and probably very few of them are translated into English. As a suggestion, remember, this is all very new stuff. And like anything that is brand new, one must use it with certain caution. I am positive you will learn something from it, as long as you can commit to walk the path, pushing through any uncomfortable feeling that might come in the beginning, until you break through it."

"Certainly," she answered. "Thank you so much. I must go now. You are not the only doctor whose papers are overdue here. I will bring your book back next Friday. It was truly a pleasure meeting you, and I wish you all the success in our humble school."

"The pleasure is all mine. I will see you soon."

Cecilia nodded and left for her own office, still puzzled by the sequence of events leading that particular book to end in her hands. She placed it on the corner of her desk, determined to finish the report she was going to submit to the Department of Public Education. She pulled sheets of paper and the box of ink pens from her drawer, not hesitating to let her ideas flow into the blank sheet.

To the Secretary of Public Education, Señor Juan Fernandez.

I was honored to be sent to Europe, by the Government of Argentina, as a physician and a professor, to study everything pertinent to the progress of the education of the women, especially to observe the schools dedicated to the formal training of nurses, in addition to the schools dedicated to domestic economy and domestic labor, in the countries that I had the pleasure to visit.

Upon my return, I presented to the Director of the Public Assistance a study about the institutions for nurses in Europe. It is with great pleasure that I can inform you that, from the report of several European educators and doctors, the similar institution that I have founded here, in our country, stands at the equivalent level of the British schools, where the teaching and the training of nurses are role models.

Unfortunately, the School of Nurses in Buenos Aires had stopped functioning during my absence. Nevertheless, I found this incident not only as an opportunity to reinstall the school with some improvements and modifications on its curriculum, but also as our chance to establish the National Association of Nurses. This premier organization will represent the interests of our registered nurses, with the foremost goal of improving the quality of health care for all.

At the International Congress of Women held in London in 1899, presided over by the Countess of Aberdeen, Lady Isabel Gordon, and where I was honorably elected vice-president, I made a moral commitment to organize, in our republic, the National Woman Council, an organization that must be kept linked to the International Woman Council. After great effort and the valuable cooperation of a team of professionals, I am pleased to announce that the National Woman Council has now been successfully installed. Our goal is the federalization of the diverse associations that benefit women, those that support and stimulate the woman's tasks, cooperating for the improvement of homes, for the elevating and advancement of women, as a factor that demonstrates the progress of humanity.

Since 1900, I have also been reporting to the State Department of Education with several articles regarding the institutes for the blind that I visited in Edinburgh, London, Paris and Vienna. I was especially impressed with the Royal Blind Asylum, the School of Edinburgh and the National Institute for the Young Blind in Paris.

I have noticed that all those great institutions are well set up, thanks to a network of philanthropists that assure the funds for the success, and thanks also to their own society and government, who take pride in helping those in need. With the information I send annexed, it is my hope that we can find a way to replicate here what I have witnessed in Europe. I trust that our Government continues to count on me and many other community leaders and colleagues, for the development and improvement of our society.

Sincerely,
Dr. Cecilia Grierson

The bell rang shortly after she finished, announcing it was two o'clock in the afternoon, closing time for the school on the weekends. Cecilia placed the letter in the drawer, where several other manuscripts were stored in a brown large envelope. She almost forgot the book about dreams on the corner of the desk and, for a moment, she had second thoughts on bringing it home. She should rest that weekend. But being more curious than tired, she grabbed the volume and walked out.

After having a light dinner, Cecilia sat down in the rocking chair in her bedroom. A cup of tea and a scone brought from the bakery that morning rested on the tabletop by her side. She inhaled deeply, as if she was getting ready to open a Pandora's Box. *What are the chances I would start this day waking from a nightmare, to finish it with a book about the interpretation of dreams, by the respectable Sigmund Freud?* she thought.

She opened the book, noticing a handwritten inscription on the flyleaf: *To my friend Giuseppe, I leave you the words of the Greek philosopher Epictetus: 'All external events are beyond our control; we should accept calmly and dispassionately whatever happens.' However, as individuals, we are responsible for own actions, which we can examine, control and change through rigorous self-discipline and courage. May you always have the wisdom to know the difference between the controlled and uncontrolled events that surround your beautiful life.*

The signature below was unreadable, and for a moment, Cecilia wondered who had written such a touching, personal note.

She went straight to the third chapter. "Dreams perform important functions for the unconscious mind and serve as valuable clues to how the unconscious mind operates; dreams are scientifically meaningful mental phenomena; dreams allow people to express unconscious wishes they find unacceptable in real life." She repeated the phrases, her eyelids eventually getting heavier and heavier as the minutes passed by. "Unconscious wishes they find unacceptable in real life; all dreams serve to fulfill our deepest desires, but they often hide which desire it is."

She decided she should just read the book first, as if studying it, without trying to analyze her own dreams. But it did not take too long for her to start dozing off, so she changed into a light cotton nightgown, planning to continue reading on her bed. She soon fell into a deep sleep, the book resting on top of her chest.

That night, she finally rested. Her dreams this time were peaceful. She dreamed she was still living in Entre Los Rios. She was the only person at the family ranch, but not for a moment did she feel lonely. On the contrary, she found serenity as soon as she stepped into the family library. Even in her dreams, she was happy among the books. Somehow, that place brought a certainty that everything and everyone were in the right place, at the right time, for a purpose.

Chapter 2

"The immensity is everywhere...
The plains, the woods, the rivers are all immense;
And the horizon is always undefined...
Making it difficult to tell where the land ends
And the sky begins."
(Domingo Sarmiento)

Entre los Rios, 1859-1874

Cecilia spent her early childhood on the family's ranch, named La Estancia Bella Vista, or The Beautiful View, in the province of Entre los Rios. The ranch was a large plot of land, used to raise cattle and sheep and to farm wheat and corn. Cecilia's paternal grandfather, William Grierson, a passenger of the sailing ship Symmetry, was among the Scottish colonists who had arrived in Buenos Aires in 1825 to settle the first Scottish Colony of Santa Catalina—Monte Grande. From then to the middle of the 19th century, William Grierson's sons began to acquire tracts of land throughout the grasslands of Argentina, the Pampas, commonly known as the Great Plains. They established a prosperous business of trading primary goods such as hides, fat and grains, in exchange for manufactured products that crossed the Atlantic from the newly industrialized Europe.

The family's ranch thrived thanks to the prodigious work ethic, determination and support of the inhabitants. Contracted *gauchos*—the skilled Argentinean cowboys, usually of mixed European and Indian ancestry—tended to the care of the cattle and were responsible for the property defense against anyone who would dare to invade its lands, while Scottish and other European immigrants were responsible for farming, household functions and crafts.

La Estancia Bella Vista was originally a tract of one hundred thousand acres granted to Cecilia's grandfather a few years after his arrival in Argentina. The land became an El Dorado that enticed the Grierson family and the Scottish immigrants of the region into this flourishing lifestyle. It resembled a green oasis, like a European country transported into South America, surrounded by a yellow-brown plain of thick, flat grass that seemed endless. Cecilia thought it would stretch without limits, towards the infinite. Only a few trees and an occasional wire fence broke the line of her sight.

She and most of the servant children spent their time at the main house, called *la Casa Grande*—a one-story brick home, commodious without being ostentatious. Built around 1850, the house was covered in white plaster and stood with grandeur in the center of the land, encircled by paths of reddish pebbles. Its tall windows allowed the sun to brighten and warm all the rooms in the morning, while a gentle breeze cooled the interior in the evening, bringing with it the sweet scent of musk. Apple, pear and citrus trees grew in an internal patio, and even a small chapel stood in the back, as a place of gathering and worship.

An upright piano in the living room offered a great source of entertainment for the adults and the children, while the modest library became Cecilia's favorite place in the house. From the age of four, the girl grew into an avid reader. With her independent mind, she learned to question and constructively argue rather than be passively molded by others.

She lived the first six years of her life in this bucolic microcosm, which in her mind seemed to be the entire universe. She loved nature, especially the birds and the horses. The younger children, whom she enjoyed playing with and caring for, often called her *la feroz Amazona*, the fierce Amazon, because of the way she could control and ride the horses of the ranch. Even the servants learned to admire the dexterity and charisma of the young girl. She enjoyed sitting and talking with men and women of different ages, reading them books, telling them all kinds of tales.

At the long mid-day siestas during summer, when all the workers had a deserved break from activities, Cecilia listened to the immigrant stories, especially those about crossing the ocean from the Old Continent to the new one. She could not distinguish the fine thread between what was real, what was imaginary and what was legend, but in fact, the differences (if they existed) would not matter. Her heart, her mind and her spirit were free to run, just like the land in front of her own eyes.

At night, her mother used to read her stories, some from the classic books they owned, but most of them tales made up at that exact moment by Jane herself. Cecilia would fall asleep after minutes and she would dream about wild horses crossing rivers, or about the *gauchos* in their red ponchos, singing improvised melodies in an unfamiliar language that only a tender heart could understand. She would dream of people of different colors sitting by a firepit, sipping *cimarron*, the traditional caffeine-rich green *maté*, through a *bombilla* metal straw, while some would be dancing and clapping their hands under a starry immense sky.

In 1865, when Cecilia turned six years old, her father thought she should receive a proper education, so she was sent to attend English and French school in Buenos Aires. Because the family kept their house in the city, Jane was able to move there with Cecilia and Maria Eugenia, while John remained on the ranch. The Constitucion Railway had finally opened, facilitating travel between the rural areas and the city.

The next four years would elapse without major incidents, except for an outbreak of cholera, followed by a yellow fever epidemic. In those two circumstances, Jane and her family returned to their safe oasis in the pampas, where life still flowed smoothly, regardless of the political fluctuations that could be sensed here and there.

But by the year 1870, a revolution caused a civil war to break out in the province of Entre los Rios, leading to the death of General Jose Urquiza, one of the most influential politicians at that moment and a close friend of the Grierson family. A disastrous effect to the family's agribusiness followed, and Jane and the children were forced to move back to La Bella Vista Estancia. Cecilia would never know, but this was the beginning of a cascade of events that would not only mark her life forever, but would test the resilience of her character in the years to come.

Only two years after their return to the ranch, tragedy mercilessly knocked at the family's door. John Robertson Grierson died unexpectedly, at the young age of forty-four. Cecilia was only thirteen years old. Being the oldest child of her family, she felt compelled to help her mother and their ranch workers as much as she could. Because she always loved to tutor the children of the land, she begged her mother to let her teach, even when she did not possess the proper title or degree.

Despite her youth, she helped her mother run a country school inside their own house. She worked as a teacher but, being still a minor, her salary was paid to her mother. Cecilia's vocation and native ability to instruct were so impressive, it could not pass unnoticed by those around her. So, as the family gradually overcame the misfortunes, Jane sent Cecilia back to Buenos Aires to attend the Girls Normal School, under the constant care and love of her governess, Dona Maria Eugenia.

Chapter 3

"Walking with a friend in the dark
is better than walking alone in the light."
(Helen Keller)

Buenos Aires, Summer, 1902

Cecilia woke up to a knock at the front door that scared her and made her feel disoriented. The clock hands pointed to eleven, and for a moment she wondered who could be there so late at night. But the glimmer of sunlight through the window shutters made her realize it was actually a new day. The knocking continued, making her yell, "I am coming!"

"Who is this?" she asked, before unlocking the door.

"Cecilia, it is me, Estella."

Cecilia opened the heavy carved wooden door, covering her eyes with one hand, trying to block the bright sunlight from blinding her. "Oh, my dear, is everything alright? Come in." She opened her arms to hug her friend.

"Yes, everything is good, how about you? Sorry, I decided to show up without notice. Were you sleeping? You aren't sick, are you?"

"I was sleeping but, no, I am not sick. I didn't realize how tired I must have been. I guess I slept like a stone last night, I don't recall a thing." Cecilia laughed at herself. "Do you want something to drink, or eat? Where is Pedro today?" Pedro Gutierrez, Estella's husband, worked for the railway company, spending most of his time traveling to different provinces of Argentina. Cecilia guessed he was out of town again.

"Pedro decided to see the horse race at the Jockey Club with some friends from the fire department, which I didn't mind. The man deserves some time alone with his fellows. And so do I!"

"I am glad you came to see me. I actually asked about you yesterday, when Professor Martin found me at El Molino."

"Oh, Martin! He was inquiring about you last week at our art meeting. I could sense a nostalgic tone in his voice," Estella said, waiting for a reprimand from her friend.

"I know, he told me," Cecilia said. "I am so sorry. I feel I have been neglecting my friends lately."

"Maybe you have neglected us just a little bit. But I will forgive you, as long as you spend this Sunday with me. Do you have any major plans for this afternoon? I am getting hungry and we could have a picnic kind of a day, outdoors of course. Botanical gardens, maybe?"

"I guess I have no choice other than say, yes, let's do it." Cecilia laughed. "Let me change and put my hair up. We must stop at the French Gallery for some cheese, ham and bread then."

"Perfect. But you always have a choice. Simply say no, if you don't feel like doing it."

"I was joking about not having a choice," Cecilia replied, walking toward her bedroom.

"What are you reading now? I see a thick book on your desk over there," Estella shouted.

"Oh ... I didn't even realize I brought the book to the front room. Last thing I remember I was reading it on my bed. But that is a story on its own. I can talk to you about it at the gardens."

The two women had very different personalities, but they had become close friends after Cecilia treated Estella years ago at the Hospital de las Clinicas. When Estella was in her early twenties, she had suffered a miscarriage that almost took her life; she had to have a hysterectomy, leaving her and her young husband devastated. Because Cecilia was still a medical student at that time, she was allowed only to observe the surgical procedures, although she could care for post-operative patients. Just a few years older than Estella, Cecilia felt incapacitated for not being able to assist with the surgery.

The day afterward, she had asked permission from the obstetric surgeon to be in complete charge of Estella during the recuperation period. She wanted to do whatever she could to help the young couple, especially Estella, to regain a sense of normalcy. Neither woman could imagine that, in the midst of such tragedy and loss, a friendship would bond them for the years to come, transforming their lives.

As they set out on the forty-five-minute walk to the botanical garden that Sunday morning, the weather was pleasant, slightly cloudy, leading to a nicer temperature with a soft breeze blowing from the Plata River banks. They admired the architecture of their city, pointing to the new facades of the buildings that reminded Cecilia of her time in Paris. Residential buildings with carved wooden heavy doors and massive bronze hardware gave the city a solid feel.

"Can you believe we've seen so much transformation in our city over just the last twenty years? When that first steamer, Le Frigorifique, arrived with frozen meat and vegetables from France, it brought some amazing changes for the country," Cecilia said.

"Yes, I actually remember how people were very skeptical about the cargo of that ship," Estella said. "Everybody was talking about it. Mothers were scaring their children, telling them to stay away from the port and from all the food that could not be traced to a local farm."

"It was hard to believe that foods preserved by cold could be brought safely all the way across the ocean, but once it was proved, that turned out to make a huge difference in life, didn't it?"

Cecilia was referring to the first transatlantic vessel containing a refrigerated plant, developed by French engineer Charles Tellier. The voyage to Buenos Aires was an experiment, almost a stunt, to demonstrate how well refrigeration could preserve perishable foods. The results revolutionized the entire economy of Argentina. Previously, the nation's plentiful cattle had low export value—limited to hides, fat and salted beef, the latter sold primarily to feed sailors and slaves on long voyages. The new refrigeration system meant the entire cow could be commercialized for export; soon, livestock and agriculture would be as important as silver had been in colonial times. With this influx of wealth, the country could import more goods affordably, and Buenos Aires began to develop in accord with residents' extravagant visions of the progress seen in Europe. And waves of European immigrants, arriving daily in Puerto Madero, continued to revolutionize the city's culture and spirit.

Estella had never traveled abroad, and for that reason, she always encouraged Cecilia to tell her stories about the places she had visited, about how people lived. Despite the superficial differences found in various countries, Cecilia was starting to conclude that humanity shared the same basic needs: love and acceptance, peace and beauty, security, health and prosperity. Therefore, she thought the people here weren't much different than the Parisians, Londoners or the Scottish. At the same time, they had their own singularities; they clearly had their unique culture.

Argentina had fewer natives than any other country in South America, since the indigenous populations had been dominated and pushed to marginal and inhospitable regions. On top of that, after the abolition of slavery, the African-Argentine population also declined sharply due to wars, mortality rates and epidemics. It was commonly said that the Argentines "descended from boats," since two-thirds of the capital city's population were of European descent. Buenos Aires housed the third largest concentration of Spaniards outside Madrid and Barcelona, and more than forty thousand Britons, at one point, lived and invested largely in the city. So, in a way, how much different could the Argentineans be from those fellows living in Europe?

Buenos Aires was becoming a translation of Europe, revealing itself in a plurality of styles. And if, until the end of the nineteenth century, the city had lacked in modernization, now commodities like the sewer system, public transportation, telephone and electric lines were distributed throughout. Large streets were paved and well-lit and the aristocratic classes built opulent houses in eclectic styles. Landscape architects designed parks, and grand public buildings were raised following the Beaux Arts guidelines. The city must have one great park to be matched to Central Park, Hyde Park, or the Bois de Boulogne. It must have a grand opera and a hippodrome, a botanical garden, a zoo and a tree-lined walkway along the river. It must have fine museums and a leading university. The citizens of Buenos Aires needed these. And they would have those needs met, no matter what.

"Do you want to know something that is very unique to us?" Cecilia asked Estella, rushing her friend to cross the street.

"Our friendship?" Estella guessed.

"That is a good one," Cecilia laughed. "But I was referring to the uniqueness of our city."

"If I had to guess, I would say the colorful houses built from salvaged wood and corrugated metal containers in La Boca. But maybe you have seen something similar in Europe."

"I doubt they have that kind of patchwork neighborhood. I actually have never seen anything like La Boca either. But I was referring to those corners." She pointed to the intersection of Avenida Santa Fe and Callao.

"The *ochavas*?" Estella sounded a little surprised.

Indeed, every corner of every street block in Bueno Aires was blunted, or chamfered. The buildings on corners had a diagonal edge, which the locals called *ochava*. The name probably derived from the word *octava*, since the part lopped off was thought to account for an eighth or so of the corner lot, and it was also a reference to the octagonal shape the four corners of the intersection formed when viewed from above. The city was built on a grid, like New York or Barcelona, but this one refinement, the diagonal edges, multiplied by hundreds of street intersections, fundamentally altered the cityscape. In other cities that were laid out in grids, streets intersected at a sharp, monotonous angle—but in Buenos Aires, each corner consistently became a meeting point for four separate uses, whether shops, cafés, bookstores, or even residences.

"Exactly," Cecilia said. "Our intersections become a destination itself, filled with interesting, meaningful things."

Estella turned around, noticing that in one corner there was the French market. Across from it stood a hat store. On their right side, they saw a haberdashery, and on the other side, a barber shop.

"It seems those corners are really appealing and, in a way, they might act as safety features," Estella commented. "I can see some corners could easily allow muggers to lurk around, if it wasn't for the presence of those *ochavas*."

As they stepped inside the French Gallery, a young salesman greeted them as he restocked jelly jars in the shelves behind the counter.

"*Buenas tardes*, ladies. Please let me know how I can help you. We just got this homemade orange marmalade and we have fresh baguettes, croissants, Roquefort and Brie in the back. But if you are here for something more feminine, fancier, or more playful, I can show you the new boxes of lavender soaps and jasmine perfumes that came directly from Grasse, France. I've heard their scents are magically irresistible."

"Magically irresistible, is that right?" Estella asked with a smirk, willing to engage in a conversation with him. Cecilia, feeling pressed for time, interrupted them.

"We are definitely taking the croissants and the Brie. That's it for now," she said sharply.

"Yes, ma'am," the boy replied, running towards the back of the store to get the items.

"We should check the perfumes, have some fun, Cecilia," Estella whispered.

"We should get our food and have a picnic kind of a day in the gardens, darling. That seems more appropriate and hopefully more fun than flirting with a nineteen-year-old boy. Besides, I don't need perfume from Grasse at this moment."

Cecilia paid for the small groceries and the two of them continued their walk to the Botanical Gardens.

"Can we have our lunch by the Roman garden?" Estella asked.

"If that is your favorite spot, then we must."

The Botanical Gardens, inaugurated a few years ago, had been built to evoke the grandiose and exotic dreams of the Argentineans. Housing the mansion of a French architect hired to design and landscape the area, the grounds featured three distinct gardening styles, including a Roman, a French and an Oriental garden, in addition to an abundant collection of local flora and other plants from the Americas. An art nouveau greenhouse that contained thousands of tropical plants had received recognition in the Paris Universal Exhibition in 1889, and without doubt, this was one of the most beautiful structures ever seen by the locals.

The two friends chose a spot to spread their thin blanket underneath the shade of a majestic ombu tree, overlooking a fountain. A bronze statue of Mercury, with wings on the hat and heels, stood a few feet from them, as if predicting a message from the gods would soon be delivered. As hungry as they were, they devoured their sandwiches without talking, appreciating the tranquility of the garden, the chirping of the birds, the sound of the wind whispering secrets to the trees. Estella, mouth still full of cheese, wiping the corner of her lips with her fingers, finally began the conversation.

"So, what happened to you yesterday?" she asked. "Did you spend all night long reading a new book? It'd better be a good one."

"Yesterday, I woke up after a weird dream that follows a pattern. It comes and goes, repeating itself over and over, from time to time," Cecilia said. "And to my surprise, I ended up going to the college, where by kind of an accident, I met a new professor from the Neurology Department. The book you saw, *The Interpretation of Dreams*, belongs to him. And the author is no less than Sigmund Freud himself. Giuseppe Moretti, the new professor, noticed my interest in the book and let me borrow it for a week."

"Did you spend the entire night reading Freud? I hope it helped you understand your dream."

"No, I read only a few parts and it brought me more questions than answers. I did not try to find the solutions for my dreams, not right away. But the book might help in shedding some light into the unconscious activities of our minds. That can potentially explain the recurrence of those dreams. The basic claim is that a dream is a fulfillment of a wish, or a repressed wish. But the thing is, I honestly don't wish anything that is happening in the dreams I have."

"So, if I understood you, consciously you may not wish what are you dreaming about, but subconsciously, there could be something hiding there," Estella said. "And that might not be something necessarily horrible. After all, I believe we all wish we had something extra, something that we desire but we can't have, or don't have, at a conscious or subconscious level. Maybe we all sometimes wish we were someone else too. We just don't like to admit it, but I think that is almost normal, isn't it?"

"It might be normal. But that doesn't seem to be the case of my dreams. Whenever I have those dreams, I am just the opposite of myself. I can feel, even in the dream, how pitiful the whole situation is and I still don't do absolutely anything to change it. It is as almost as if you know you are heading towards a brick wall at full speed but you are powerless. There is nothing you can do to prevent the catastrophe from happening. You just brace yourself and wait for the impact. Then I wake up. Sad, tired, hopeless, feeling I am half-alive, half-dead ... I hate that."

"That is horrible. You have the right to be very distraught. What specifically are you dreaming about, my friend?"

Cecilia knew this question was coming and for a moment, she thought that maybe she should just change the subject. The dreams were related to a distant past and she did not really feel related to it anymore. She was mentally at peace, or so she thought. She had consciously accepted it, forgiven it, prayed for it, moved on. So why all that, right now? But she knew, at this point, there was no return. She could not hide this part of her life from Estella. Maybe, by talking about it to someone she trusted, those dreams would leave her once and for all. And that gave her some hope. Hope, maybe that was all she needed.

She closed her eyes briefly and then opened them as she finally found the words to begin. "The dreams are about a man with whom I had an intense, but short, relationship decades ago. In the dreams I am always pitiful, I am always begging for his love and attention. Meanwhile, he always keeps a cold attitude towards me. He looks at me, but it feels as if I don't exist. Sometimes, it is like he doesn't see me at all."

She looked away from Estella's sympathetic face for a moment before going on. "In the dreams, somehow, we're always working together, or we are the only two people in a familiar place. Regardless of the location, I am always running after him, trying just to talk to him. But no matter how much effort I pour into the situation, at the end, he just turns around and walks away, leaving me speechless, confused and deeply sad."

Estella patted her shoulder gently and sighed. "It seems you were in love with him, and you might still be carrying him inside your heart. That might be why you are still dreaming about him."

"I am sorry to disappoint you, but you are wrong. The worst part is that I was never truly in love with him. I liked him very, very much, I must admit. I had and I still have great respect for him, although I haven't heard from him since the day we broke apart. I wanted him to love me and for sure I wanted to be able to surrender myself and love him fully in return. But deep inside, very deep inside, I could always hear an intuitive feeling in the back of my head—a voice saying, 'Do not let yourself fall in love with him.' And surprisingly, I didn't."

Cecilia paused a moment before adding, "So, of course I was sad, maybe even depressed after the end of our relationship. But I didn't fall into despair. I understood that was part of the game called life: one day is blissful and we are delighted with laughter, the next day is miserable and we are soaked in tears. But since the world does not stop spinning in order for us to recompose, we eventually must learn to get up and recover, as promptly as possible."

For her, there truly seemed no reason to revive the past. Therefore, she never thought about Jacques or what had happened between them, except in those brief moments right after waking up from those dreams.

"Would you like to tell me the whole story, Cecilia, about what happened?" Estella asked, reaching out to hold her hand.

Cecilia looked her friend in the eyes and, taking a deep breath, she went back to her college years.

Chapter 4

"The heart was made to be broken."
(Oscar Wilde)

Buenos Aires, 1885-1889

Cecilia had reached her fifth year of medical school at the University of Buenos Aires, where she was the only female student who had ever been allowed to enter the College of Medicine. She had spent more than two semesters studying histopathology and the microscopic analysis of human cells. She diligently followed the techniques of the laboratory technician, Thomas Lovett, who taught her how to prepare the thin, high-quality sections of biological tissues, mounted on glass slides after being appropriately stained to demonstrate normal and abnormal structures. Fresh biological tissues are usually very delicate, easily distorted and damaged, and manually preparing them required not only expertise, but also patience, traits abundant in Cecilia's nature.

So, when the laboratory technician resigned, Cecilia boldly wrote a letter to the dean of the college, suggesting her own name as a replacement. In fact, by that time she had already honorably completed all the basic medical disciplines and the greater part of the clinical subjects. In addition, the majority of the professors considered her one of the best students, which gave her additional confidence.

Quickly accepted, she became an unpaid, volunteer histopathology assistant; at the same time, she was an intern at University Hospital. But at the end of 1886, she was forced to leave the laboratory position, because the city was struck, for the third time in that century, by a cholera epidemic.

The Secretary of Public Assistance requested the collaboration of all medical students, who had their normal classes and routines abruptly interrupted. As a response to this health emergency, several sites inside and outside the university were improvised to be refuges for the sick. One of these places was La Casa de Aislamento, an isolation medical house that eventually was turned into a hospital.

There, Cecilia worked intense hours, assisting the doctors. For weeks, she knew little sleep and few baths, losing track of day and night. Nevertheless, she managed to keep her spirits up. If fear is contagious, so is hope, she told herself.

And it was in the middle of one of those exhausting days that she began to devise a plan to educate the nurses, since there was no formally trained staff who could take care of the patients. She was convinced that the best way to provide relief to patients who suffer is to place caring people by their side—empathetic people who can understand the patient, who are capable of collaborating with the doctors in the fight to regain health. Months after this outbreak, the idea that started in the middle of a chaos turned into reality, as Cecilia founded the first School of Nurses in Latin America, while she was still a medical student.

Finally, at the end of April 1887 when the cholera cases were reduced, Cecilia was able to return to her position as a histopathology assistant and to her internship at the University Hospital. As soon as she stepped into the laboratory, she was surprised to see a new face. Jacques Copplet, a French-Argentinean biologist who had recently returned to Buenos Aires, in a collaborative exchange between the Parisian Ecole Normale Superieure and the University of Buenos Aires, had his own desk, in the middle of the lab.

For a moment, Cecilia thought she had lost her job to some foreign, good-looking, tall, blondish male professor. As the first female student, she had grown used to the threats and even bullying from some students and a few professors, those who would comment that there was no place for a woman inside a medical school, those poor souls who would be glad to see her simply packing and leaving. Trying to keep her sense of humor as much as possible, she had adopted as her motto "*Res non verba*." Actions speak louder than words.

Since she had learned to avoid taking anything personally, she refrained from asking him sharply, "Who are you, and what are you doing in the middle of my lab?" The young man, as if he knew this was Cecilia's territory, rushed toward her, introducing himself.

He was not there to take her place, but the opposite—he had come to help, bringing new technologies that could speed the process and increase the quality of histological preparation and analysis. During the cholera outbreak, the government had decided to raise the investment in all fields that could potentially help in the diagnosis and control of infectious diseases, and for that reason, the university brought physicians, pharmacists and biologists from all over Europe and from the United States. And Jacques Copplet happened to be one of them.

Jacques soon won not only her friendship, but also the trust of her professors and her classmates. Only twenty-eight years old, the same age as Cecilia, he was brilliant, devoted to teaching and hungry for learning. He carried himself with an elegant composure and confidence that could almost make others jealous, until the moment they talked to him, until the moment they knew him a little bit more, when they found the genuine, simple, caring person behind that broad, perfect smile.

It was not difficult to become a friend of Jacques. And that was what Cecilia always highly valued. They shared hours in the laboratory, discussing all kind of topics, from life in Paris to the ethics and politics of mass vaccination; from the scientific articles published by Robert Koch to their own religious beliefs.

She would never forget a written prayer she found lying on top of Jacques' desk: "Posterity will one day laugh at the foolishness of modern materialist philosophers. The more I study nature, the more I stand amazed at the work of the Creator. I pray while I am engaged at my work in the laboratory." One day she was repeating those same words to some of her classmates at the cafeteria, when Jacques himself walked up behind her, clapping and saying, "*Magnifique*! *Magnifique*! Louis Pasteur will be so proud of you when he learns you have spread his prayers into the New World."

Cecilia laughed, her face turning red, not disguising her embarrassment for having memorized the words of the note she'd copied from her dearest friend. Meanwhile, her eyes gazed at the shiny golden ring Jacques wore on his right hand.

He was engaged to a distant French cousin who lived in Strasbourg. He never talked much about her, and Cecilia did not inquire about her either. Occasionally, Cecilia wondered if he and his fiancée shared the same affinity, the same compatibility and chemistry they had developed. But she did not allow those thoughts to dwell in her mind for too long, too afraid to put their friendship at risk. So, while she was attending medical school, they always kept their relationship respectful and strictly professional. If they were starting to have any emotional feelings towards each other, beyond friendship, they both hid that very well. Even from themselves.

***

At the beginning of 1889, when Cecilia graduated at the age of thirty, the entire College of Medicine took certain pride in sharing that emotional moment with the first female physician of their country. In her thesis, a manuscript of more than one hundred pages, Cecilia dedicated her work to the memory of her parents. She listed all the members of the College of Medicine and Pharmacy, with special acknowledgements to Maria Eugenia, to her friend Amalia Koenig and to Jacques Copplet, who was sitting in the first row at the commencement ceremony.

Before starting her thesis presentation, she shared a few words with the audience. "Like almost every student who leaves the classroom, I had a dilemma in choosing the topic for my thesis, among all the lectures and investigations we have faced throughout the years of medical school. It is a challenging task because we have to be extremely careful in adding anything new to the truth that has been already conquered. Because of my gender, I spent most of my clinical hours at the Women's Hospital, where I practiced medicine for six years, following the scientific and ethical conduct of that excellent medical center. For that reason, I chose the field of obstetrics for this evening's discussion."

Cecilia continued, "In my humble vision, one of the greatest signs of human ignorance is to merely believe in somebody's words, instead of believing in their concrete actions. I will soon speak just about what I have witnessed and learned during those six years of my career and the focus of my clinical research, but it is my hope that, at some point in life, you can also witness what I have accomplished. Before starting in the subject of obstetrics, please allow me to express my sincere feelings.

"As the first woman honored to step up on this graduation stage, it is my wish that my words can fuel those who will follow this path after me, in the near future. The difficulties that I have faced during my career were much less than what I expected. I only have words of gratitude to every single one of my professors and to all of my classmates. The great majority of people I know have been attentive and caring, like brothers who have adopted a sister. I would not be here if it was not for their teaching, camaraderie and support. I could not dedicate my thesis to all of those who have helped and encouraged me in my career, this noble fight for science and for life, because there would always be someone left out, someone that I should be thankful for. Nevertheless, I would like to emphasize my profound gratitude to all of you, my mentors and my friends, for all that you have taught me and selflessly shared with me. In the words of the Irish playwright Bernard Shaw, I will close this part with his thought: 'Progress is impossible without change, and those who cannot change their minds cannot change anything.'"

Shining with tears, Cecilia's eyes briefly locked with those of Jacques, seated in the front row, and for a moment, she could only hear the pulsating beat of her own heart. A standing ovation followed her speech, and that was the second time Jacques applauded Cecilia. This time there was no ring on his finger.

The graduation banquet and the ball lavishly celebrated the successful conclusion of the academic year. A concert by the senior students of the School of Lyric and Scenic Art entertained the new doctors, professors and their guests. Cecilia did not mind being the center of the attention that evening, and after a series of photographs and even a brief interview she gave to a local newspaper, Jacques finally was able to congratulate her, handing her a box neatly wrapped in golden paper, tied with a green satin ribbon. A sealed envelope lay under the bow.

"Congratulations to my favorite doctor of all time," Jacques said, smiling. Leaning close to her ear, he whispered, "I am a very lucky man. Among all the places I could have ended when they transferred me to this university, they had to reserve me a chair at the laboratory of the only dazzling woman this school ever had."

For the first time she could remember in years, Cecilia was speechless. When her mind and her heart returned to a less hectic pace, she could only say, "Now you left me without words." She kept her eyes on the beautiful gift, her fingers caressing the smooth satin ribbon.

"Then don't say anything. I hope you enjoy this simple gift. I ordered it from Perugina, Italy, from a successful entrepreneur, a friend of my family; she reminded me of you. I must confess I took certain pride in the wrapping. The golden paper symbolizes prosperity, love, and wisdom. The emerald green is the color of medicine, and symbolizes growth, renewal and well-being. And inside the box, there are sweet treats, something that I would like you to enjoy. So, do not open it now. I will see you tomorrow, if you would like to meet. There is a note with the place and the time inside the envelope. I will be there, at the location stated, regardless of your decision." Jacques planted a quick kiss on her cheeks and left, without turning back.

Cecilia could hardly wait to get home to open her gift and the envelope, although she told herself she was no longer an excited little girl who couldn't control her emotions about a surprise gift. But sometimes, logic and rationalization do not work, no matter how much effort you put into it. Still, her instincts warned her to proceed with caution. She knew that the human heart is one of the toughest working muscles in the body. She had studied its layers; she had seen its beautiful mosaic of cells stained in purple, fuchsia and blue under a microscope. She knew well how unique the structure is. How restlessly it works day in and out. Nevertheless, in its essence, the heart is as fragile as a crystal vase. She knew that for sure, not from words, but from experience, because her own heart had been broken in pieces before.

That night, alone in her bedroom, she carefully unwrapped the tin box. Amid the chocolate truffles filled with hazelnuts, she found several love notes. "In dreams as in love, all is possible." "Being deeply loved by someone gives you strength; loving someone deeply gives you courage." "Passion dazzles lovers; love unites them forever." "Lovers can live on kisses and water." With shaking hands, she broke the seal of the mysterious envelope, revealing a card with an entrance ticket neatly folded inside.

"Congratulations, dear Cecilia. May God grant you the desires of your heart, and make all your plans succeed. Meet me at the Constitucion Station, at one o'clock. No delays. Polo Tournament at Hurlingham Club starts sharply at three. Jacques."

That night, Cecilia could not sleep. She tossed and turned, her heart racing from time to time. She could not believe all she had lived in one single night. Despite the fact that women were practically barred from the medical school, she had managed to obtain her degree as a physician, after six years of dedication and strenuous work. She was officially a doctor now. The first female doctor in the entire country. Would there be boundaries for her impetus, for her dreams, for her passion? Passion ... was that why her heart was pounding inside her chest? She asked herself those questions, wondering what the future would hold.

Then she laughed. "A polo tournament with Jacques Copplet is what you have tomorrow, Dr. Cecilia Grierson. And that is as far ahead as you are allowed to know," she murmured, closing her eyes again.

***

When Cecilia arrived at the train station, she found Jacques at the main entrance, impeccable in a light gray suit, a blue silk ascot, polished black shoes and a straw boater hat with a grosgrain band. She thought about complimenting his elegance, but instead she said, "You left me yesterday without words. So, I guess I won't say anything, Mr. Copplet."

"The least you can do is make me laugh, Doctor."

"You'd better stop this doctor thing, or you will be watching your polo tournament alone!"

"Don't threaten me," Jacques said.

"Don't force me," she replied, giggling. "I am actually very excited at the chance to watch a polo match. Thank you for this opportunity. I didn't know you liked horses, much less polo games. I thought only the British and true Argentineans were into this."

"True Argentineans? You know there is no such thing, darling. My grandfather was born in England. He and my father used to attend polo games at the original Hurlingham Club in London, and that's how I ended up loving the sport. I am so glad the British brought the game to the western continent. I really missed it during the time I lived in France."

"One more reason for you to love this country, monsieur," Cecilia said playfully.

"Among all the other reasons I love this country, indeed."

They boarded their coach for the short ride to the outskirts of Buenos Aires. Cecilia turned her face towards the window as she noticed the changes in the landscape, reminding her of the journeys back to her *estancia* when she was a child.

"I almost forgot how beautiful this land is," she said, pointing out. "It looks like the sunlight is dancing through the tall grassy leaves, turning them into a field of gold." She turned back to Jacques, thinking she could ask him about the absence of his engagement ring, but before she spoke, he asked if she had liked his gift.

"Of course. I love it," she said, smiling.

Soon they arrived at the Hurlingham Club, an imposing sports club built in a traditional English style, covering an area of seventy-three hectares, featuring two polo fields, a cricket pitch, a golf course, stables for more than fifty horses, and a pristine new clubhouse. Cecilia noted that the club was predominantly a male domain, although there were a few elegant women, most likely wives, walking arm-in-arm with their husbands, giggling from time to time, holding their hats in a charming way when the wind wanted to blow them away. For a moment, she felt slightly awkward to be there, not sure if she belonged in that place. She wondered if she might be a little jealous of those women.

"Are you all right, Cecilia?" Jacques asked.

"Yes," she lied. "I guess I'm just overwhelmed by all the excitement of the last few days."

"I understand. It seems you are melting also. Come with me. Let me get you something to drink before we head to our seats. Have you ever been to a polo game before?" He offered her his white cotton handkerchief.

"Thank you. A drink sounds perfect. I have never been to a polo game before, although I love horses. I used to ride them with Papa when we lived in our ranch, but that was decades ago. After I entered medical school, I could not find time to step outside the city, and with the passing of my father, I never had a chance to ride horses again."

"I am so sorry about your father, Cecilia." Jacques paused for a moment, trying to choose well his next words. "If you would like, at the end of the game, I can talk to Mr. Walter Dawson. He is one of the founders of this club. I am sure he will let you see some of the horses. Maybe we can even go for a ride. If you would like to, of course. Do you think you can still ride?"

Cecilia's eyes brightened, not hiding her excitement. "I am sure I can ride. I am probably rusty, but that is not an obstacle." She was suddenly now laughing, forgetting the moments of insecurity and doubts she had not that long ago. She could see a spark of happiness in Jacques too, and she decided to just enjoy that moment. She sipped her cold tea, letting the ice cubes touch her lips, cooling her gently.

"Tell me something," she said, while they were heading back from the cafeteria to their seats. "How do you know about this place? Where did those tickets come from? This is too sophisticated for me ... so thank you again, for bringing me here."

"You are so funny. You probably just forgot that you are a doctor now. There is nothing too sophisticated for you anymore, my dear. The world is in the palm of your hand," Jacques replied, laughing.

"Is it so? I am still the same person I was yesterday, and the day before. The only difference is that now I have a diploma in my hands."

"And sometimes, a piece of paper in your hands makes the entire difference in the world," he replied. "Look over there." He pointed to their left side. "The players are about to enter with their best ponies."

"Ponies? They look like huge horses to me," Cecilia said with amusement.

Jacques gave her a serious look, then exploded in a laugh. "I told you in the beginning, the least you could do was to make me laugh ... and, girl, you got that," he continued. "The pony part was definitely funny. But please, whatever you do, do not call the equine animals on the polo field horses. In the world of polo, they are referred as ponies, even though they are horses by height. I am not quite sure why they are called ponies. Maybe because they are very agile. They are trained to not be afraid to bump into other animals, and not to be shy at the ball or mallets swinging near their heads."

Jacques explained the dynamics of the game, one of the oldest sports in the world. Two teams of four players each, using mallets with long, flexible handles, would drive a wooden ball down the field to score points between two goal posts. "The match will have four plays, or chukkas, lasting seven minutes each," he said. "The umpire over there will soon start the game, throwing the ball between the two teams. When one of them scores, the teams will change ends, helping equalize any ground or weather advantage."

"That sounds fair," Cecilia commented, noticing Jacques' excitement and familiarity with the sport.

"Fair play, camaraderie, gentlemanly conduction and ethics. Those are the values praised here," he said, this time gazing at Cecilia.

"Those are the values that should be praised all over the world," she replied, turning her face to the pitch where the game had already started.

At half-time, the spectators were invited to wander all over the field for a bout of divot stomping. Cecilia thought that was a bizarre but funny sight, and she couldn't help but laugh at the scene. Most of the gentlemen, including Jacques, removed their jackets and hats, running to the pitch, smoothing the surface of the grass with the soles of their shoes. "Come on, Cecilia!" Jacques shouted from a distance. "Show us how to stomp a heart away!"

"I don't know how to stomp a heart away!" she yelled promptly. "And I don't see any ladies over the pitch either. Plus, I don't think I am dressed with the appropriate shoes," she continued, giggling, remaining in her seat.

Polo was definitely an intriguing game, full of action, tactics and fast pace. A skilled sport that required mastery, where movement was constant. The ball moved, the horses moved, all the players were in motion all the time. It was a great combat sport, definitely not for the faint of heart.

That summer afternoon ended up being more relaxing than she had expected, with a mischievous sun poking through some clouds from time to time, warming the field of grass. A light breeze brushed her hair, bringing memories of her childhood in Entre los Rios. The sounds of the men playing and laughing in the pitch somehow reminded her of the children she grew up with at La Estancia Bella Vista. Suddenly, she missed those moments. She missed her parents. Her mother had passed away two years ago. She would have loved this place. Her parents should have been there with her this weekend, celebrating life, celebrating her graduation. *They left too soon*, she thought, looking jealously into the blue sky, as if the heavens had robbed her of the family she loved. Absorbed in her own world, she did not notice when Jacques returned to her side.

After the match, champagne, French wine, English tea, coffee and biscotti were served at the clubhouse, where Jacques introduced Cecilia to a small circle of friends and acquaintances. He was suddenly interrupted by a small hand pulling at his jacket, and a child's voice was heard from below. "Uncle Jacques, Uncle Jacques!" A boy in knee-length shorts and suspenders, about seven years old, was standing at his feet. Jacques immediately swept the child into his arms, spinning the little boy in a three-hundred-sixty-degree circle. Cecilia, surprised, admired the scene.

"Leonardo!" Jacques' exclamation made the little boy eyes glitter. "I was wondering where you could be! What great mallet action we witnessed today!"

The boy, hanging onto Jacques' neck, spoke very fast, with a hint of a French accent. "I loved it, because our team won, *oui*, we won!" Jacques smiled in return, looking at Cecilia's puzzled face.

As if anticipating her questions, he placed the child down, bending to be at his height. "Leonardo, let me introduce you to Dr. Cecilia Grierson. She is a very good friend of mine."

"How lovely it is to meet you, Leonardo. Between us, you can call me Mrs. Ceci," she replied.

The boy politely replied, "Nice to meet you, Mrs. Ceci," but he immediately ran away, getting lost in the crowd.

Jacques explained that the child was the son of a good friend of his, William Lacey, from Quebec. If Mr. Dawson was the brain of the polo club, Will was the right arm.

"The little boy seems to adore you, and vice versa. That was lovely," Cecilia said.

"Yes, we bond very well," he replied. "Now, please, follow me. I would like to introduce you to Mr. Dawson." He guided Cecilia through a sea of guests and polo players.

Walter Dawson was a typical English gentleman, in his late fifties, with a perfect groomed gray hair, high cheekbones and a mouth that did not show much of a smile. But as Cecilia spent the next half-hour talking to him and his wife, she was both pleased and relaxed in their company. They were also delighted with Cecilia, congratulating her for her career that was just starting. She was taken by surprise when Mr. Dawson asked her to follow him.

They walked over to a mahogany podium, located against the back painted wall, where stained-glass windows filtered the sunlight in a playful effect. The club treasurer requested the attention of the guests, while a bottle of champagne was popped. He proudly raised his glass to toast the winners of the match—and to recognize the presence of the first female physician of the country, Dr. Cecilia Grierson.

Cecilia squinted her eyes at Jacques as if asking, *Why did you put me in the spotlight?* He simply replied with a smirk, raising his bubbling glass in return for cheers.

Following the toast, Mrs. Dawson asked Cecilia if she would like a tour of the club, and she promptly accepted, leaving behind the men and their conversations on the latest finances and politics. Mrs. Dawson brought her to a large terrace, a space that was always opened for balls and parties. She insisted that, although they all enjoyed pompous celebrations, the club was created mainly for the gathering of family and friends. For that reason, various rooms nearby offered more discreet and intimate settings, such as the Billiard Room, the Bridge Room, and the large Reading Room, with its sunny bow window and comfortable velvet armchairs.

As the ladies stepped outdoors, Mrs. Dawson explained how the club was born, and how lucky they were to have met a fine, educated gentleman, a biologist, like Jacques Copplet. The club, the first of its kind in the country, was created just few years ago. John Ravenscroft, an Englishman, initially wanted to bring together all the British subjects living in Buenos Aires, so they could socialize and practice every imaginable sport. Ravenscroft's pretentious dream finally reached the financial British investors, including Walter Dawson and other bankers and lenders. William Lacey, a Canadian architect and sportsman, had overseen the design. It was Lacey who introduced Jacques to the Dawsons, and because Jacques shared the same interests as her husband—nature and polo—they all became close friends.

"I always find nature is absolutely breathtaking, Mrs. Dawson. And you, your husband and Mr. Ravenscroft surely have captured the earth's stunning beauty in this club," Cecilia said enthusiastically. From the large grassy lawn to the manicured hedges and shrubs, to the red brick buildings partly covered in creeping ivy, the club combined sophistication and attention to the details, molded by the spectacular landscape of the pampas.

"The boys truly enjoy their time together here, where they can breathe and live the true spirit of the Hurlingham," Mrs. Dawson added.

"And that must be fair play, camaraderie, gentlemanly conduction and ethics." Cecilia remembered Jacques' words, in order.

"Exactly," Mrs. Dawson replied with conviction. "As in life, one must learn how to win, how to lose, and above all, how to play."

Cecilia suddenly noticed her companion's penetrating gaze upon her, feeling the aristocratic woman was about to ask her a personal question. Cecilia was glad Jacques himself found them in the garden, interrupting any further interrogation that might have come up.

"Mrs. Dawson, your husband is requesting your presence at the entrance. The players would like an official photograph with you both."

Mrs. Dawson excused herself and said goodbye, explaining that she would probably leave the facility soon. Cecilia noticed only a few guests remained inside the clubhouse, and she wondered if they should also leave. Nevertheless, Jacques invited her to visit the stables.

"Can we walk up there?" Cecilia was surprised by his familiarity with that entire place.

"Yes, we can. I told Mr. Dawson that you are a horse lover, so he gave me permission to take you there. Carlos, the stableman, should be there by now."

Cecilia paused briefly, looking back to the guesthouse, having second thoughts about walking around the property at that hour.

"Come on, we don't have all the time in the world," Jacques said, offering his arm. She hesitated momentarily, but she could not refuse such a nice gesture. Her arm embraced his, suddenly sending shivers down her spine. She hoped he didn't notice it.

They walked in silence for a few minutes. Cecilia was tempted once again to ask about Jacques' engagement. She was sure all his friends at the club had seen him with an engagement ring. She wondered if he had talked to them about his distant cousin, his French fiancée. And now Cecilia was there with him, in public, walking arm in arm, Jacques displaying his affection to her without shame. Maybe she was overthinking. *He is just a gentleman. That is why he belongs to this club and why he is so cherished among everyone. You do not have the right to spoil this moment,* she told herself. Jacques, if he was uncomfortable with the quietness between them, did not display a trace of that on his face. His serene expression was almost intriguing.

"Do you come here often?" Cecilia finally broke the silence.

"I actually do, usually on the weekends, to give a hand to Will," he explained. "Then sometimes I stay at his cottage, depending on his working plan. There are still too many things they need to build here. Their goal is to expand the club functions to include tennis courts and an indoor gymnastic complex."

"That is truly impressive. What a team of entrepreneurs you all are. Mrs. Dawson seems to be very proud of all of you. She spoke highly about you and your friend, and how lucky they are in finding educated men like you two."

"There is no such thing as luck," Jacques responded. "Luck is nothing but an event that happened that we all think it was exceptionally great. But luck, per se, it doesn't exist. There are only probabilities. There are only possibilities. And I believe we are blessed with good things. Sometimes, or a lot of times, we are even blessed with bad things."

"Blessed with bad things? I never thought about that. I would call that a curse, then. But I don't believe in curses either."

"Then neither you should believe in luck. Luck and curse are the opposite sides of the same coin. An imaginative coin, I would say."

Cecilia was starting to feel entertained by their philosophical conversation. She commented in a casual tone, "You are right. Then I simply must have misunderstood you yesterday evening."

"Too many good things happened yesterday evening. Refresh my poor memory, please." Jacques sounded intrigued.

"I thought you whispered in my ears that you were a lucky man. A lucky man for being placed in the middle of my laboratory when you arrived in town, years ago." She insisted on emphasizing the words "my laboratory."

He laughed, throwing his head back, his cheeks slightly flushed.

Cecilia, joining him laughing, continued, "To think that you left me speechless yesterday, because of a mere misunderstanding about the coincidences the universe sometimes plays with us. But, if the least I can do is to make you laugh, I believe I got that part right."

"You are something, Cecilia. Coincidence, hmm?"

"Yes. I don't believe in luck either. I would say just cosmic coincidences, sometimes."

"I like that. Cosmic coincidences ... There is no such thing as luck. Just some cosmic coincidences."

They arrived at the stable, still laughing. Carlos, the stableman, greeted them by nodding his head. "Good evening, Mr. Copplet, Dr. Grierson." He paused for a second, surveying Cecilia with critical eyes. "Mr. Dawson asked me to show you some of his finest horses. I wish you were here a little bit earlier, because the sun will be setting soon."

Cecilia looked at Jacques and was getting ready to say something in reply, but Jacques sped up to catch Carlos, who was already a few feet ahead of them. The men mentioned something to each other, but she could not understand them.

The stableman sighed, handing Jacques a heavy key chain, and as he left, he said harshly, "I will be back at half past six to lock the place. Be careful with Zeus. He is not in a great mood today, Mr. Copplet."

"Neither is he," Cecilia whispered to Jacques as soon as she reached him. "What is the matter with the man?"

"I don't know. But honestly, who cares? He has no power to ruin the end of this day."

Cecilia smiled in agreement.

Like anything in the club, the stable area was immense and brand new. It included sandy and lush grassy paddocks, where horses had appropriate intervals of pasture time to rest and rejuvenate, and large, clean stalls providing access to shelter.

Cecilia closed her eyes, deeply inhaling the fresh, crisp air. The smell of hay, salt, grain and wood, all seem to be combined as one chemical element, a component of her childhood, rooted in her brain, her heart, her soul. Some animals were huffing with their presence, and chewing noises could be heard in the very far back. "It might be feeding time for those babies," she murmured, letting her thoughts speak louder than she intended, caressing one of the horses.

"Do you want go for a ride?" Jacques asked, while tying up the horses, preparing to place the saddle pad on one of them.

"You must be kidding me," she replied.

"Do I look like I am kidding? I don't think so," he said without interrupting his task. Although Cecilia enjoyed his confidence, she wondered if he was going a little bit too far. He was acting as if he owned the place. Soon, it would be dark and Carlos would be outraged if they went missing with a horse or two when he returned.

"Do you want go for a ride or not?" Jacques asked bluntly.

"I do, but—"

"Then what are you afraid of? We will go just around the paddock and towards the golf course. It's not that far. We will be back by the time grumpy Carlos is back."

"You are trouble, Mr. Copplet. You are so trouble."

Regaining her reassurance, she caressed her horse, smiling at the thought of a brief adventure. Jacques moved towards her as if to help her mount, but Cecilia quickly walked to the opposite side, climbing onto the animal's back before Jacques could reach her.

"Impressive for someone who hasn't ridden in years, Doctor."

"You are funny, Jacques. My father used to say that once you know how to ride a horse, you will always know how. I am just making sure he was right about that."

"Sure. But don't go crazy. Not yet."

Cecilia sighed, deeply appreciating Jacques' company and care. They rode side by side, the animals trotting slowly, taking them around the paddocks.

"Oh, my goodness, how much fun this is," she exclaimed after a few minutes. "And how different the world can be when seen from just a few feet above the ground. It gives you a totally different perspective."

"It feels good, doesn't it? I love this place. I love those animals. They are intelligent, they are strong, they have self-control," Jacques replied.

"Yes. But on top of all those admirable qualities, they are well trained too. Just like us. Without proper training, even the most intelligent human being can lose their track and purpose in life."

"That is so true." Jacques paused, reflecting on that saying. "Follow me here on this path. I want to show you something."

"I thought we would be back soon, Mr. Trouble," she nervously responded. She followed his horse, increasing the pace a little to not stay too far behind.

"Are you all right over there?" Jacques asked, turning his head from time to time to check on her.

"I am just fine, sir. Very fine, actually." Cecilia contemplated the view, taking in all she could: the green oasis, the horses, the movements of the tall, handsome man riding in front of her. The colors in the sky were changing from blue to a pink-orange hue, like a painting coming to life, and the sounds of thousands of crickets were growing in intensity. Once again, she thought about her childhood at the ranch, about the rides with her father, the stories her mother told her, about the sounds of the birds she loved. Looking at the sky, she was thankful for that magnificent sunset.

Jacques slowed down and Cecilia followed, the path turning slightly narrower after a curve that led to a grove. They came to a halt where a small lake appeared in front of them, reflecting the last rays of sunlight. White wildflowers danced with the gentle wind, while the first star, shining like a diamond, made its solemn appearance in the sky.

"This is so beautiful, so peaceful," she said, contemplating the golden glow spread in the horizon.

Jacques quickly dismounted and walked toward her horse, asking her to remain seated. He pointed to the sky, and she followed the tip of his finger up.

"Star light, star bright, first star I see tonight. I wish I may, I wish I might, have this wish I wish tonight."

Cecilia started giggling at the sound of the old saying, a nervous type of laugh that Jacques recognized right away.

"You are beautiful when you are nervously laughing, did you know that?" he asked, not expecting any answer in return.

He raised his arms to help her dismount from her horse. She accepted his assistance with an uneasy smile, but his hands purposely slipped about her waist, pulling her against him. Holding her firmly, he inclined his face forward, kissing her lips lightly, softly, tenderly.

She backed for a moment, surprised, still held by his strong hands. She was out of breath, her trembling hands holding his face gently away from her.

"Jacques." She could barely speak, a rush of blood coursing wildly through her veins. His face was just a few inches from hers, his aftershave scent, a mixed citrus with a trace of bergamot, fogging her thoughts, while the crispy, fruity taste of the champagne on his lips remained on her tongue. "What are you doing?" she asked shyly, blushing.

"I am simply kissing you."

"You might have drunk too much." She turned her face away, trying to rationalize the situation without hurting his feelings.

"Do I act, talk or look like I am drunk?" He was still holding her tight, their bodies connected, her heart pounding. She could feel his torso pressing against her chest, his lean, athletic, firm body telling her, without words, how he felt about her.

"No, of course not." She paused, embarrassed, trying to catch some air. "Jacques, I just don't want this to be just ... one night. To be ... just this. I don't want us to be engaged in something we will later regret."

She sounded stupid, she thought. No, she did not mean that they would have to marry and live happily ever after. That was not what she meant. She just wanted ... an abiding and comprehensive love. A meaningful relationship. Preferably, a stable relationship. And somehow, she did not even know how to start one. She had never lived through one before. But she knew this for sure: she did not want to be kissed by him for one evening, and for the next day, to have it be over.

She hadn't forgotten he was engaged not too long ago, and she had never had a chance to ask him what really happened. Somehow, she felt vulnerable being in his arms, getting involved with him. It seemed so sudden, so unexpected, so fast, so familiar.

But she could not think much, not for so long. She was in the arms of the man she adored and admired. She was being kissed by her best friend, a man who understood her, respected her and made her happy since the first day they met. Jacques, ignoring her talking and her perplexity, started to kiss her again. She could no longer help but surrender to that moment, now holding him and kissing him in return. His fiery mouth claimed hers, their bodies vibrating to the furious, un-explainable rhythm of their needs.

Holding her face, kissing her all over, Jacques whispered, "It is not going to be just one night, my love."

They remained locked in each other's arms, for an amount of time that seemed immeasurable, as if nature and time conjured to hold that moment still. There was no past nor future, only the present, with a blaze of emotions consuming both of them. Cecilia knew the danger of being alone with a man, but the desire burned in both, and she soon struggled with other feelings and thoughts that she longed to discover.

One of the horses suddenly neighed, startling Cecilia, breaking the spell, separating the two lovers.

"We should go," she finally said, feeling dizzy and lightheaded, checking on the horses.

They rode back in silence, her mind filled with a turbulence of emotions. Painful confusion, desire, longing, fear, pleasure. Her thoughts rioted out of control, her heart, still racing.

Carlos was waiting for them with his arms crossed and a frown. Cecilia knew her red face was a display of a romantic encounter mixed with embarrassment, but once again, Jacques did not make much of the situation.

"*Mi amigo*, Carlos! I am deeply sorry for making you wait. It is all my fault. Please accept my deepest apologies. Here, few cents, for a beer or a bourbon this weekend, a small token of my appreciation for your work and understanding."

Carlos did not need to say a word; his accusatory eyes towards Cecilia said it all. She swallowed dryly, trying to ignore his coldness, while he placed the money in his pocket. Jacques helped with the horses and they locked the stable, leaving Hurlingham behind.

As they were waiting for the last train to take them back to Buenos Aires, Cecilia finally confronted him. "Jacques, can I ask you a question?"

"Any one, any time," he said, his eyes fixed on her.

"What happened to your engagement?"

He did not answer immediately, and for a moment Cecilia blamed herself for the possibility of finishing a splendid day with a bucket of icy water on everyone's head. But she could not afford to spend a miserable night with that question inside her mind, on top of every other thought she already had.

"We kind of broke off few months ago."

"Kind of?" Cecilia shrugged, trying to sound indifferent to his answer.

"I wrote her a letter, months ago, telling her it was over. It was somehow a difficult decision. Our families are very close in France, and she is a beautiful, good, young woman."

Cecilia felt a twinge inside her stomach.

"I said kind of, because I feel I need to travel over there, to talk to her face to face, to give my apologies to her family, knowing that they will hate me forever, most likely," he added. "But I won't blame them. They have the right to be mad about all this. All I can say it is what happened is nobody's fault. It is not a premeditated action; it is not a crime. Life simply happened. And it happened that I developed feelings for you over the last years."

Cecilia looked straight into his eyes, and this time, she reached out to him. Cradling his face with both hands, she brought him to her lips, kissing him earnestly.

They spent the next two months together, as much as their agendas allowed. They were both very busy, between his work at the laboratory, Cecilia's brand-new private medical office, and her teaching at the School of Nurses. They met each other primarily on the weekends, when they often attended operas at the Teatro Colon or strolled the tree-lined avenues along the Plata River, before enjoying each other's company in the city's many cafes. It was in one of those cafes that Jacques told Cecilia one afternoon that he had bought the ticket for France.

The Exposition Universelle of 1889, the world's most famous fair, was being held in Paris, and after much thought, he'd come to a conclusion that this would be a perfect time to combine work and his personal business on one journey. The ship would leave Puerto Madero in two weeks, arriving in Rouen, France, after roughly twenty days. From the coast of France, Jacques would board a train to Paris and stay there a few weeks before heading east to Strasbourg, where he intended to officially dissolve his engagement.

An apprehensive sensation crept into Cecilia's core, but she tried to dismiss it with a positive comment. "I wish you the best and the safest trip. I wish you the best time in Paris. I can see your face glowing with excitement about attending the World Exhibition. I am this close to being very jealous," she said, showing her thumb and first fingertip almost touching each other. "But I won't feed that evil thought, knowing that you will return here, happy and overflowing with knowledge." She did not know what to say about Strasbourg, so she left that part out of the conversation.

***

During the following weeks, Cecilia worked intensely, taking interest in helping the Therapeutic Institute of Medical and Mechanical Gymnastic, founded by the Swedish physician Dr. Ernesto Aberg. There, Cecilia learned the concepts of Gustav Zander's system, a therapeutic method using special machines to help stimulate biological tissue to repair and be restored after injury or damage. Doctors prescribed this form of exercise to promote healing and rehabilitation, especially for tendons, muscles and bones. Treatment also included therapeutic massages, and Cecilia developed a profound interest in this field, bringing the teachings of kinesiology to the School of Nurses.

One afternoon, she was happily surprised to see a letter from Jacques under her door. The envelope, with a stamp from Paris, contained several pamphlets about the Universal Exhibition, including a beautiful print of an imposing wrought-iron lattice tower. Her hands trembled with excitement as she read the letter:

Dear Cecilia,

I am finally in Paris, after a smooth, but long journey overseas. I kept you in my dreams at nights, and the image of your beautiful smile kept me company during daytime. It is so good to feel the earth under my feet, stepping on solid ground. I am overwhelmed to be in Paris, at the centennial of the French Revolution. It feels like the entire world is here, celebrating with us the principles of Liberté, Égalité, Fraternité. Freedom, Equality, Fraternity. As the world also celebrates the promising years of industry, art and social ideals, I wish you could be here to witness the grandeur that progress has brought us. This year, they say there is a revolution in Paris. A revolution where no shots were fired, no buildings were torched, no palaces were looted. This year, the revolution is on the Champ de Mars and on the Esplanade des Invalides. It is a revolution where past and future fight a world of ideas. Iron battles stones. Javanese ritual music defies the siege of a German orchestra. Electricity triumphs over gas.

The tallest manmade structure in the world stands now here, on the Champ de Mars. It is the symbol of the Fair and serves as its gateway. I wonder if one day, this will be considered the symbol of an era. Entitled La Tour Eiffel, the tower is the summit of art, beauty, creativity and modern engineering. As the base pillars are oriented with the four points of the compass, I almost feel like it has been purposely built to represent a massive instrument of navigation, encouraging people to travel around the world, literally or symbolically, exploring the unknown. It is an iconic structure that, although it is supposed to be removed in twenty years, most likely its recognition will stand for the generations to come. It amazes me something can be made aesthetically so impressive and appealing with a new material like puddled iron.

However, not all the city's inhabitants are as enthusiastic; some conservative Parisians are actually outraged by what they call a metal horror three hundred meters high. Some writers, painters, sculptors and even architects have been protesting against this monument, arguing that it is not only a useless landmark, but it also goes against the classic taste of France. I found it beautiful, and I totally agree with the sound words of Gustaf Eiffel himself. "The tower will be the tallest edifice ever erected by man. And why, something admirable in Egypt becomes hideous and ridiculous in Paris?" Life is always full of polarity, but in a way, we should be thankful to that. That not everyone agrees with everything. How boring life would be if everyone always agreed! Contradiction brings challenge, challenge brings new ideas, new ideas bring new theories, new theories bring new philosophies. And in that eternal struggle, the world continues to spin, moving always forward.

Countries from around the world meet here to show their achievements and lifestyles. One can visit an exotic Aztec temple in the Mexican pavilion, and hours later, can be mesmerized by the replica of The Bastille. People marvel at the African bazaars and villages, after cheering the live performance of Asian theater and dance.

The Argentina Pavilion has earned highest marks from the international jury. Our pavilion has a central cupola, surrounded by four smaller ones, with classic bronze statues on its corners that blow the trumpets to the four winds, representing the agriculture and navigation. With its iron pieces, stones and blue tiles, we have built a porteño palace in France, where above it, the Argentinean sun shines. Adding to our accomplishments, one of our naturalists, the paleontologist Florentino Ameghino, won a medal for his book, entitled "The Contribution to the Knowledge of Mammalian Fossils in the Argentine Republic."

My dear, I hope you are doing well. I hope to see your beautiful face upon my arrival in Puerto Madero in the next few months.

With love, Jacques Copplet

***

Jacques returned to Buenos Aires in the middle of the spring. Cecilia had made arrangements for another professor to cover her classes that day. She planned to see just a few patients who required immediate attention, freeing her afternoon to meet Jacques at the harbor. The long platform of the port, recently carved out the mud banks of the Rio de la Plata, teemed with people eager to meet their relatives, spouses and friends.

Another ship from Italy had arrived earlier, and the commotion of the migrants could still be felt. A pretty young woman sat crying alone in a corner. A harbormaster approached her and pointed to a wooden door, where the young lady soon disappeared into an office. When the officer walked in front of Cecilia, she interrupted him, politely. "Excuse me, sir. Is everything all right with that young lady?"

The officer surveyed Cecilia slowly, from head to toe, as if he was insulted by such a question from a strange woman. "Everything is fine. It seems her fiancé just passed away in town, and apparently the news did not arrive in Italy in time to save the poor soul from the journey overseas. That happens every day here." He walked away, leaving Cecilia with a tightness in her chest.

She wondered how her ancestors had arrived in the port decades ago and what had driven them to leave a relatively stabilized life in Europe. She hoped they were greeted differently than the woman she just saw, in a much more amicable way. How hard it must have been to arrive in a foreign land, speaking very little of the language, and have to start everything literally from scratch, she thought. How brave all those men, women and children truly were, and how fortunate she was. In a way, despite all her battles, life was still easier for her, compared to many others.

The steamship from France finally arrived and a swarm of people looked up, waving and calling out names, as the passengers started to disembark. The expectation of seeing Jacques again made her chest swell, but she told herself they would have all the time in the world to be together after that, so there was no need to rush to beat the crowd. Minutes passed, and almost an hour later, only a small cluster of spectators remained at the quay. Recalling the young lady crying in despair over the loved one's death, Cecilia fought hard against a bad premonition. A stranger leaning against a wall had been watching her, and his glance made her even more nervous. The same officer walked by her again, and she managed to speak to him again.

"Do you know if there are any more passengers on board?" she asked, trying to maintain a calm tone in her voice.

"I believe by this time all the passengers are out." He paused, as if taking pleasure in seeing her face turning pale. Finally, he added, "But some passengers sometimes are detained because of customs or for medical reasons."

Cecilia, taking a deep breath, was about to ask how much more time would be expected for this, when a tap on her shoulder startled her.

"Looking for someone, Doctor?"

She turned around, sighing in relief when she heard the familiar voice. She contemplated Jacques for a moment, surprised to find differences in him. A close-trimmed beard and mustache made him look slightly older than when she last saw him. He held his tanned face with the chin high, displaying his usual elegance. His sparkling eyes fixed on hers made her blush. She wanted to hold him in her arms, but something made her stand still, waiting for him to take the first step.

"You almost had me worried, stranger," she finally said, trying to be casual.

"I am so sorry for letting you wait. I was helping this old French couple with some paperwork and translation. Apparently, the elderlies brought too many edible goods in their luggage, and the officers were giving them a hard time. It is so good to be back," Jacques finally said, quickly kissing Cecilia's cheeks.

She felt tempted to ask him how the journey was, how he'd enjoyed Paris, what he had seen and experienced in the cultural capital of the world. But his silence made her hold her inquiries. He must be exhausted, she told herself, while they were waiting for a tram that could take them to Jacques' lodging.

"Dona Maria Eugenia is going to prepare some soup and vegetables this evening," Cecilia said. "I am thinking I could help you with the luggage and then let you rest. You look exhausted. If you like, she and I can stop later at your place with some food. Or you could join us at our house, whenever you're ready for a meal."

He held her hand, bringing it to his lips, kissing it. "Thank you. I can stop later at your house, if you don't mind."

He lived in a small apartment that belonged to the university, consisting of a bedroom, a small area that served as a kitchen and study room, and a bathroom. Jacques invited Cecilia to come inside with him, but she was still worried about the repercussions of a single woman being alone in a male faculty member's apartment. In fact, nobody at the university knew about their relationship. Although she was no longer a student, she still had plans to continue her post-doctoral career. She was a professor at the School of Nurses. Jacques was still the main coordinator of the histopathology laboratory. The last thing that Cecilia wanted or needed at that moment was something to ruin their careers. Against her will, she refused his invitation, refraining from being alone at his place, even when what she wanted most was to spend the rest of the day in his company.

That night, she was surprised that he did not show up for dinner at her house. Once again, she thought something was odd. Dona Maria Eugenia did not make much of the absence of Cecilia's friend. Cleaning up the dining table, she murmured, *"Mi cara niña, los hombres no cambian, solo cambian los nombres."* My child, men don't change; the only thing that changes is their names.

Jacques remained quiet for the next three days, which almost killed her. But everything changed when she arrived at her office one morning to find out that someone had left her a beautiful bouquet of red roses. It was from Jacques, with a note of apologies for his absence since his return and for his unacceptable conduct in missing the invitation for dinner at her house. He had overslept and been completely overwhelmed by a series of meetings and reports he had to present at the university right away. He requested a dinner that night at the Restaurant Esplendor, the most elegant fine-dining restaurant in town. She would be just as happy if he had invited her to eat *empanadas* at the corner bistro, she thought. It wasn't about the place where she was going. It was all about the man she was going with. The thought that Jacques deliberately took the time to analyze his own behavior made her happy; she was glad she wasn't the only one perceiving a certain distance between them.

At dinner, they talked for hours. Jacques brought all his contagious enthusiasm from the Paris Exhibition, from the display of the phonograph to the sculptures of Auguste Rodin. When he finally said it was her turn to tell him the latest news, she laughed, saying the only thing new in her life was the kinesiology project, where she was studying and implementing the mechanics of body movements to promote health. She told him, smiling, that most likely all those ideas and inspirations started at the Hurlingham Club, on that evening when she was riding behind Jacques—where she could contemplate and admire the eloquent motion of the man on horseback.

Three months passed, and Cecilia almost forgot about the singularity of the day he arrived from France, as life and their relationship returned to normal. One evening, she told him that she would stop at his laboratory the next day. She had a tissue biopsy taken from one of her patients, and although the surgeon was confident about his diagnosis, Cecilia requested a complete histopathologic analysis of the specimen. Since her graduation, she no longer worked at the university laboratory, and Jacques now was fully in charge.

"Did you operate on a patient yesterday?" Jacques asked, surprised.

"No, of course not. You know they won't let a female doctor hold a scalpel to operate on a patient. Unless that patient is dead," she replied, with a sigh of annoyance at the reality of the facts.

"They are a bunch of stupid blind people, darling."

"No, they are not stupid, much less blind. They are full of knowledge and they know exactly what they are doing. They are just afraid and scared that women will take their place, or worse, will compete with them at the same level. There is plenty of space in this world for men and women to work side by side, without killing each other, without the need to perpetuate medieval superstitions. Now they blame the way the society is, its values and traditions, but that is all nonsense. They will say that is none of my business, so for now, I am just content in assisting the surgical procedures."

The next day, when Cecilia went to the laboratory to drop the tissue specimen, she slowly turned the doorknob, pushing the door open. Surprised, Jacques walked straight to her, sweeping her off her feet, spinning her in a hug.

"I hope you don't greet everyone who walks into your workplace this way," she said.

"No. Just you, Doctor."

He carried her in his arms and seated her on the top of one of the empty lab benches, then returned to the door, making sure it was locked this time.

Cecilia started to jump to the floor, but he reached her before she could glide off. "You're not going anywhere," he said, holding her gently, but firmly.

He began kissing her neck, her body shivering at his touch, a shudder of electricity traveling through her spine. He kissed her lips fiercely, with intensity, with passion. His tongue explored each space inside her mouth, overpowering her helpless senses. She wrapped her arms around his neck, entwining her fingers in his blond hair, longing for a connection, exposing her vulnerability. They shared a labored breathing, and she could feel his heart beating fast and faster, racing against her breasts; she could feel his body burning in desire for her, as much as her own body desired him.

"Jacques," she whispered, her voice trembling as her entire body was. She could let him go, but she didn't want to; she kept her arms around him, holding him. "We are both going to be in deep trouble if someone here sees us together. We cannot mix work and pleasure like this. We both came this far, but I won't let you, me, or anything jeopardize our lives."

"Doctor Cecilia," he said, gasping for air. "Life is too short to be taken so seriously," he whispered into her ear. "I say, once in a while a mix of work and pleasure is perfectly fine. We are not jeopardizing anything. Besides, you have called me Mr. Trouble before, apparently for no reason. So, we might as well justify the nickname you gave me."

She was about to laugh when a sudden knock at the door made her jump to her feet.

"Mr. Copplet," an unfamiliar deep voice from outside said, giving Cecilia chills. She smoothed her dress and picked up an atlas of histology that was on the nearest shelf. Taking a seat in a chair by a small cabinet in the far back corner, she could partially see the door from that spot.

The knocking continued, this time stronger. "Mr. Copplet, telegram for you. It's from overseas."

Jacques straightened the collar of his spotless white shirt and checked his trousers before answering, "I am coming."

Cecilia watched him opening the door halfway. She could not see the visitor, so she thought they were relatively safe. But after a few minutes, when Jacques simply backed up, locking the door again, without turning around, a paralyzing fear struck her. Somehow, the image of the young lady crying at the port came back to her mind, and the cold words of the officer echoed inside her. "The fiancé is dead. That happens every day, all the time." An avalanche of emotions poured over Cecilia, while Jacques remained still, at the door.

When she finally managed to reach him, her gentle touch on his shoulder startled him. His face seemed drained of blood, and the warmth of his body had suddenly vanished.

"Jacques ... what happened?"

Still holding the white paper in his shaking hands, he walked away from her, to the back of the room, silent, without looking at her. Standing in front of a window, arms crossed, he stared off into the distance, far beyond the walls of that room.

"We need to talk, Cecilia," he finally said, his voice cracking.

She felt he was trying to choose his words, but no matter how much he tried, she intuitively knew there wouldn't be anything gentle to break whatever news he had to tell her. She simply braced herself for the worst.

"Francoise is expecting a child. She is five months into her pregnancy."

Cecilia stood frozen. At that moment, the only thing that crossed her mind was that she was going to lose consciousness. She felt her airways collapsing, her throat suddenly constricting. The laboratory suddenly turned into a centrifuge; everything spun out of control. A subtle noise inside her head prevented her from hearing words intelligently. Thankfully, she saw the chair nearby, so she could fall into it.

"What is he talking about? Why is he telling me this? This must be a nightmare and I must wake up." She heard her own voice, the only thing clear inside her. She could see his lips moving, articulating soundless words. She felt like throwing up, but there was nothing inside her to come out. Suddenly numb and cold, she could not even feel her hands, her arms, her legs. Her entire body uncontrollably shook and she thought she was going to enter into a state of shock.

Somehow, though, she managed to recognize the truth. She had seen this before. It could be a joke, a very cruel prank—but it wasn't. *You have seen this story before, and you know this is no fairytale*, she told herself. *This is no romance with a happy ending. This is just* déjà vu, *as the French would say with such eloquence. It is a tragic story, and you are the central character. Again.*

Cecilia remained seated, trying to get the strength to just leave. She heard Jacques' version of the story, bits and pieces of an irrational puzzle: "Francoise must have planned that really well, because when I arrived at her house, her parents were gone for the weekend, leaving her alone. She was very cordial, to my surprise ... there were wildflowers on the table, bottles of wine. She said we were adults; we should still be friends. She poured too much wine for herself; I ended up drinking too much too. I cannot blame her for seducing me, I should have refrained from staying with her, but I didn't ... I ... I don't know why. I am not in love with her. It was just a night of wild lust."

Just a night of wild lust, Cecilia thought, still unable to speak. *Of course, it was. It is always only one night of lust. Only a moment of desire.* She could not feel anything, as if her body was anesthetized. For a moment, she actually worried about herself. *I don't hate him. I don't hate her. I don't feel like crying. I don't feel like laughing. I don't feel like yelling at him, or hitting him, or killing him. I don't even feel like asking him why. Maybe I am just dead. Maybe that is how dead people feel. Nothing. Absolutely nothing.*

When she finally had the minimal strength, she rose from the chair. Not trusting her unsteady legs, all she wanted was to get away from that place. This time, she would not walk aimlessly to the riverbanks. This time, she promised not to cry out, hoping for death. Because she had done that before; she had walked that walk before. And now she knew it was not worth it. All she wanted now was to leave all that behind.

She walked to the door, opened it and turned back, looking at Jacques for the last time. He remained still in front of the window, his back to her. She wondered if he was crying, but that would not change their reality, would not change anything. *Tears. They have no power in changing the facts. They are just an escape valve when your heart cannot hold the emotions inside.*

Her last words were dry, but sincere. "I hope you marry her and I wish you a happy life. I hope she makes you happy, as much as you once made me happy. It's all a fair game. In life, one must learn how to win, how to lose, and above all, how to play."

On that dreadful day, Cecilia told herself she did not even love him. Therefore, she could care less if their relationship was over. And somehow, she believed in herself.

Chapter 5

"Even when everything seems to be falling apart, it is up to me
to decide between laughing or crying, staying or going,
giving up or fighting;
because I discovered on the uncertain path of life,
that the most important thing is to decide."
(Cora Coralina)

Buenos Aires, Autumn, 1902

Since the weekend she had talked to Estella, almost a month ago, Cecilia actually felt better, as if a weight had been lifted from inside her soul. She was definitely sleeping better. She even found herself excited again by the La Boca Fire Department's invitation to organize a new series of speeches on accident prevention and first aid. It reminded her of a few years ago, when she first started helping and teaching the firefighters the basic health principles applied throughout the Red Cross, of which Cecilia was an active member.

She recalled the day she suggested that alarm bells, similar to the ones used in the fire brigade, should be integrated into the medical ambulances, to expedite the transport of caregivers and patients in emergency situations. Until that time, only fire and police vehicles were equipped with sirens, and the idea of expanding that device to the ambulances finally took wings when Cecilia wrote a proposal to the Public Health Department.

Colorful fall foliage draped the city and the days of sweltering heat were now fading, especially in the evenings and early mornings, making this time of the year Cecilia's favorite season. After the meeting at the fire department, she walked back home, enjoying the last rays of the sun reflected by the metal sheets that covered the houses of La Boca, the oldest neighborhood in town. Located at the mouth of the Riachuelo River, La Boca was the entry point for immigrants, and with its massive presence of Italians, the area felt like a little piece of Italy tucked away in South America.

Barefoot children ran around and yelled, talking in different idioms. Despite their differences in ages, they all seemed to get along, playing in the small, narrow alleys. On a nearby field, a group of teenagers played soccer. The small dirty ball seemed to foster the creativity of the boys to dribble past obstacles and make quick decisions, pushing themselves forward, towards the goal. "Oh, the simple pleasures of youth," Cecilia sighed as she crossed the walkway.

She slowed her steps when she noticed an older man, still in his work overalls, painting the side of a house in a brilliant orange hue. Cecilia did not think the man was aware of her presence nearby, until he spoke with a heavy Italian accent, *"Le gusta el color, señorita?"* Do you like the color, young lady?

"Yes. It is a bright, warm choice for sure," she shyly replied, caught off guard. "I was wondering why the orange now, when the sides are already painted in green."

"Por qué?" The man returned the question with a question, laughing. "It was the only leftover paint from the marina, where a few boats were painted last week. We cannot afford to be wasteful here, señorita. We reuse everything, until the last drop."

"I see. That is pretty smart. For sure it is a practical way to assure you always have a rainbow outdoors." Contemplative, she pondered whether it was Paul Cezanne who once said, "We live in a rainbow of chaos." She could not find the answer right away, but she found the thought surprisingly appropriate. So, wishing the man good luck, she continued her journey across the town.

After dinner, Cecilia put together her brushes, the palette, and a blank, primed canvas. The art group would be meeting on Saturday evening, and she thought about starting a new piece. Maybe a landscape. She kept in mind the lake view she had seen through the window in Chillon, the medieval castle in Switzerland that she'd visited three years ago. She remembered clearly the humbling sensation when she saw the magnificent splendor of the Le Dent du Mid, or Tooth of the Moon, the multi-summited peaks in the Chablais Alps. The power of the scenery, the combination of the mountains with their white tops covered in snow, resting against the banks of the sublime Lake Geneva, made a deep impression on her soul. The turquoise-blue smooth surface of the lake reflected the cloudless sky, while the crisp air from the mountains and the lush forest around filled her spirit with a certainty that the richness of the universe is always at hand, especially for those who have the eyes and the heart to perceive it.

Inspired by those thoughts, she grabbed a charcoal pencil and a paper pad, and started sketching it. The View from Chillon. That would be her first landscape project. She had painted still-life canvases in the past, following a more realistic technique, seeking an accurate representation of the object. Maybe because of her training as a physician, precision, attention to details and predictability were all familiar territories. Professor Antonio Mancini had been trying to convince her to loosen up the brush strokes, allowing spontaneity and boldness to permeate her work.

"You are very talented, Cecilia," he'd once said. "I like how well you manage the light and the shadows, how you make an object tangible, real. I always tell my students: creativity knows no boundaries; there are no rules. But that being said, I know you can do more than what you are showing. You can be much more than just a classic pupil who knows how to paint a flower in a vase. You have been to Europe. You have been to Paris. You have seen the works of Monet and Renoir.

"You know exactly what I am talking about," he told her. "You have sensed where the world is going, how movement, light and modernity are affecting every inch of our lives. That is where we are heading: to a future where we can capture a glimpse of moment in time, with color providing definition, instead of precise, dark outlines. Recreate a sensation in the eyes of those who view your work, rather than delineating the details of the subject, and you will bloom."

Cecilia went to bed, her thoughts drifting from the Chillon Castle to Antonio's words; from the colorful houses at La Boca to the impressionist paintings she saw in France. Colors and lights formed the common denominator. Colors and lights were everywhere, pulsating energy, life. Until the darkness of the night finally engulfed her, making her sink into a fitful sleep.

That night, Cecilia dreamt of a place covered in white tiles that reminded her of a hospital surgical room. There were several empty shelves on its walls, and a large, empty wooden table in the middle of the room. The place looked desolate, sterile and cold, yet it seemed familiar. She knew she had been there before. She saw a door in the far corner, also painted white. And as if she was sure of what waited for her on the other side, she opened it without hesitation. Abruptly, the scenery shifted, and she found herself in a long, dark hallway of the medical school building. Someone was walking in the distance. Cecilia tried to ask the person to wait for her, but her voice would not come out.

She turned back, realizing that the door she'd opened was gone. Behind her, the corridor was pitch black. The person, who seemed to be a man wearing a hat, was now striding even farther away. Cecilia ran, trying desperately to reach him. When she finally could grab his shoulder, the man turned around.

She tried to identify him, but his face looked blurred, as if smeared with burnt sienna mud. She still could not talk, but her thoughts were clear, as if her words could reach his mind. *Jacques, why can't you wait? Why can't you stay with me?* But the instant she had this thought, the man just changed direction, vanishing into the darkness.

Cecilia woke up in the dark, lying still in the bed. The familiar heat crept through her body, drying her mouth. Her head started aching again, but this time, she did not want to ask herself the reasons for the dream, nor for the desolation that afflicted her soul. Suddenly, she felt too weary to try to be strong. She surrendered herself to that moment, letting the salty taste of her tears roll over her face, drying on her lips. Her blood pounded in her veins, her body and mind in a turmoil that no reason or science could explain. She remained in bed awake until the first rays of the sun brushed through her windows, announcing the beginning of a new day.

As tired and restless as she was, she was glad it was Friday, usually a busy day at the hospital. She would just bury herself in work again, because if you let your mind wander aimlessly, demons would just creep into it, making your life a living hell. There is no vacuum inside the mind, and she knew it was up to her to decide what she would fill her mind with, what she would allow to rush into it. She might not be able to control her mind while she slept, but for sure she did not have that excuse when awake.

So, for the first time in years, Cecilia took a deep breath, accepting the dreams and the pain they momentarily brought. She'd tried so hard to fight them before, with no success, adding more frustration and suffering than the dreams themselves. She kept inhaling deeply, and effortlessly pictured Jacques in a landscape painting, a smooth hill, somewhere in the French countryside, surrounded by green trees and purple stretches of perfectly aligned bushes of lavender. The same light from the sun that was entering her room now extended there, with Jacques, brightening his way, warming his soul.

She imagined a beautiful, violet wave of serenity, calmness and grace suddenly enfolding him, and somehow, a little of that peace finally reached her heart. And almost as a prayer, she closed her eyes and whispered, "Wherever you are, dear Jacques, I wish you peace, happiness and above all, love. Because love is the beginning, the middle and the end of all things. It's the only reason life is always worth living."

***

Cecilia arrived at a quarter past seven at the hospital and Antonia, the nurse on call, greeted her at the floor entrance. "Good morning, Doctor Grierson. You are way early today. Are you all right?"

"Good morning, Antonia. Is there any reason something would be wrong?"

"No, I suppose not. Sorry for asking," the nurse replied, lowering her eyes.

"No need for apologies. Anything new from last evening?"

The nurse showed her the log list of the patients, most of them suffering from some comorbidities that were getting stable at the moment. "I will start my round of visiting the patients immediately, so you'd better follow me," Cecilia said, aware of her slight impatience.

Finally, around ten o'clock she had a little pause, allowing her to stop at the break room for coffee. As she sipped her black, steaming drink, a familiar face poked through the open door.

"Good morning, Doctor," Estella said, carrying a newspaper in her hands.

"Estella, what a surprise. Are you back here to work?"

"No, not yet. But I was on call last night, so I decided to stop by before heading home. You look tired, my friend. Is everything well with you?"

"It's the second time someone asked me that question today. And the day has barely started. Whatever it is, it must be stamped on my face," Cecilia snapped.

"Well, they say the eyes are the windows of the soul. And your eyes are bleary. Maybe it is allergies. Or maybe you're just tired. I hope there's nothing wrong with your soul. That is all. And I hope you are not working yourself to death either, as you have done in the past." Estella tried to make the comment sound casual, but Cecilia did not smile or reply.

"Look what I found in the social pages of the newspaper today — the announcement of the autumn ball. It states the names of Antonio Mancini and Martin Francisco as the organizers."

Estella dropped the La Prensa, one of the country's most prestigious newspapers, onto Cecilia's desk, opened at the social section. On the right page, the title was "It takes more than two to Tango. A night of music, dance and glamour." The article would have caught Cecilia's attention, except for what she saw on the adjacent left page, which made her face turn pale.

Below the headline, "Alone we are strong. But together, we are stronger," a large black-and-white photo showed a tall, well-dressed, dignified gentleman, smiling, shaking hands with a younger fellow. The caption read, "The successful agreement between the distinguished lawyers Lorenzo Bianchi and Nestor Fernandez was sealed at the Cabildo this Thursday, finally bringing the branch of Bianchi Law & Associates from Mar Del Plata, to Buenos Aires." Cecilia moved her face closer to the paper, staring at the man in the photograph, completely ignoring Estella and the reason why she'd brought the newspaper there in the first place.

"I hope you are not in trouble with the justice, my friend." Estella finally broke the silence, noticing how Cecilia's expression worsened after she saw the newspaper, her eyes frozen on the article adjacent to the one Estella thought was the most important. "You are shaking and there's not a drop of blood in your face. What is the matter with you and the lawyers? The young gentleman in the picture could be a keeper. He is charming."

Cecilia drummed her fingers on the tabletop for a few seconds, shaking her head in disbelief. "We will talk about it later, Estella," she said, suddenly getting up from her desk. "I might admit today I am not really in my best mood, but I can assure you whatever is afflicting me is nothing major, nothing serious. By the way, can I keep the newspaper?" She was still holding it, trying to keep a detached expression. "I'm afraid I have to run to the college as soon as I am done with my morning patients, and I will be at the neonatal unit this afternoon. Are we still having the art meeting tomorrow?"

"Yes, of course. You can keep the newspaper. I brought it thinking you would like to read what Antonio had written. It was never my intention to scare you. You look like you have seen a ghost. Or maybe even two," Estella joked. But again, she got no reply. "I'll see you tomorrow, my dear. You know where to find me, if you need anything. Please, get some rest after here." She hugged Cecilia before turning and walking away.

"Thank you," Cecilia muttered under her breath, a minute or two too late for Estella to hear it.

She folded the newspaper, placing it carefully inside her portfolio. She took the coffee cup with trembling hands, swallowing the cold drink in one gulp. Exiting the breakroom, she rushed through the hospital hallway, searching for the nurse, with a determination to continue her work. She found Antonia at the triage area, where two other medical residents were taking turns evaluating the new patients.

"Is there any doctor responsible for the morning shift today, or am I the only one?" Cecilia asked, a tone of urgency in her voice.

"We have Doctor Gutierrez, and Doctor Lopez is in surgery."

"Let me review the log of the patients again and, quickly, tell me exactly what do we have here with those who were already screened," Cecilia demanded.

"Two mothers dismissed last week are back with signs of infection and heavy bleeding. The infants seemed to be doing all right, although one baby is back with very yellow skin and eyes—it seems to be jaundice. One woman is complaining about swollen lymph nodes in the groin area, sore throat and fatigue. We suspect she might have syphilis, but of course, we are not sure about it. She needs a full examination. An elderly lady might be just malnourished and dehydrated. She seems very confused, her vital signs are off chart, but we could not find anything determinant for a major condition—"

Cecilia interrupted the explanations. "Malnutrition and dehydration can be major underlying causes of death; one should not take them lightly. We have to find out why she is dehydrated, if that is the case. The patient with suspected syphilis must be examined in the floor above, where we isolate and treat patients with infectious disease, in case she has contracted something contagious. I will see the three women and the infant right now, while you get a room on the second floor. Assuming Doctor Gutierrez is not in surgery, he can handle the rest of the patients for me this morning. I have to run to my office at the school right after seeing those patients. I will be back in the afternoon, at the neonatal unit."

"Yes, Doctor Grierson. I will look for Doctor Gutierrez and let him know he is in charge until you are back."

Cecilia finished examining the patients before noon. Once she had established a diagnosis and a treatment plan, the nurses and the interns would be able to manage the majority of the cases. Grabbing her purse and her portfolio, she walked to the college, her mind still locked on the newspaper image she had seen early that morning.

He looked so different now, she could barely recognize him. But the shape and contour of his full face, the sensual lips, the half-deceiving smile ... yes, that was him. Lorenzo Bianchi, with his immaculate attire and elegant poise. Definitely Lorenzo. She sighed. What was the last time she'd seen him? 1878? Yes, of course. She should never forget that. Exactly five years before her admission at the Medical School. How many things had changed since then, she thought—how many things had happened in a quarter of a century.

She suddenly now remembered the countless nights she went to bed thinking about him, tracing his face mentally, in hopes maybe she would dream about him, giving her heart and her mind the feeling that he was real, still near at hand. But she never dreamed about him. Not even once. *What year did I finally stop trying to find you, to bump into you, just to see your face one more time?* she asked herself, unable to find an answer. That she would not remember. Because it took a long time for her to stop thinking about him, trying to forget him. It felt like an eternity, a lifetime.

Fortunately, it was the school lunch break and the medical building was pretty much empty, with the employees, students and doctors gathering at the cafeteria. She locked herself into her office on the third floor, unfolding the newspaper at her desk. She started reading the full article now, slowly, as if savoring each individual word. "The prestigious lawyer from Mar Del Plata returns this week to his beloved capital, along with his wife, Rebecca Bianchi, and their children, to sign a new agreement with the local authority in law, Dr. Nestor Fernandez, finally bringing the branch of the office Bianchi Law & Associates to Buenos Aires. Dr. Lorenzo Bianchi will continue to directly manage and work at his main office in Mar Del Plata, but he has appointed Dr. Fernandez to preside over the administration of civil and criminal law in Buenos Aires."

The article praised Lorenzo for his move, especially because he had declined several invitations in the past to work in Buenos Aires. It ended with quoting the words of Lorenzo: "I love Buenos Aires, but

Mar del Plata is the city I chose to call home. I know how strong I am in what I have been doing for my country during those countless years and I see the same strength in my colleague and friend Dr. Fernandez. But together, we are definitely stronger. It's a pleasure to share the law office with such a noble man. I entrust him to take care of the citizens of Buenos Aires, bringing us the peace, the justice and the order we so much crave." At the bottom of the page, the name of his firm, with the addressees of the offices at the two locations.

"Oh, for God's sake, Lorenzo!" Cecilia rolled her eyes, shaking her head after a deep sigh. "Did you really end up the interview for La Prensa talking as if you are one hundred percent certain sure of what our population so much craves? Really?" She let out a laugh, her eyes still fixed on his picture. "I could barely recognize you today. You look vastly different from what I kept in my memory," she continued, talking to the photograph in front of her.

He had definitely added few extra pounds to his figure. And he had lost most of his beautiful, smooth, thick black hair. She wondered how hard that must have been on him, considering how extremely vain he'd been. Yes, he looked vastly different from what she kept in her memory.

But I am sure I am different too, she thought. *The thing is, I know for sure I have improved some. At least I am not that naïve teenage girl you once met.*

Cecilia paused for a few seconds. So ... Rebecca. She remembered that name from the last time she'd been with him. *The one you chose to be your wife, the one you chose to be the mother of your children. Do you remember? You were the only one talking at the end of that evening. For both of us, of course.* Cecilia stopped her train of thought, noticing the sound of her heart beating fast against her chest. *Lorenzo Bianchi. If you weren't a lawyer, you would make a great comedian.*

On an impulse, she opened the drawer of her desk, pulling out the ivory box of fine writing paper and a black pen. Without hesitation, she started pouring her thoughts into words, her neat, elegant handwriting transforming the blank sheet of paper into a written work of art:

Dear Mr. Lorenzo Bianchi,

You probably do not remember me, because it has been a quarter of century since the last time we met and spoke. At that time, we were mere students, taking Latin classes together at the University of Buenos Aires. We were young, dreaming about ruling our world in greatness, freedom, balance and equity.

Today, I was deeply glad to see your name in La Prensa, in the article that praises your name and all the great achievements towards what we once dreamt.

Congratulations on your new endeavors. I always knew you were destined to excel. I always wished you only the best of life. It brings me immense joy to see a glimpse of all you have accomplished.

It is my sincere desire this letter will find you and your family well in Mar del Plata. I also hope you are still reading poetry, like the good old times. Just because you once told me that poetry opens the doors to endless possibilities.

Respectfully, Cecilia Grierson.

"Life is a stream
On which we strew
Petal by petal the flower of our heart;
The end lost in dream
They float past our view,
We only watch their glad, early start.
Frightened with hope,
Crimsoned with joy,
We scatter the leaves of our opening rose;
Their widening scope,
Their distant employ,
We never shall know.
And the stream as it flows
Sweeps them away,
Each one is gone
Ever beyond the infinite ways
We stay alone
While years hurry on,
The flower fared forth, though its fragrance still stays."
(Amy Lowell)

Cecilia folded the letter carefully, taking her time to crease the folds back and forth, as if she wasn't sure what to do next. *It is just a letter. Letters are meant to be sent, meant to be read,* she finally thought, placing the sheets in an envelope. Out of prudence, she decided to send it with only the addressee stated on the outside. But the urge to give Lorenzo the opportunity to reply made her get the letter out. Unfolding its pages, she wrote her home address at the bottom of the last sheet.

She read the correspondence a few more times, finally sealing it inside the envelope, pressing the engraved crimson stamp on it. A perfect letter G, the initial of her last name, added a subtle element of personal distinction to the envelope, pleasing her. Suddenly, her face lighted up with delight and wonder. How would Lorenzo react when he opened this? Would he be upset, cold or indifferent? Would he remember her, just to treat the letter with disdain, throwing it in the trash underneath his desk? Or would he burn it? Would his face flush if his wife was with him? Or would he look in her eyes and say, "It's nothing important"?

Cecilia would not have time to go to the post office that day, but there was no need to rush. After all, she had lived very well the past twenty-five years without any contact with Lorenzo Bianchi. She checked the time, realizing she should head back immediately to the hospital. As troublesome as the day had started, she did not feel hungry, or tired. In addition, her headache had suddenly vanished.

Chapter 6

"Life beats down and crushes the soul
and art reminds you that you have one."
(Stella Adler)

Buenos Aires, Autumn, 1902

When Cecilia arrived at the Casa LaValle, the informal art meeting had already started. She even thought about not going there, considering how late she was, but she felt awful at not honoring her words to Martin and Estella. In addition, she realized she had been working too hard the last few months. She deserved a small rest. The studio was more packed than she remembered last time she was there. Some people were just carrying on conversations, while two or three amateur artists painted at their easels. She spotted Estella in the back, talking with Antonio Mancini, the owner of the house, and a dark-skinned man that Cecilia did not recall ever seeing before.

"Señorita Cecilia!" Martin walked towards the entrance as soon as he noticed her at the front door. "It is so good to see you again. I was wondering if you would still come."

"I'm sorry for being so late. Patients don't have time to choose when to be sick, you know. What is going on here tonight? It's a full house!"

"Well, our meetings have been very popular lately. Since there is no formal *Accademia* for arts in this country and the government hasn't yet paid serious attention to the great artistic movement now growing among us, I feel it's almost our duty to convert our houses into *casas museos*, or museum-houses, offering the public easier access to the different forms of arts," Martin said. "Lately, in every meeting, someone is bringing a new guest, an interesting person with new perspectives on how to express life to its fullest, through art. Tonight, for example, we are honored to have Mr. Ezeiza here. He is a musician. A *payador*, to be more specific."

"A *payador*? One of those wandering minstrels of the plains?" Cecilia looked around the room to see if she could recognize any man who suited the role—someone who could sing or recite lyric or heroic poetry during an improvised performance, usually accompanied by a guitar. "If I had to guess, I would say he is the gentleman speaking with Estella, over there."

"Exactly. Estella has monopolized the poor man from the moment he got here," Martin replied jokingly. "Let me introduce you to him; you will like him a lot."

Estella paused her conversation as she saw Cecilia approaching the group and gave her friend a huge hug. "I am glad you made it! You look fabulous today, by the way. Have you met Mr. Ezeiza?" Holding Cecilia's hand, Estella did not wait for an answer.

"Mr. Gabino Ezeiza, this is my friend, Dr. Cecilia Grierson. She is a physician, the founder and the director of the School of Nurses in Buenos Aires. In theory and practically, she is my boss. The best one I could ever ask for."

Cecilia slightly shook her head, as if she was asking everyone to disregard Estella's exaggeration and the titles associated with her name. "Sometimes, you have to take half of what this lady tells you, Mr. Ezeiza. It's a pleasure meeting you."

"The pleasure is all mine, Doctor Grierson," he replied.

"Please, just call me Cecilia, I insist. I've heard you are a poet and a musician—is that right?"

"The most incomparable one in the art of *payar*, to be more precise," Antonio Mancini added.

"That is what they say, Señora Cecilia. As you know, sometimes one must take in consideration half of what people say," Ezeiza humbly answered. They all laughed and requested him to tell them more of his stories, his passion for poems, music, and improvisation. Above all, they were all there to hear more about tango.

Ezeiza, of African-Argentinean descent, carried himself in a way that evoked wisdom and simplicity, with dignity as well as an exceptional sense of humor. Cecilia was immediately drawn to his personality and his sharp mind that enabled him to answer challenging questions in any situation. She was aware that among the first tango singers and composers, there were the balladeers, the *payadores*, a name derived from traveling musicians from the gaucho stock.

"Mr. Ezeiza, I have heard that *el payador* is considered a wizard of the words, a kind of shaman of a tribe, one who can cure the yearning of the audience's souls with the power of his words. Is that true?" Antonio asked.

"Mr. Mancini, my success depends on a quick and smart answer," the singer replied. "I will tell you my words cannot cure. Actually, no words can cure anything. The only thing that can cure is your own ability in believing in the cure. It's your own faith that is responsible for such a miracle."

Cecilia started applauding, followed by Estella, Martin and other guests who had joined the group. "Crafty answer!" someone teased with enthusiasm.

"Mr. Ezeiza, I believe it was Socrates who once said: It is not the wisdom that enables poets to write their poetry, but kind of an instinct or inspiration, such as the one you find in seers and prophets, who deliver all their sublime messages without knowing exactly what they mean. Do you agree with that?" This time, the question came from Martin.

"My dear friend, I will answer your question with another question. Or a series of questions. A poet is an artist. A musician is an artist. A painter is an artist. A sculptor is an artist. An actor is an artist. Caring for the sick and poor requires a doctor, a nurse with a creative soul, therefore they are artists. We are all artists here. And we carry inside us both wisdom and inspiration. Without wisdom, art is dull. Without inspiration, art is dead. And who wants dull, dead art? My question is: Where do we get our inspirations, where do we, artists, get our ideas? What is the driving force behind our creations? People have been making art since the beginning of human history for a myriad of compelling and complex reasons. But to me, deep inside, we all know exactly what message we want to convey. We'd better know what we want to convey. Because without knowing it, any kind of art would be meaningless."

"Well said, Mr. Ezeiza. Well said," Cecilia repeated, impressed. "We make art to communicate, to claim a status, to stir emotions, to transcend the material world. A venue in which people can project, play out and satisfy their feelings."

Another round of applause followed. Then Estella spoke up. "Mr. Ezeiza, you live and grew up in the neighborhood of San Telmo, the place they say the Argentinean tango was born. It's growing so popular today. Would you tell us a little about how it developed?

"It seems the word tango was first used to describe the music and dance events organized by the slaves, but I can tell you, our tango is a historical and cultural testimony of the complexity of our country," the musician exclaimed. "Tango was born out of our effervescent socio-cultural setting, in the murky suburb of San Telmo, a place that embraced millions of immigrants: Creoles, artisans, sailors, textile workers, *payadores* like me. The working class. Italians, Spanish, Hungarians, Jews, Slavs, who soon joined the freed slaves, the native Indians and the Argentineans from the pampas. We lived in squalid apartments called *los conventillos,* where families and individuals rented rooms but shared the service facilities. Usually the rooms opened to a large patio, where the *conventillos* parties started, where the tango was born. Today, those parties are still happening, allowing the tango to grow, to change and evolve."

The people of San Telmo had shared a destiny of disillusionment and despair, from which the music emerged, representing a desire to escape, Ezeiza said. The songs were about sadness, nostalgia, loneliness, distance. But they were also songs of loyalty and brotherhood in adversity.

The dance followed as a natural completion. The gauchos who abandoned their nomadic lifestyle brought the *payada*, the folk poetry, which evolved and joined the *habanera*, the dance from Cuba, where the man advances and the woman retreats. That led to the *milonga*, a type of Spanish festival where people spent the night alternating between singing and dancing. And from the port of Buenos Aires also came the *candomblé*, an African dance where couples dance separately, but very close, in sensual movements.

"The tango is truly a melting pot of ethnicities and cultures, merging into a unique style of music and dance," Ezeiza said with a beaming smile.

"It seems the music gave the immigrants the opportunity to indulge in nostalgia for a happier past, to have a moment of pleasure in the present and to dream of a better future," someone added from the back.

"And we can all definitely relate to that," Cecilia replied. "It seems the soul of our city is expressed through these songs—a universal lyricism, nurtured on eternal feelings like melancholy, nostalgia, sensuality, passion, anger. That is what tango is all about. It is about all of us."

Estella stared at Cecilia's spontaneity, a mixture of pride and surprise in her eyes, and more applause followed.

"Ladies and gentlemen, talking about tango, I would like to invite all of you to a ball at the end of the autumn season," Antonio announced. "The Teatro Victoria will be holding the event at the end of May, and it is with immense pleasure that I can assure you they will include the tango. I am positive about this because the tango baroness, the talented Mrs. Eloisa D'Herbil, has composed some songs specifically for the ball, and she is one of the special guests for the occasion."

"That is compelling." Estella's eyes sparkled as she looked at Cecilia. "A tango, a ball, a woman composer. All under one roof. That will be an historic event! I wonder how the public will react to all that."

"Who cares about how the public will react? It is about time they get used to this," Cecilia casually replied. "This is just the beginning. The beginning of a world transformation. Old and new ideas, aspirations and attitudes simply in a total metamorphosis."

***

The next week when Cecilia returned to Casa LaValle, she found less discussion and more hands-on art work. Estella quietly worked on a portrait of a boy. Estella always carried a sketchbook and from time to time, between hospital shifts, she did some drawings. Cecilia wondered if the child could be one of their patients, or an allusion to the child Estella had lost. But Cecilia refrained from asking her friend the question, giving her the freedom and privacy to just paint.

Martin concentrated on a still life he had set up on his table. A transparent vase filled with water and sunflowers was carefully placed against a blue velvet cloth, whose chroma varied depending on the flickering of the oil lamp that stood nearby and how close you were to the light. The work was still incomplete, but Cecilia contemplated it with admiration, the contrast of the colors reminding her of the flag of their country—blue, white, golden yellow. The colors of the bright sky, the peaceful clouds and the rising sun.

"How do you like it, my friend?" Martin asked without interrupting his strokes.

"It's intriguing," she answered. "I was wondering how hard it must be to paint the glass, something that is transparent, colorless, and keep it real, tridimensional. You are truly talented, able to make it so realistic."

"Sit down," Martin said, pushing a stool underneath the table to Cecilia. "Most of us start out floating on some type of talent, but you know what? Talent is like a muscle. It must be exercised on a regular basis to keep it supple. In order to fine-tune any talent, any skill, exercise is always required."

"I see. Where did you start, with this painting?" Cecilia asked, still staring at the sunflowers and the vase.

"Just as a clear mind prompts clarity and manifests the universe energy around it, the glass, which is clear in nature, reflects the color of its surroundings. So, with the blue background, the base of the vase will also be blue, a little bit darker because of its thickness. Then you must know where your source of light is. The light. We are always looking for the light. The brightest speck will be drawn in the place where the beam touches the glass. The light will pass through, dissipating a little bit before striking the other side. This will be the overtone, a big spot of diffused light, much less intense than the speck. Finally, you consider the thickness and shape of the vase, making light and shadows more intense on those areas. Next, you just fill your vase, with whatever you desire."

"In this case, you and Van Gogh chose the stunning, happy sunflowers." Cecilia smiled.

"Exactly. What are you planning to paint next? I see you brought a sketched canvas." Martin backed away from his canvas, squinting at it as if searching for a detail he'd missed.

"I might try to loosen it up and paint a landscape," she replied. "I have in my mind this beautiful memory, a view from a castle's window in Switzerland. But I am worried I will be disappointed if I try a different approach. You know I am always using small brushes, tied to the very little details as if I want a perfect photograph of my subject. At the same time, I am a little tired of that. I think if I start working on broader, looser strokes, painting will be even more enjoyable, and at the same time, more challenging."

"Well, take a look around you and remember Mr. Gabino Ezeiza last week. There are no rules here. Only freedom, spontaneity. Try it. You will never know what you can accomplish until you try. In order to grow, you must try new things. And most likely you will mess it up. You'll most likely hate the process and even your painting at the end."

"One step closer to a frustrating situation," Cecilia joked.

"Perhaps. But you know what? When you're done, you will have at least three options. You can cry like a child, stomping your feet in a tantrum, yelling because the end result is abominable. Or you can start all over, covering the canvas with new oil, leaving the old images that you do not like behind. Last, but not least, you can keep the messy work, observe it, learn from it and move on to next piece, where I am certain a bit of improvement will be incorporated. That is how we eventually master it." Martin grabbed his palette, now mixing cadmium yellow oil with cobalt blue, creating a vivid green that immediately gave life to the sunflower leaves on his canvas.

"Honestly, I am not worried about the first option," a confident Cecilia replied.

"Neither am I. That is not you. And I am totally fine with the other two options, if you so choose one of them. That is the beauty of the oil painting. Just like life, it can be malleable. And just like life, it is full of little imperfections."

"You speak words of wisdom. You've convinced me to try a new approach. You are really good at this." She thanked him with a smile.

"We are all good at something, don't you think? By the way, am I good at painting or convincing you about something?"

Cecilia chuckled. "Both, I would say."

"If that is the case, would you go to the ball with me? I promise you your patients will remain absolutely fine, if we can steal you for just a few hours on a Saturday night. But if you cannot go or do not want to go with me, I am fine too—I have learned to take no as an answer, and I have realized it does not kill me at all."

Cecilia's eyes grew wider, partly surprised and partly admiring his boldness and spontaneity. "Fine. Since you have assured me my patients will be all right, I'll go with you. That will be fun. Thank you for the invitation. I cannot promise anything else other than my company, since I am not a good dancer. But if you swear you are good with that, the evening will be a pleasure."

"Your company, that is all I am asking, Doctor Grierson."

"It's Cecilia. Don't forget that," she replied, getting back to her easel.

Chapter 7

"Be patient toward all that is unsolved in your heart
and try to love the questions themselves, like locked rooms
and like books that are now written in a very foreign tongue.
Do not seek the answers, which cannot be given to you
because you would not be able to live them.
And the point is to live everything."
(Rainer Maria Rilke)

Buenos Aires, Autumn, 1902

Clara Gomes, who was Estella's niece, had become Cecilia's housekeeper after the passing of Dona Maria Eugenia. She was now eighteen years old, and due to family issues, including the tragic death of her uncle who had helped raise her as a father, the girl had had to quit school twice, making her one school year behind. Cecilia had agreed to hire the teenager under the strict condition that Clara would attend school in the mornings and keep good grades. At first, she'd thought the girl should go home every evening, but safety concerns arose, and they'd agreed she would stay overnight during the week, occupying the room that Dona Maria Eugenia had used for years.

That early morning, Clara set the breakfast table with Cecilia's black coffee, bread and jam. She left the envelope with the official justice stamp facing down, wondering if Cecilia would notice it had been tampered with. The letter had been delivered the day before, frightening the girl to her core. She thought about her uncle's death and the events surrounding it, and immediately wondered if her job, or much worse, her family and herself could be in danger. Apparently, the letter itself brought no threats, but the fact that she had violated the privacy and trust of her employer left her uneasy. Furthermore, the letter's contents provoked a storm of desire and a curiosity that she had never experienced before.

"Good morning, Clara," Cecilia said as she stepped into the dining room, then realized the room was empty. Noticing the envelope on the table, she caught her breath as she saw the justice symbol, the blindfolded woman holding a sword and a balancing scale. She wondered why the girl had not given it to her the night before.

"When did you get this, Clara?" Cecilia held the envelope in her trembling hand, bringing it to the girl's bedchamber, where she was dressing to go to school.

"Good morning, ma'am. I am so sorry; I didn't realize you were up. About the letter, it was delivered yesterday, by the time I returned from school. The envelope ended up accidentally in between the books I was carrying. I totally forgot about it until I saw it this morning. I am so sorry, Dr. Cecilia. Please forgive me. I hope the few hours delay I have caused does not bring any major consequences." Clara's voice cracked, her head down, avoiding Cecilia's gaze.

"That's fine, Clara. I know I hardly ever have any personal correspondence sent to home; I'd rather use my work address. But in case we get any more mail in the future, please do not forget to place it immediately on my desk."

"Yes, ma'am. I will be more careful next time."

"Have you had breakfast yet? If not, come and join me. We must not be late this morning."

They ate breakfast awkwardly in silence. Cecilia remained in shock she had actually received correspondence back from Lorenzo's office. She did not see his name nor his address on the envelope, but the postal stamp from Mar Del Plata was an indication that the letter could only be sent by him. Clara's mind seemed somewhere far from that room too, but Cecilia did not make much of it.

As tempted as Cecilia was to open the envelope, she simply carried it with her all day long, managing to restrain her urges until late at night, when the house was quiet and she was certain she would not be interrupted. Still astonished by the line of communication she had suddenly reestablished after all those years, she sat in her rocking chair. Inhaling deeply, she started reading his pleasing longhand and a jolt of tremor ran through her body.

Dear Cecilia,

What a delightful surprise to come to my office, to find a letter from you on my desk!

How are you, how have you been? How is your family? Are you married? Engaged, perhaps? Do you have children of your own? Are you still teaching at the Normal School for Girls in Buenos Aires?

You might be overwhelmed by so many questions coming from me, all at once, like a suddenly torrential rain at the end of our long summers. But this is what happens when we let years pass by between us, without any contact.

So, where should I start? First, thank you for the letter and for your encouraging words about my successful career. I opened my own law office and I have been practicing as a lawyer since I graduated at UBAs. I thought about applying for a post-doctoral degree, but I did not see the need for that, as my office has been very busy since the first day. I have several clients, friends and government contacts that have begged me to move to Buenos Aires, but my family insists on staying in Mar del Plata. So ... I democratically let the majority win. Recently, the opportunity came to join forces with my colleague Nestor Fernandez, the reason why now I also have a second branch of the office in the capital.

I have two adorable children. My oldest son, Mateo, just turned eighteen. He is finishing the secondary school level and is thinking about following my footsteps, applying for law school. Maria Angelica, my daughter, is only fourteen. In a way, she reminds me of you, because she likes to teach children. She already assists the Spanish and Italian teachers at a private elementary school nearby. She has confessed that she would love to have an opportunity to study law, although my father and I have told her women are too emotional for judicial duty. In addition, I am not aware of any law schools that accept women as their students at this moment. Therefore, she will be better off choosing another career. Or finding a suitor as great as her father, which will be obviously quite impossible. As for Rebecca, my wife, she takes care of all of us and helps with the financial account of her father's importing business, so she has her hands always full.

But tell me about you. I want to know everything about you. EVERYTHING. You are probably still lean and tall. I could compare you to a speckled hummingbird, feeding on the nectar of flowers, consuming the food in little bits and pieces, here and there (that was probably the secret of your elegance). Have you traveled outside Buenos Aires? Do you still have family members in Entre Los Rios? Any hobbies? I can see you are still inclined to poetry. What is your favorite one? Do you like American poets? It gives me immense pleasure to know I had a great influence in your life. Yes, that is right. I know you will deny it until the day we die, but you started reading and enjoying real poetry because of me.

By the way, I am still waiting for the German chocolate cake you had once promised to bake for me. As you notice, I haven't forgotten.

Please, send me a picture of you. I want to see your face. I want to know what you look like now. I don't have any plans to return to Buenos Aires for the moment, but next time I am in town, we must have lunch together. Meanwhile, we will definitely keep in touch by letters. I will finish for now, leaving you with Edgar Poe.

Take this kiss upon the brow!
And, in parting from you now,
Thus much let me avow –
You are not wrong, who deem
That my days have been a dream;
Yet, if hope has flown away
In a night, or in a day,
In a vision, or in none,
Is it therefore the less gone?
All that we see or seem
Is but a dream within a dream.

Respectfully yours,
Lorenzo Bianchi

Cecilia re-read the letter several times, pacing her room, back and forth, in a mixed state of confusion and delight. She found herself completely caught off guard. Lorenzo's letter was something she had never imagined receiving, something that never crossed her mind. Somehow, he seemed much lovelier now than in her memory, making her uneasy. Walking to the small wooden cellarette in her living room, she poured herself a small glass of brandy. She sipped it slowly, as if it was a homeopathic medicine, one of those remedies usually taken in small dosages to stimulate the healing process. Thankfully, this was Friday, so Clara had gone home.

"Are you serious, Lorenzo? Are you serious?" Cecilia repeated aloud, in complete disbelief. She took the letter into the dining room, pulling up a chair, her elbows now resting on the table, one of her hands supporting her head. She did not know if she should get mad or happy. She had the right to be utterly furious. After all, the last time they talked, he'd abandoned her ruthlessly, treating her with cruelty and disdain. Now, out of the blue, he decided to reappear in her life, writing as if they had been best friends since childhood.

What the hell, Lorenzo? she thought acidly. After a quarter of a century, he continued to be the most unpredictable man she'd ever met. He was supposed to reply with the same coldness he'd shown when leaving her—or at most, with a simple cordiality, keeping the proper distance, considering they were both grown-ups now.

Her anger flared and she wanted to crush the letter. *But, no... you have to demand that I send you a picture. You have to know what I look like. You have to know absolutely everything about me, of course. Everything. Why? Why the curiosity now? Who cares how I look? Why would you care?*

For a split second, the thought of a possible revenge crossed her mind. Based on Lorenzo's words, demonstrating such an interest in her life, she could easily lure him with her charm. Even though not the most glamourous woman around, she knew she possessed a singular, simple beauty, not only of the physical kind, but mainly with emotional and intellectual appeal. They shared a connection before, and it would not be totally impossible to rekindle it once again. In a way, his letter was a sign that despite the years that had elapsed, he clearly remembered several personal details of their brief time together as if it was yesterday.

She could seduce him with impressive, powerful written words, just to see how far he would go, how he would act, what he would do. Maybe this time he would truly start to feel something for her. Something real. Something extraordinary, remarkable, something that he could not logically describe. Something he might have experienced before, but had totally forgotten its taste or its rhythm. Something that once experienced, he could not live without, much less get rid of. And when she realized that the time had come, because she would realize it, she would simply vanish. Just the way he did, twenty-five years ago.

The light from the chandelier caught the silver beads of the family rosary hanging on the wall, making it twinkle for a fraction of second, interrupting her thoughts. Somehow, the face of her mother appeared clearly inside her mind, Jane's gentle words whispering, like a melody, into her ears: *Love those who have hurt you. Let them always bring the best of you. Never the worst. Never give them the pleasure of bringing you down to their level, but the opposite. If they are blind, they might not know what they are doing. For that reason, may your light always shine, as bright as it can be. Because even a blind person can perceive light.* Cecilia sighed, dismissing that inner voice by shaking her head.

Suddenly she got up, and reaching into the back of her armoire, she grabbed her wooden keepsake. As soon as she opened the box, a pungent smell of mothballs permeated the air, tickling her throat, making her cough. Old diaries and journals that once were her confidants, allowing her to pour out her heart, lay inside the box, the thoughts and feelings mummified by years of darkness and isolation. She had not written anything like that in years. Now, she wrote only for the sake of science, for purposes of education and progress. But since her graduation night, she had not written anything for her own sake, to vent, to record her own history. Staring at the box, she wondered why she would need to keep a record of her history at this point. Placing the letter and the newspaper article on top of one of the diaries, she quickly closed the box, pushing it into the very back of the wardrobe, where it belonged.

By the time she went to bed, she could practically recite Lorenzo's letter by heart, still stunned, unable to make anything clear out of that situation. She lay motionless for hours in the dark, mesmerized by the thought that he had not only sent her a poem, but had emphasized the last part. All that we see or seem is but a dream within a dream. What was he implying?

"All that we see is a dream; all that it seems is a dream. All is a dream within a dream." She repeated those words to herself over and over, like a soothing lullaby in her mind, until she finally fell deeply asleep.

***

The autumn ball was less than fifteen days away and although Estella was fretting about outfits for her and Clara, Cecilia had her mind set on keeping things simple. They stopped at The Beau House, a French atelier whose owners, Mr. and Mrs. Beaufort, kept a refined and exquisite collection of women's garments, from lingerie to corsets, gowns and laces, making them one of the finest couturiers in the country.

Clara was content with her French rose-and-white satin dress, trimmed in pink flowers. She was extremely thankful that Cecilia had convinced Estella to take her to the ball, which would be her first time at such a social event. Meanwhile, Estella was still having alterations made to her own dress, already chosen weeks before, a sapphire blue silk two-piece gown covered in black tulle, studded with beads and sequins.

As Cecilia gazed at a black dress displayed on a mannequin, Mr. Beaufort approached her, requesting her to follow him to the back of the store. "I have reserved something special for you, Doctor Grierson. I believe it will be livelier and suit you much better than that black dress."

The shimmering, sage green silk gown he showed Cecilia struck her as a vivid work of art. Simplistic in design, yet extravagant by the choice of materials that were carefully selected. A sheer overlayer enhanced the solid lamé underlayers and the hidden lace flounce at the hem added a sense of luxury.

"For sure you will make an entrance in this dress, Doctor Grierson. Would you like to try it?"

"Undoubtedly, it's the most beautiful gown I have ever seen," she replied. "I guess I cannot refuse the offer to try it."

"I shall ask my daughter to help you with the attire," Mr. Beaufort suggested.

When Cecilia stepped out from the dressing room, the entire atelier stared at her. The seductive gown fitted her silhouette perfectly, as if it was custom-made for her, and its low décolleté displayed a hint of feminine cleavage.

"You look stunning," Estella told her. "It never gets old how you have the incredible talent and capacity of pulling the most beautiful things out of the blue. It is like the universe truly conspires in your favor, my dear."

"She simply makes the ordinary look extraordinary," Clara added.

"Oh, you two stop it!" Cecilia's cheeks flushed. "The gown is so precious, it can easily transform anyone into a beauty queen."

Pleased with her reflection in the large gilded mirror, she knew she did not have to look further for anything else. Maybe just a quick stop at the French Gallery. A mist of perfume from Grasse would definitely be the final touch.

The day of the ball arrived and Cecilia had made arrangements to meet Martin at the Victoria Theater, along with their friends. Martin and Estella had tried to persuade Cecilia to let one of them pick her up at home, to no avail. She adamantly intended to go unaccompanied, joining them in front of the theater. She needed time alone to just enjoy herself, the moment of solitude before a main event giving you a chance to realize there's a purpose to all the hustle and bustle that is about to come.

The theater entrance teemed with men and women dressed in their best attire. A long row of imposing, gleaming carriages continued to drop off more guests, while police officers directed the traffic, assuring the safety of the evening. Above the crowd, in the façade of the building, the statue of Apollo was surrounded by the muses Euterpe, Clio, Terpsicore and Thalia. The sculptures appeared to be delighted with the festivity. For the first time, Cecilia realized that the Greek god of healing and medicine, Apollo, was also the god of music and poetry. The thought intrigued her. With her eyes still fixed at the building, she abruptly bumped against the back of a tall man in a black tuxedo. The resemblance to Lorenzo paralyzed her.

"I am so sorry, ma'am. I did not notice you behind me. Forgive me if I scared you," the stranger, turning to Cecilia, apologized.

"No need for apologies. It was all my fault, walking without paying attention to the direction I am going," she replied, relieved that her mind was just playing tricks on her. She spotted Estella, Pedro, Clara and Martin in the far right near the stairs, and regaining her confidence, she walked towards them.

"*Buenas noches*, my friends. I hope you are all having a great evening," she greeted the group.

"Doctor Cecilia, you look beautiful, just like my wife had advised me," Pedro replied first, planting a light kiss on Cecilia's hand. He always used her title before her name; she had given up on getting him to change.

"It seems I have not seen you for years, Pedro. I'm so glad you are in town this weekend, sharing this moment with us. Look at Estella. Isn't she radiant?"

"Well, I am just trying to keep up with you, my dear," Estella said, hugging her friend.

"We definitely need to do this more often. You all look stunning." Martin bowed with a warm smile on his face. "Shall we go in?"

"Where are the Mancinis?" Cecilia asked.

"Antonio and Isabel are already inside. They wanted to make sure the Baroness D'Herbil has all her needs met before she walks onto the stage," Martin explained as they climbed the steps of the theater.

"Is the baroness actually playing the piano tonight? I've heard about the successful charity event she organized to benefit the cholera victims decades ago, when she was only twenty-one." Cecilia stopped talking suddenly when she realized how insensitive it was to bring up the subject of cholera, which years ago had taken the life of Martin's young wife.

But Martin did not seem to be negatively affected by the comments and continued the conversation, avoiding any awkwardness between them. "She is playing tonight. I am surprised you haven't met her yet. You two have a lot in common."

"Is that so? I wonder why."

"You both are talented women, determined not to bend yourselves to please the norms. You follow no social prescriptions. You are both intellectuals and art lovers, yet you strive for simplicity, humility. You share this unrelenting passion for what you do, as if medicine, music and charity are the fuel that runs in your veins. You challenge the traditions of an era where women are not expected to be part of a revolution."

"I was not aware I was part of a revolution," Cecilia replied, slightly perplexed.

"I believe you are. You two are. The revolution of creating a presence, of making a statement. A revolution where the weapons are wisdom, knowledge, discipline, kindness and good deeds. Acts of pure love. A revolution of ideas that is manifested in the form of art: music, poetry, literature, paintings."

"I never considered the different forms of arts as being components of a revolution, but instead, as being part of our culture." Cecilia paused briefly, wondering about the revolutionary term. "I am not a revolutionary," she concluded.

"In our eternal search for our own identity, I believe we are simply looking more inward, caring less about what is socially and po litically correct. Because what is considered correct today might not be necessarily correct tomorrow. History not from a distant past has shown us that. And I believe we are finally grasping this idea. The uncertainty of the future forces us to fight, in the present, for what we know is noble, what is right and what can bring benefits for the majority today. So, if you believe the baroness follows this line of thought, then you are absolutely right about us: we have a lot in common."

As they walked into the lavish theater, Cecilia realized the grandeur of that venue. To accommodate more than six hundred guests, the seats on the first floor had been removed, clearing the space below the stage for dancing. Against the lateral walls, the seat boxes were reserved for the dignitaries, where Antonio Mancini and his wife stood.

"Dr. Cecilia Grierson, Señora Estella, Clara! I was wondering why it took so long for you to come in. You must be Pedro, Estella's husband," Antonio opened his arms, a typical Italian sign of welcoming, hugging everyone. "Let me introduce you to my Nicaraguan friend, the greatest Ruben Dario. He is a poet, a journalist and a diplomat. He is writing a series about what is happening in the world of music and art this fall. You all arrived just in time—the photographer was about to snap a picture of us, before the musicians start taking their places." Antonio requested everyone to squeeze in and smile for the Brownie cardboard box camera that appeared in front of them.

Shortly after, Antonio took the stage to introduce to the audience El Trio Rosa de Oro, consisting of three talented young musicians: a guitarist of Spanish descent, a *mestizo* flautist and an Italian violinist. The piano was reserved for the baroness. Eloisa D'Herbil was born in Spain, but because she spent most of her years in Cuba, she considered herself a Cuban. Upon her entrance, she received a standing burst of applause, before taking her seat in front of the majestic Steinway.

Cecilia wondered how four very different individuals, from the four corners of the globe, would harmonize in the songs to come. One could almost picture a Babel tower in one's mind. She could hear a few whispers here and there and could feel the inquisitive looks of some guests, as though wondering if something good could actually come out from that stage. But to the audience's delight, the first melodies were frisky and lively, expertly played. A mixture of provocative rhythms from polkas to the *habanera* and the *milonga* immediately filled the hall and some couples began to dance.

The musicians allowed their enthusiasm to flow smoothly, as if Eloisa D'Herbil, the leader, knew very well they should not start the night with a sensory overload; they would not start with the tango right away. But when the tango finally arrived, it stayed. The audience, as though sensing an unquenchable thirst of their soul, quaffed it with a new passion.

The tango. Its music, felt in the heart, melted the audience in an emotional experience. Its romanticism, fused with vigor, brought together energy and tragedy, roughness and sophistication. The dance created a synthesis of the extremes that surround and embrace the human being: masculinity and femininity, connection and separation, spirituality and elegant sensuality, nostalgia and a sense of belonging. In the rhythmic tides of the music, men and women rose and fell, much like the ocean whose waves rolled upon the coast, bringing to South America its people—the essential ingredient of that artistic meld.

"Your contemplative look makes me wonder if you would like to dance, Cecilia," Martin murmured.

"I thought we had a verbal agreement with a non-dancing clause on it," she quickly replied with a smile.

"Oh, yes. We had indeed. But I was just informed that it is against the law to remain seated the entire night at a ball. Especially when the music is so tempting."

"I do not know how to dance the tango," she returned.

"Well, that's not a problem, because I can lead. It will not be hard for you to follow. Also, tango is highly improvisational. It might require just a little bit of magic, a little bit of willingness to try. It does not require a choreographer, much less a professional dancer. Come, let's try." Martin stood and extended his arm, waiting for her.

She did not want to go, but it did not feel right to say no to Martin either. So she stood up, feeling a little awkward and tense. He clasped one of her hands and placed the other on his shoulder. He whispered, "One, two, three," near her ear, making her heart skip a beat. The last time she danced so close to someone had been a waltz with Lorenzo at his house, both of them humming the notes of Vivaldi. "One, two, three," pause. "One, two, three ..." Transported to a past far away, her mind revived all the emotions and the love she once shared with Lorenzo.

With her eyes closed, she let Martin carry her with subtle movements, guiding her back and forth, a gentle pressure from his open hands on her back. The tango, just like her at that moment, was both happy and sad. A world of contradictions and paradoxes somehow coexisting in a perfect harmony. A torrent of emotions burst through her heart, as she danced the melancholy of a happy memory mixed with loneliness. She hoped Martin could not sense those feelings, but that night, she learned that, in tango, people dance who they are. They become transparent. Their deepest selves, their need for connection, their experiences of life's losses and gains surface, mercilessly, all at once.

When the musicians finally stopped for a break, Cecilia quickly excused herself, freeing from Martin's arms. As she walked to the restroom, her eyes blinked back a few tears, preventing them from spilling out.

She returned recomposed and undaunted. With a lifted mood, she thanked Martin for the opportunity to dance. She was glad for the brief intermission, a moment to chat with him and Estella.

"Everyone looks thrilled to be dancing, especially the women—have you noticed?" Cecilia inquired.

"It's fascinating," Estella replied. "Women dancing tango ... a woman playing tango. People of all different colors, races, cultures are dancing here tonight. The elite. The working-class people. The anarchists. I am sure there must be at least one or two conservatives in the house too." She laughed.

"Tonight, the floor and the music connect us all, entwining our flesh and souls. The floor and the music give us permission to move, to feel, to embrace one another, regardless of our gender, religion or level of education. That is powerful. That can leave me speechless," Martin said.

Cecilia chuckled. "You? Speechless? I do not think I will live to see that happen, my friend. You have always something to say. Something filled with wisdom. A word at least." They shared a good laugh.

After the show, Antonio Mancini walked the group to Eloisa's dressing room, where they remained talking for a good while. Undoubtedly, the night had been a great success. Thanks to the skills and finesse of the baroness, the tango might have more compositors from that point on, and above all, it would have a chance to ascend the social stairs, from the poorest slums of the southern outskirts to the glamorous theaters and ballrooms of the northern neighborhoods. Eloisa confessed she had written several tangos, most of them without revealing her real name as the author. She did not care that other musicians—meaning male artists—took the credit. She knew her work. And she knew she could not hold the gift of tango to herself; it belonged to the people. "The tango belongs to the world," she corrected herself.

Despite her social status, she was still seen by many as an eccentric old widow. So, by keeping her name partially hidden, Eloisa D'Herbil saved herself some trouble, allowing her music to travel much farther. Sometimes, one needs to stay behind the curtains, in order for the show to go on. And she was happy with that. "Being happy means the feeling of plenitude. The feeling you reach when you are capable of laughing or crying, with the same intensity, in accordance with what the circumstances dictate," she told them. And that was the second great lesson Cecilia learned on that night.

Chapter 8

"There is only one happiness in this life,
to love and be loved."
(George Sand)

Buenos Aires, Winter, 1902

The day Cecilia found the picture of herself in the La Prensa was the day she decided to reply to Lorenzo for the first time. The newspaper article that contained the photo was a continuation of the one published a month ago. This time, it was entitled "Tango reigns in Victory," an allusion to the successful night at the Teatro Victoria. Cecilia was surprised to see her image in print, standing beside Clara, Martin, Antonio, Isabel, Estella and Pedro. The image displayed the elegance and happiness of the group, including Cecilia's radiance. After buying an extra copy of the newspaper, she cut out the article and photo, attaching the clipping to the letter she had just written.

Dear Lorenzo,

I can assure you I was totally in awe by your letter, much more than you were astonished with mine. I was not expecting anything of that nature, but even after a quarter of a century, you continue to be a man full of surprises.

I am doing quite well. I have been living in Buenos Aires since the time we met. I have not been back to Entre los Rios, as my family sold the ranch years ago. My mother decided to join my father in heaven, while my brother moved to Scotland, where we still have a few relatives.

Too many things have happened in my life in the last twenty-five years... First of all, I am now a physician. I stopped teaching at the

Normal School for Girls once I got admitted as a medical student at the University of Buenos Aires.

I always had an inclination to continue my studies towards the biological sciences. But when my best friend, Amalia Koening, fell ill, I was committed to study medicine. In the suffering of my dearest Amalia, I found the strength and inspiration to be admitted at the College of Medicine, with the sole ambition to find a cure for my friend's chronic ailment. She suffered from a mysterious illness, enduring the pain and life limitations with a smile and good cheer. I can recall her desire to see the ocean, her craving to capture the nuances of the sky, framed by her window, always opened, surrounded by hundreds of petunias.

I clearly remember the time she bluntly asked: "Why don't you seriously study at a university?" As if the task was something as simple as someone crossing the street to reach their destination... But I looked into her serene eyes and I earnestly told her: "I'll do it. For you, Amalia. To heal you." Thinking back now, maybe I also thought that, burying myself in the study of medicine, I would also find a way to heal my broken heart.

I remember how many people did not believe I could rise above the circumstances. But look at a few other women of our time. Look at Florence Nightingale, who has laid the steppingstones of the Red Cross. Look at Marie Curie, the radiation researcher. From the struggles and obstacles in their lives, one can conclude with optimism: the circumstances? We do the circumstances.

In order to apply to medical school, I had to return to the Latin classes taught by Professor Larsen. Do you still remember him?

In the winter of 1882, I decided to write a letter to the College of Medicine, explaining my situation: "Graduated by the Normal School of Buenos Aires, with the superior title of teacher, I would like to apply for admission to the medical school, knowing that I am still taking the prerequired courses of Latin." I knew women were barred from studying medicine at the nation's four universities at that time. But I was also aware there were no laws prohibiting women from applying to them either. My mother used to say: "Knowledge, my dear, is a powerful thing when you must navigate against a turbulent ocean."

I faced entrenched opposition to my enrollment in medical school in 1883, and was asked to provide written justification for my wish to become a doctor. Despite the bureaucracy and difficulties, my relentless persistence finally got me into the College of Medicine. Those initial years were not the easiest. Not because of the massive classes I had to attend, nor because of the sleepless nights at the hospital or in front of the books. But because of the harsh criticism of some students and even some professors, those who insisted on disqualifying my outstanding work simply because of my gender.

When my Amalia suddenly died, part of me died with her. At that time, my beloved governess, Dona Maria Eugenia, held me tight, whispering: "Each one carries inside of them a Lazarus, a person who is just waiting for Christ to say: stand up, come forth! If every day we die a little bit, every day we must resurrect a little bit." Dona Maria Eugenia, who took great care of me since I was born, knew I was going to dedicate my life to study medicine, to help the sick, to teach others how to heal, regardless of the impotence we all face in front of death. That is the burden of medicine, and one who embraces this beautiful profession must cope with that for the rest of their lives. On that day, I learned we are not able to save all from death, despite our greatest efforts, despite our purest intentions. But daily, we can help save each other from the prejudices, from the injustices, from the disparities, from the pain and the loneliness that afflict us all. When we cannot offer them a cure, we can always offer them our shoulders, our ears, our hearts.

So, when you told me your daughter wants to apply to law school, my heart rejoiced. At the same time, I was disappointed to learn that her own family has not encouraged her to follow her dreams. I strongly believe that, if your daughter is as intelligent as you are, she must not be a slave of absurd generalizations, such as the one her father and grandfather have stated: that "women are too emotional for judicial duty."

It is my sincere desire that one day, people will leave behind old prejudices in order to properly advance.

Once again, I hope this letter finds you and your family well. I will finish now, with the words of Joan of Arc.

One life is all we have
And we live it as we believe in it.
But to sacrifice what you are
And to live without belief,
That is a fate more terrible than dying.

Sincerely,
C.

This time, she placed the letter inside the envelope with a growing confidence she had not noticed before. Perhaps she could start to maintain a casual, decent relationship with the man who once was her friend, once was her first true love. She still did not grasp all the repercussions of this new encounter with her past, but deep inside, she found herself happy with the simple present. Once again, she mailed the letter to Lorenzo's office, the red wax sealed with the imprint of G on the back, the only external form of identification.

***

They say winter symbolizes hardships, discontentment, anxiety and dormancy. But they also say for every rule, there must be an exception out there. So, that winter was one season of exceptions that Cecilia happily lived.

In the following days, in the few free hours she had in the evenings, she continued her painting, "The View from Chillon." As she attempted to depart from the classic realism, this time she banished all the browns and earth tones from her palette, using a limited range of other colors. She focused more on texture, light and brush stroke. "The quality of the light is more important than the intrinsic color of the object," she repeated at times to herself. As Martin had taught her, she started with the tree foliage and the flickering, sun-dappled light that she vividly remembered seeing from one of the windows of the chateau.

So far, she was enjoying the new endeavor. Especially because at this time of the year, the trees in her city had already lost all their leaves. They always seemed to shiver, as if their bark could not provide them much protection. So, to Cecilia, painting the summer view of Chillon was a perfect contrast to the bare trees and the gray fog that was starting to linger day and night around Buenos Aires.

That same winter, Cecilia took on other new challenges when she established the Society of Housework Education. Observing that women could never be totally free from their homes, she sought to better organize the teachings of domestic economy as a science, adding the recognition that household tasks also demanded structure, prestige and honor. As industries were developing strict operating rules in order to maximize their profits with fair benefits to the employers and employees, Cecilia believed that family dynamics should not be centered only around sentimental love, but also on solid and practical established instructions, bringing benefits to the entire clan. This would range from how to raise healthy children to the basics of child education, domestic finances, nutritional cooking, social etiquette, principles of sanitation, gardening, sewing and handcrafts.

She discussed those subjects at the first meeting with Estella and two other friends, Ernestina de Nelson and Dr. Elvira Lopez. "Just like political decisions have consequences in the entire country, so do household decisions," Cecilia told them. "And when those decisions are multiplied by thousands of families, their habits and expectations will affect not only the business community, but also the environment and eventually the social life of the nation."

Led by Cecilia, the goal of the new organization was to link all women with a common aspiration: education and instruction, supporting the evolution of ideas that could strengthen their nature. This social movement could improve women's economic situation and morale, based on equitable rights, favoring families, and as an extension, improving society.

***

One winter evening, after a productive day at work, Cecilia arrived at home to find the familiar envelope on her desk. Once again, other than her full name in the slanted handwriting, the only form of identification was the symbol of justice stamped on the back. Her breath heaved in her chest and her throat constricted as she opened the letter.

Dear Cecilia,

There are no words left for me to express how proud I am of you. You have grown to be a formidable, an incredible woman. You have always been. Never forget that.

You are even more beautiful now than when we met. Definitely time has been more generous to you than me. What is the shade of the gown you are wearing? It looks stunning.

Is the young gentleman by your side on the photo your husband? He is a very lucky man to have you by his side. The young lady to your left has also a fresh charm. Is she your friend?

As I read the article you sent me, I found a remarkable coincidence: my father is a friend of the family of the baroness Eloisa

D'Herbil. We used to visit them, at her house, where she always bestowed upon us the gift of her music. It quite surprises me she has now an inclination to the tango. Back then, she kept her repertoire strictly to classic music. At least that was what she played for us. We used to kindly call her "the Chopin in skirts."

Do you still play the piano, Ceci? (Can I still call you Ceci? After all, I knew you way before you became a doctor.) I haven't played the piano as much as I would love to. I blame lack of time for that. But thank heavens, my daughter plays it for me. She loves it too. I am always attracted to a woman who knows well how to touch one key after another in the piano, unlocking its beauty, causing vibrations in my soul.

How funny you had to take Latin classes again with Professor Larsen! He was one of a kind with his sarcastic humor and intelligence. I guess he and I shared those characteristics, which I insist on calling qualities. Yes, of course I remember him. We hung out together at a few cafes at the end of some of our classes. To tell you the truth, he once confided to me how interesting you were. But when I suggested that he invite you for a tea or coffee after our class, he quickly replied he was a married man. I honestly could not find any harm in a married man inviting a young woman for coffee or tea. Assuming he would take you to a public café. At least to start.

So, were you the only girl at the College of Medicine? I hope you did not have to go to school disguised as a man, in order to be left alone and in peace. I cannot picture how hard things must have been for you. But knowing your determination, passion and dedication, on top of your intelligence, you would naturally succeed in any career you chose. Most likely you have opened the doors for other future ladies to simply follow in your footsteps. You have already opened my eyes and made me reflect upon what I said to my daughter about her future. It is my hope that, if she can accomplish a third of what you have already accomplished, my heart will be overjoyed.

Where are you working now? Do you have your own private clinic? I hope I am never ill when I am in the capital, but it is good to know that I will have someone I can trust, to take good care of me, in case I need it. I can trust you, can't I? Would you take care of me?

My family doctor here keeps telling me I must lose some weight to keep my blood pressure under control. He must be right. After all, I chose the best physician in town to be my doctor. But I never listen to him. I should say, I listen to him, I just never follow his direction. Nobody tells me what to do, much less what not to do. Life is too short to restrict yourself from the few pleasures like eating and drinking very well. I will never give up on those delights, among a few other ones.

What delights you, other than medicine and poetry? Talking about poetry, shall I finish today with another great one? Specially for you,

Carpe Diem

Do not let the day end without having grown a bit,

without being happy,

without having risen your dreams.

Do not let overcome by disappointment.

Do not let anyone you remove the right to express yourself,

which is almost a duty.

Do not forsake the yearning to make your life something special.

Be sure to believe that words and poetry

it can change the world.

Whatever happens, our essence is intact.

We are beings full of passion. Life is desert and oasis.

We breakdowns, hurts us, teaches us,

makes us protagonists of our own history.

Although the wind blow against the powerful work continues:

You can make a stanza. Never stop dreaming, because in a dream, man is free.

Do not fall into the worst mistakes: the silence.

Most live in a dreadful silence. Do not resign escape.

"Issued by my screams roofs of this world," says the poet.

Rate the beauty of the simple things.

You can make beautiful poetry on little things, but we cannot row against ourselves. That transforms life into hell.

Enjoy the panic that leads you have life ahead. Live intensely, without mediocrity.

Think that you are the future and facing the task with pride and without fear.

Learn from those who can teach you. The experiences of those who preceded us in our "dead poets", help you walk through life.

Today's society is us "poets alive."

Do not let life pass you live without that.

(Walter Whitman)

Sincerely, L.B.

Cecilia stared at the pages of the correspondence, in deep contemplation. Lorenzo's affable response to her letter was more than her heart could take. Maybe, once again, she was overthinking. Reading between the lines, in the empty spaces that were freely given, filling them with the desires of her own heart.

At the same time, no one needed a degree in etymology to understand the content of the letter. Lorenzo's words were plain and clear. He wrote that she was a formidable woman. She was and continued to be an incredible one, according to the verb tense he chose. He reiterated she should never forget that. He not only noticed her beauty, but also pointed out how time had worked in her favor.

He expressed not only his desire to trust her, but also his need to know if she would take care of him. How was she supposed to take care of him? As a physician? As his friend? As his lover? No. She would never be his lover—she quickly dismissed the thought. Could he be playing tricks with the words? Undoubtedly, he was a brilliant lawyer, gifted in his knowledge of language and literature. Could he be the one luring her with charming sentences and poems, to a secret world of possible non-return? The loving sound of his letter aroused in her a curiosity—to find the truth of what lay not only in Lorenzo's heart, but also in her own.

Cecilia brought the letter to her piano in the main room, taking a seat on the bench. She stared at the glossy ebony and ivory keys, impressed, as always, with how her fingers would still naturally fall into play. She allowed her fingers to glide gently over the instrument. Like Lorenzo, she hadn't played it in a while, with the same excuse that he had brought up, lack of time. Or more honestly, a lack of desire to play music, she concluded. But now she found herself suddenly thinking about Eloisa D'Herbil. And Chopin. She imagined Lorenzo mesmerized by the beauty and charisma that the baroness radiated.

Grabbing the partiture music book and paging through it several times, she finally found what she was looking for: "Fantasie Impromptu," by Frederic Chopin. It was an advanced piece, rich in polyrhythms and fast finger work. She knew she would not be able to play it properly, but she decided to learn at least a piece from that repertoire, practicing it every evening from that day on. Her eyes suddenly filled with tears when she heard the first few notes of the music. She sensed she was mourning for a love she knew she could not have.

Cecilia deliberately tried a few other songs, less complex ones that she still could remember from her youth. Beethoven's "Fur Elise" was the last one. She lost track of time as her fingers flew over the keys, the sweet sound of the melody filling the house. She was startled when she finally rose from the bench and turned around. Clara, in her white nightgown, was standing, leaning against the wall, her arms crossed, embracing herself. Her angelic young appearance reminded Cecilia of what once she looked like. The exact time in her life when she'd fallen so deeply in love with Lorenzo.

"It's beautiful, Doctor Cecilia. Sorry, I was just observing you, I didn't mean to scare you," the girl said.

Cecilia casually rubbed her teary eyes. "Oh, I did not know you were still up, my dear. Sorry for waking you up. I got a little bit emotional earlier and decided to find out if my fingers were still able to hit some of those keys."

She reached out to take Clara's hand. "Why don't you come with me—let's go brew us some tea before we retire to our rooms. We must finish this joyful evening with the sweetest taste of tea and honey in our mouths, soothing and warming our bodies."

It was considerably late by the time Cecilia went to bed. But after tossing and turning for an hour or two, she realized she would not be able to fall asleep any time soon. She got up and read the letter again. Sitting at her desk, she decided to write back.

Dear Lorenzo,

You made me smile with your affable letter and charming words. And I must say I loved the poem. The present sometimes seems to overwhelm my senses, but as Whitman has said, we should remind ourselves constantly to "Be happy, be happy." Seize the moment, be happy. Therefore, here I am.

I have just left my piano's bench and I am currently determined to learn the challenging and wildly difficult piece of Chopin, Fantasie Impromptu. As if fate had brought that music now to me, I find interesting the freestyle, improvised sound we can detect when we listen to it carefully. An improvised fantasy! What a genial composition to match the current moment we live in.

Talking about improvisation, music and your response about the baroness D'Herbil, I must tell you she continues to sweep our hearts and souls with a quality of music that transcends words of explanations. She had the power to connect us all with the beautiful tango she presented. And as I had the opportunity to talk to her at the end of her performance, she would correct me: it is not necessarily that she has the ability to connect us. It is the tango itself that does that. Both the music and the dance offer people a refreshingly sensitive human rapport, allowing us to realize that we all have the same needs, including the need of each other.

I have been learning to admire the tango as a nest of sweetness, a natural, innocent style of art with a touch of mischief, beauty, passion, improvisation. And of course, poetry. Tango offers us the freedom to bypass external differences that so often separate us in daily life. The more I exposed myself to the tango, the more I visualize it with inner layers, ready to be discovered, ready to be peeled off, with an unconscious rapture that eludes me. Just like the world is a place of infinite layers, so is the tango. Life gives us buoyancy and tautness, a subtle complexity in which complementary conflicts always coexist. And the tango somehow summarizes those emotions, capturing those life moments.

To quench your curiosity, I am not married, nor engaged. About the gentleman by my side in the picture, he is a friend and one of my painting instructors. The shade of my dress? It was a sage green, an earthy grayish-green, like one of the herbs that we use in the dishes, with woody stems and grayish leaves... As for the young lady with "a fresh charm," as you have described, her name is Clara. She lives with me. She is the niece of my best friend, Estella. Estella was the one who pulled me out of the hospital to attend art meetings, where I am getting more exposed to paintings, music and art in general. For a year now, I have been experimenting with oils on canvas, sketching and painting some still lifes, adventuring now in a landscape.

As much as life is busy and we find ourselves always so entangled in our routines, I am coming to a conclusion that those who are always nagging about their lack of time are those who perform much less. It is far more beneficial to separate a small fraction of our time to ourselves, to be in contact with our inner self. It is in those beautiful moments of solitude that we usually heal, get more creative, more productive, more in tune with the Universe, which is constantly reminding us of our noble purpose in living.

In my few moments of spare time, I am working on a painting, a view from the Chateau de Chillon, a castle I visited in 1899, during my first trip to Europe. I was honored to be sent to participate on a panel at the International Council of Women in London. After that, I attended classes at the Sorbonne in Paris, and then took some time off to visit Switzerland. Chillon, nestled in an exceptional panorama of the Swiss mountains and Lake Geneva, is one of the most beautiful places I have ever been. Maybe because it is an island castle. Maybe it is because of the awe-inspiring contrast between the mountains covered in snow, surrounded by the azure, serene lake. Or perhaps it is because it has a feel of a secret place. Maybe because Chillon simply has the ability to touch someone's soul. I might not have the answer to why I was so captivated, but I hope that I can express, in my humble painting, the feelings I experienced while I was there.

I am currently working on several projects. I used to have a small private office, located on Suipacha Street, but I decided my time would be better employed if I did not have to worry about the administrative aspects of running my own business. Therefore, nowadays I only see patients at the Hospital de las Clinicas. My specialization is gynecology, so most of my patients are females, and a few are children.

My affection for teaching still remains. During the years of the cholera outbreak, when the hospital was in deep need for nurses and while I was still a medical student, somehow I was drawn to a group of young ladies interested in volunteering and helping take care of the afflicted. Estella was among those first volunteers. Noticing that they needed some serious formal training, I started small meetings at the University in the evenings, where I reviewed with them the basic aspects of biology, anatomy, first aid, nutrition and pharmacology. Little by little, the meetings attracted the attention of the Dean of the College of Medicine, who suggested and appointed me to officialize the program, creating the first School of Nurses in the country, where I still joyfully teach and oversee.

Now you have an overall idea of the simple things that delight me: medicine, poetry, travel, books, music, art. Oh ... and don't forget, a good cup of tea! I almost left my heart in London, not because of their royalty and their high standards of education, but because of their art in serving tea. The British afternoon tea, started by the Duchess of Bedford, serving finger food, composed by bite-sized sandwiches and savories followed by scones with jam and clotted cream, is truly a bliss, at the end of a working day. An opportunity or a good excuse for gathering or relaxing, while one can appreciate a light meal. I must agree with you: Eating and drinking are a few simple pleasures of life that one should well appreciate. With moderation, I must add. After all, balance is the key to everything.

It is so late; I must go to bed. I should apologize for such a long letter, that might be keeping you away from all the important things you must attend and care for. Your last poem was very suitable. Therefore, I will finish now with another one, which I found in a small bookstore by the Seine in Paris.

Have you ever followed a butterfly's erratic flight?
Or gazed at the sun into the fading night?
You better slow down
Don't dance too fast
Time is short
The music won't last.
Do you run through each day on the fly?
When you ask, "How are you?"
Do you hear the reply?
When the day is done, do you lie in your bed
With the next hundred chores running through your head?
You'd better slow down,
Don't dance too fast.

Time is short
The music won't last.
When you run so fast to get somewhere,
You miss the fun of getting there.
When you worry and hurry through your day,
It's like an unopened gift...
Thrown away.
Life is not a race.
Do take it slower
Hear the Music, before the song is over.
("Slow Dance," Unknown author)

Carpe diem. And remember to always find time for the things that make you feel happy to be alive. Play your piano and above all, hear the music, my dear.

Sincerely, C.

She went to bed right after sealing the pages inside the envelope, smiling, falling sound asleep very shortly.

In a week, she found another envelope on top of her desk. Astonished at how fast Lorenzo had replied, she carefully opened the envelope, and after unfolding the pages, she noticed this letter contained no heading. No personal names or dates were written. No formal salutation or greetings either. It was simply a straight dart into her heart.

So, you are back into my life.

At the right moment, at the right time. Because they say there is a time and season for everything under the sun. A time for keeping your distance, a time for kiss and tell. A time to put your head down, when you can't keep yourself around. A time to weep, a time to smile. A time to plant, a time to sow. A time to cheer, when we see one's way so clear.

So, you have arrived. With your wild enchantments, with tender words, handpicked for me. A joyful celebration of life. A silvery ray of moonlight streaking on a dark night.

You have arrived. Bringing with you, the beauty of your nature, your boldness and strength, courage and daintiness, travels and dreams, deliberately delivered to me.

You have arrived. To set my boat free, to throw my sails against the wind.

Sometimes I wonder why you are back. Sometimes I wonder if you have ever left.

Could it be, if you left, that now you are back for a revenge?

But I refuse to accept that such a loving soul would be capable of such a horrific act.

By the inquisitive style of your writing, by the careful choice of your words. For the poems that you select, they lead me straight to your heart, as one would surely expect.

Do you know why Chillon had such an emotional effect on you? It is because I was there before you. I have set my eyes on the same mountains you have; I have admired the peaceful waters of the Lac Leman, as the locals refer to their lake. My elbows have rested on the same massive stones your elbows have touched, as we both leaned on some of the window parapets. I have contemplated the majestic scenery that now you paint.

Perhaps you felt not only my presence while you walked through the chateau's countless passages and corridors, but also the touch of Lord Byron near its dungeon, where the Genevese monk François Bonivand was imprisoned.

Do you know the story?

The protagonist is an isolated figure who brings strong will to bear against great sufferings. He seeks solace in the beauty of nature, and he is a martyr of sorts to the cause of Liberty. Byron writes that the prisoner almost gives in to grief, but he is revived when he hears the singing of a bird outside his window. It reminds him that there is beauty and hope in the world. So, he clings to that thought and survives. Years later, the guards arrive to set the prisoner free. But he has been incarcerated for so long, that he does not know what to do with the freedom he now is given.

I was wondering if you have heard the singing of a bird outside, my dear?

(I love the fact that you were the first one to call me "my dear.")

By the way, getting lost in the bookstores is one of my favorite pastimes when I am in Paris. We usually travel to The City of Light at least once a year, during the spring. Recently, we gave ourselves the luxury of staying at the Le Meurice, near the Louvre. While my wife and daughter go on a shopping spree, I take the opportunity to walk amid the locals, visiting their hidden art galleries, the small cafes, the bookstores, the street markets. In less than twenty-four hours, I usually become part of a city that is full of charm and mystery. A city that consumes me with desire. A desire for life. A desire for more. Did you feel the same when you walked the city's cobblestone streets? Did you have an inexplicable urge to be in someone's arms, hearing them whisper, in an exotic language, how much they also desire you, how much they want to touch you, how much they want to kiss your voluptuous lips, how much they want to be inside of you?

Did that give you goosebumps? Did that make your face flush?

I cherish every single word I receive from you. Fill dozens of blank pages with what you so much desire, with what my eyes cannot currently see. Tell me what I am imagining. Tell me what you are imagining. Despite the physical distance between us, we can become closer, drawn together by the power of our imaginative minds.

Be thou the rainbow in the storms of life.
The evening beam that smiles the clouds away,
And tint tomorrow with prophetic ray.
(Lord Byron)

L.B.

A torrent of uneasy emotions burst through Cecilia, almost tearing her apart. She was not sure if she should love or hate the way this liaison had been unfolding, so quickly and unexpectedly. Her heart pounded at an increasingly rapid pace, her cheeks burned and she had goosebumps all over her body. Yes, the idea of a possible revenge had crossed her mind a month ago when she first thought about replying to him. But her affectionate, gentle nature did not allow her to set foot towards the vengeance.

She suddenly dropped the letter onto the desk from her sweaty, uncontrollably trembling hands. Thinking about how Lorenzo could be so syntonized with her, she hastily rose and started pacing. She moved to the window, opening it. A wintry rush of air struck her face, tangling her hair, making it even more difficult to breathe. *Who is this man and what are his intentions?* she questioned while hugging herself.

She could not believe Lorenzo had stepped in the same place she had been in Switzerland, and the detailed story he had written disturbed her. She'd never thought she was bound to her past through her love history, but now she began having second thoughts. She sensed a parallel between the protagonist of Byron's story and her own life. Maybe they were both unjustly entangled prisoners in the affairs of this life. Maybe she was a woman in chains, trapped in relationships with men who truly never cared about her. The question that Lorenzo himself had raised remained in her mind: Would she be able to hear the bird outside, reminding her there was hope and beauty in the middle of the chaos? Could there be a bird outside, singing for her?

But the night was dark and strangely quiet, as if the cold had stolen every little bit of life that lingered out there. Shivering, with her teeth starting to chatter, she was struck by what seemed to be happening—she was again falling in love with Lorenzo. How could that be possible, when, for years, she had battled so hard to rid herself of the painful emotions this man had brought her? Maybe such feelings never truly died, unless they met a sensible explanation, a proper closure, a reason why he had abandoned her so heartlessly decades ago.

She reached to close the window, when her eyes were caught by the shimmering full moon that suddenly broke through the dense clouds. Looking up, she couldn't help giving it a shy grin. *Carpe diem, Cecilia. Make the most of the present time. Give little emphasis to the past or to the future*, she thought, finally closing the window. Getting a wool shawl from her armoire, she wrapped herself in it before going to bed.

Thoughts of her life in Paris flooded her mind. A time in a not-so-distant past when she loved, grew and bloomed, captivated by the charm and intellect of a city that has the power to truly enlighten the lives of those who experience it.

Chapter 9

"A walk about Paris will provide lessons
in history, beauty and in the point of Life."
(Thomas Jefferson)

Paris, Spring, 1899

The train carrying Cecilia had arrived precisely on time at the Gare Saint-Lazare, the most impressive, state-of-the art railway station in Paris. Teeming with energy and thunderous screeching of whistles and the crashing of metal on metal, the terminal was packed with steam, smoke and the sound of countless passengers and their companions. The place seemed way more chaotic than what she expected, based on her remembrance of the few reproductions she had seen of the works of Edouard Manet and Claude Monet, who graciously represented St. Lazarus Station in a number of artworks.

Since childhood, when she studied French at the Normal School for Girls, Cecilia had always dreamt about visiting France—Paris especially. So, when she was invited to be a guest at the 1899 International Council of Women in London, she immediately researched a way to spend at least a few months in Paris. Luckily, she found that the highly reputed Sorbonne University was offering a spring program for foreign-trained doctors in the fields of bacteriology and gynecology. Cecilia did not think twice: she wrote a letter to the university requesting her enrollment in both courses.

Dona Maria Eugenia had been worried: it was madness for a woman to travel unchaperoned, crossing the Atlantic Ocean and the Strait of Dover, adventuring in foreign lands in the name of the science. "Just pray for me that I may be useful to others. That is the whole point in doing all this," Cecilia replied, assuring her governess that she would be fine.

Now, looking around Saint-Lazare, she experienced a mixed set of emotions—the thrill of making a journey that far, the excitement of setting her feet in the capital of the world, and the nervousness of being alone in a city that was bigger and more intimidating than the courage and determination she carried inside. She almost pondered whether Dona Maria Eugenia might be right in worrying, when a porter who came to her assistance asked where her husband was.

"*Il arrivera demain*," Cecilia lied, saying he would arrive tomorrow.

"*Puis bien*," he replied, satisfied by the answer.

Cecilia had made arrangements to rent, for the next three months, a small apartment located near the Sorbonne. When she asked the porter how to get to her final destination, he offered to carry her baggage and help her board in a local carriage. Thankful for her good French and her regained confidence, Cecilia followed the man, mesmerized by everything that surrounded her.

The monumental station had several platforms, covered with a glass canopy. Sunlight warmed and illuminated its interior, a welcoming sign for those arriving. As she crossed the main concourse, she noticed that many people were astonishingly beautiful, especially the women, in elegant, colorful attire and majestic style. Others displayed a more unpleasant aspect, with sun-shriveled faces, toothless smiles and worn-out dark clothes. The contrasts struck Cecilia. But what impressed her most was their eyes. Somehow, they all shared this luminosity, as if every one of them possessed this beacon of light, drawing one's attention to know them in a personal level, to explore their world in an intimate way.

During the mind-blowing carriage ride to her apartment in the Latin Quarter, she was even pleased with the heavy traffic and congestion on the streets, allowing her more time to absorb everything that her senses could take in. Residents and visitors were indulging themselves outdoors, strolling beneath a serene blue sky, as if the Parisian streets had come to life in a state of a permanent parade. The city brimmed with charm in that sunny, brisk afternoon. The gas lampposts on the wide, straight boulevards stood in perfect harmony and symmetry in front of exquisite shops, treasure-filled markets and cafes. Trams and carriages moaned and screeched to a halt, while bicyclists whizzed by. The sound of endless construction and the distinctive smell of urban transformation filled the air.

But the view when the carriage reached the banks of the Seine made Cecilia catch her breath. In front of her eyes, the impressive Pont Neuf was about to bring her into the Ile de la Cité, the island in the middle of the river that once was the birthplace of Paris. To her left, she could recognize the splendid towers and the spire of the Notre Dame Cathedral. And to the far right, the magnificent Eiffel Tower. Along both sides of the river, open-air booksellers displayed and sold old magazines, books, posters and postcards. The city pulsated with a lively energy that she had never seen before.

The Latin Quarter reminded Cecilia of what the medieval city probably looked like, when the original students of the Sorbonne, mainly monks and theologians, roamed its narrow, winding cobblestone streets, speaking Latin. She felt an immense pleasure and privilege stepping on those stones, as soon as the driver announced that they had reached her address. The residential street featured a few buildings dating from the Louis XV period, while others were being renovated in a Haussmannian style. Street-front commerce surrounded the entrance of her building. There was a warm scent of fresh bread being baked somewhere nearby, and Cecilia could see a few pedestrians carrying their loaves under their arms, reminding her that she had not eaten anything since the early breakfast before boarding that morning.

Entering the building's main door, she stepped into a narrow corridor with doors on each side. She located the proprietor's apartment and knocked on the door. In a few moments, a well-dressed, large-framed woman appeared in front of Cecilia.

"*Bonjour*. You must be Madame Moreau. I am Cecilia Grierson, from Buenos Aires, Argentina. We have exchanged correspondence in the past about the rental of one of your apartments."

"*Oui, bienvenue*, Doctor Grierson. You are the doctor who will be taking some classes at the university, right?"

"Yes, that is correct. Thank you for your hospitality and for letting me stay in your place. In the beginning, I had some difficulties in finding a decent place near the school, someone who was willing to rent a room to a single woman. I guess sometimes they just do not trust we are human beings capable of living with dignity and with resources to pay for our own bills," Cecilia replied.

Madame Moreau surveyed her with a critical eye but did not make any further comments. Instead, she gestured to Cecilia to wait at the door, while she disappeared inside her own lodging. For a moment, Cecilia regretted being so talkative in front of a stranger. She just wanted to please and make a good first impression, but there was no need to put the cart before the horse.

"Here are your two keys. The larger one is for the main entrance door. For our safety, it must be kept locked after seven at night," the landlady warned. "The smaller key is for your apartment. Now, follow me to your accommodation, please. You can leave your belongings here; Pierre will bring them upstairs in a moment."

Madame Moreau showed her to the third apartment upstairs, a small and simple unit, bare of any decorations. But it was clean and would suffice for the next few months. In the living room, a faded crimson velvet sofa and a worn wooden table with two armchairs were all that adorned the main area. A large window opened to the courtyard below, where half a dozen tables covered with white tablecloths were paired with chairs. In the bedroom, a nightstand holding a copper oil lamp was wedged between the single bed and the wall, while an antique armoire stood across from the bed. There was a washstand for personal cleaning in the corner, but Cecilia would have to share the bathroom outside with three other tenants. No kitchen was available, but Madame Moreau offered her breakfast and dinner at the courtyard downstairs, for a modest additional fee.

"I hope you have a good stay with us, Doctor Grierson. Dinner will be served from six to eight every night. If you would like, please join us downstairs. In case you need assistance with anything, just let me know.

"Thank you. I will be down in an hour or so at the most," Cecilia replied, noticing her trunk was already at her door.

She brought her belongings in and went straight to the washstand, where she poured an ewer of water into the basin to clean her hands, face and neck. She changed into a simple cream-colored silk twill tea gown, with a high neckline and banded balloon sleeves, expecting a slightly cool evening ahead. She would not venture to stroll outside yet, as she was tired and hungry and the sun would be gone soon, so the outfit seemed appropriate for a local casual dinner. Loosening her bun, she brushed her thick hair before lying down on the bed. She closed her heavy-lidded eyes, deeply inhaling the hint of lavender from the soft pillow, falling asleep quickly.

When she woke up, the room was dark and the first stars were glittering in the sky. She wrapped her shoulders with an embroidered shawl and went downstairs, where only one young gentleman, sitting at the courtyard corner, was finishing a drink. He raised his hat and greeted Cecilia, "*Bonsoir*," as he rose from his chair and passed by her. He stopped by the double-hung door that led into another room, murmuring something Cecilia could not hear. Shortly after that, a woman who resembled Madame Moreau, wearing a starched white apron, appeared holding a tray with a glass of cold water and a fresh sliced baguette, topped with melted brie.

"Good evening. You must be Dr. Cecilia Grierson. My sister told me you are renting one of the apartments with us for the next three months. I am Sylvia Moreau, responsible for the kitchen and the cleaning of this building. We keep our menu simple and seasonal, but the food is always fresh and good."

"There is nothing better than a simple, good, homemade meal, Mrs. Sylvia. It's a pleasure meeting you."

Sylvia Moreau brought a bowl of beef bourguignon, a meat stew braised in red wine, with carrots and onion, seasoned with garlic and a garnished bouquet of fresh thyme, bay leaves and sage. Following the main course, a slice of apple tart was offered as dessert. Indeed, it did not take long for Cecilia to finish the delicious meal. Then, Sylvia brought her some guides and maps about Paris and the University District. Cecilia's classes would start in two days, so she would still have the whole weekend to explore the area and get familiar with her new environment.

That Saturday morning, after an early breakfast, she stepped out to tour the Sorbonne and its surroundings. Although most of her classes would be at the Hospital Pitie and the Hospital La Rochefocald, she was assigned to attend theoretical classes at the Ecole de Medicine during the first two weeks. Similar to the University of Buenos Aires, the Sorbonne had no main campus. Instead, scholars studied where people lived, surrounded by the working class, bookstores, cafes, patisseries and shops. Cecilia was delighted to be able to advance her career by studying not in an isolated location, but in the middle of Paris, totally connected with its citizens.

Walking towards the Rue des Ecoles, she crossed a quaint little green park and finally reached the courtyard of the Sorbonne. Showing her letter of acceptance and the voucher for admission at the main gate, she entered the Grand Hall, where the allegoric statues of Homer and Archimedes seemed to respectfully maintain the balance between arts and sciences under the same roof. The massive main lecture hall was open and empty on that morning. As she peeked inside the Grand Amphitheater, which could hold more than nine hundred students, she pondered how many students lost their concentration by just looking up, letting their minds wander through the impressive Neoclassical mural above the podium. In a world completely dominated by the male counterpart, it was almost ironic to see a woman enthroned at the center of the painting, personifying the school, while figures surrounding her symbolized the institution's ideals and major areas of study, including philosophy, history and sciences.

Before leaving the main building, Cecilia asked the concierge about access to the public library. With no acquaintances in Paris and living in a small apartment, the library would be her second home for the next few months. A place not only where books were kept to be studied and read, but mainly a place to clear her mind. A place where questions, uncertainty and negativity could be easily replaced with answers, confidence and hope.

The Bibliotheque Sainte-Genevieve stood next to the Pantheon. The exterior architecture, resembling an Italian Renaissance palace, glowed a creamy beige in the sun and shade, with its arched large windows and discreet bands of sculptures composing the façade. No sign of identification could be found nearby, but the ingenious device of inscribing the names of celebrated writers, philosophers and scholars of all nations and periods on the exterior walls gave the public a hint that they were standing in front of a temple of knowledge, to say the least. Abelard, Suger, Dante, Marco Polo, Cervantes, Luther, Calvin, to name just a few. It seemed no women made the cut, Cecilia noticed, not to her surprise.

The library housed an extensive collection of books and manuscripts related to medicine, pharmacology, law and letters, but it was a small, gray percaline hardcover book with a gilded floral pattern, on top of a cart of returned items right at the entrance, that caught Cecilia's attention. *Therese Raquin*, by Emile Zola. It was the first edition in the English language. Cecilia opened the book randomly, resting her eyes upon those words that sounded more like a prophecy than a mere coincidence. "When there is no hope in the future, the present appears atrociously bitter." For a moment, she thought about that fortunate stroke of serendipity, about how blessed she was in having this chance of a lifetime. It felt as if an unknown force was whispering an intimate secret deep inside her heart, that everything in this world, at the end, works for the benefit and growth of the human being. Intuition? She pondered whether that was the name of such insight.

Holding the book tight against her chest, she walked to the stunning reading room on the first floor, where rows and rows of study tables stood under a ceiling with intricate lace-like cast iron arches. Large windows flooded the room with sunlight, and Cecilia felt the impression of a warming, welcoming space as soon as she stepped in. After finding a comfortable seat at the corner of one of the rows, she was able to remove all other distractions from her mind, losing track of the passage of time, absorbed in the pages of her new literary work.

***

The introductory class of the postgraduate course at the Sorbonne was not limited to physicians, but opened to all those who were enrolled in the natural sciences that spring.

"Learning is a concept that is not limited to books or classes, although I will assume all of you here today came to Paris to study in our institution, to learn from our written material," began the first speaker, Professor Marcelin Bertoldini, chairman of the Microbiology Department. "But the first thing I would like to clarify here is that we are all learners. And we will always continue to be. The second thing is that knowledge is only a relative term. New theories, adaptations and audacious surmises are all pieces in the puzzle of a universe that is constantly being shifted. What is considered scientifically true today will not necessarily be true fifty years from now. At the end, as Socrates stated so well, the only true wisdom is in knowing we know nothing. But let that not be an encouragement to anybody to remain or become ignorant," he said.

"They say if advice was something extraordinarily great, it would not be given freely," he added with a smile. "Nevertheless, I always start my semester with a few recommendations: Be humble, as we are daily faced with new situations. Take as much time as you need to deliberate on a problem before making a decision and always foresee the consequences of your actions. Act on your values, never on your thoughts; learn from your mistakes. And finally, spread your wisdom with others." The speaker took a long pause, slowly sipping his water, patting his mouth with his white handkerchief, observing his audience with delight. Then he cleared his throat and continued, "Welcome to the Sorbonne. Let us make the best of what we have, let it be our aim reverently to cherish the light of knowledge and wisdom that has been bestowed upon us."

The students, a group of about fifty professionals, all rose from their seats, giving him a round of applause. Then, the professor asked them to introduce themselves and to briefly summarize their professional journeys and goals, their expectations and plans for the near future.

The class resembled a meeting of nations. French, Russians, Poles, Swedes, Germans, English and Americans constituted the majority. Cecilia was the only one from South America, but gladly not the only woman. A female chemist from Russia was also present, seated next to her husband, who was also a chemist and a foreign student. The university was open to both genders, but clearly, there were still many fewer females than males, especially in the fields of natural and biological sciences. Nevertheless, as the days passed, Cecilia noticed the Sorbonne took great pride in accommodating rich and poor, men and women, irrespective of family or geographic background, using the criteria of intellectual excellence. "Equality, Collegiality, Morality, Studies"—these were the university's rules. Or at least, these were the principles shown to the public, making the University of Paris the biggest cultural and scientific center in the world.

The spirit of camaraderie and respect remained during the months to come, but as the students were taking different classes on subjects that required undivided attention, there was not much free time left for socialization. Not that this would be an inconvenience for Cecilia, who could always find an immense pleasure in reading, studying and diving into research. But after a week dedicated exclusively to reviewing and analyzing scientific articles, it was about time to reach the streets and do some sightseeing. And undoubtedly, the life of Cecilia Grierson would be very different, if it wasn't for that Saturday morning encounter on the market of Le Bon Marche Rive Gauche.

She had no specific plans to go shopping, but on her way to visit the Eiffel Tower, at number 24 of the Rue de Sevres, she was stunned when the huge market, a building of fifty thousand square meters, materialized in front of her eyes. Inside, the space provided an elegant atmosphere of high-end products and services. Original creations and limited editions stood alongside a selection of the most beautiful objects from all over the world. The market was compartmentalized in sections for women's, men's and children's fashion, in addition to household goods and accessories. Welcome stations staffed with English-speaking personnel were spread across the building. This lavish place even included an art gallery and a reading room.

At the jewelry section of the accessories department, Cecilia stopped in front of a glass display holding a collection of Asian necklaces. Another customer, a charming, petite woman was holding one of them in her hands. Cecilia was close enough to take a look at the exquisite piece and hear the explanation by the salesman, who seemed to be an expert in his field.

"The *gau* is a Tibetan Buddhist prayer box worn as a pendant. As you can see, this one is encrusted with unblemished glossy stones like turquoise, lapis lazuli and coral, in an intriguing matrix. The container opens and closes perfectly, so it can carry printed prayers on a piece of paper inside. Would you like to try the necklace?" the store employee graciously asked, already holding a gilded mirror in his hand.

"It is a very unique, glamorous piece. I am always fascinated by Asian art and history, so my eyes were drawn to this collection. But honestly, I cannot afford it right now. Maybe in the future, if it is still available," the young woman replied, returning the necklace to its red velvet box. When she realized the proximity of Cecilia, who was clearly able to listen to the dialogue, her face flushed with embarrassment.

"I couldn't help but notice your great taste for jewelry and art. You should try the necklace, just for the experience," Cecilia proposed with a shy smile.

"Just for the experience, hmm? I don't know if that will make me happy or sad ... but I guess I will not know unless I try it," the woman replied.

"Well said for both of you," the salesman said, handing the necklace back to his potential customer.

The heirloom-quality pendant added a touch of mystical glamour to a woman who already carried an inherited classiness.

"I think it matches you perfectly," Cecilia said sincerely. "What do you think?"

"I think you are correct. And I am honestly glad I have experienced it. Did you know that the lapis lazuli is one of the most sought-after stones in use in man's history?"

"No, I was not aware of that."

"Its deep celestial blue remains the symbol of royalty and honor, gods and power, spirit and vision. It is a universal symbol of wisdom and truth," the woman added, now removing the jewelry from her neck. "Thank you again for the opportunity of trying it. It is absolutely lovely."

She returned the item again to its box and said, "Au revoir," as she walked away. Cecilia was left with a strong impression from that young lady, feeling tempted to follow her, maybe to invite her for a coffee and some casual conversation.

Without hesitation, Cecilia asked the salesman the price of the necklace. Although the cost was steep, she paid for it and asked the man to hurry so he could take it as a gift to the other customer, whom she could still see in the store.

"You must write a prayer or a quote to be stored inside the *gau*. It will bring both of you good omen," the salesman said, giving her a strip of a quality white paper, pen and ink.

Pressed for time, Cecilia was amazed she could remember an appropriate quote from Alexandre Dumas. "*Toute la sagesse humaine est resume en deux mots: attendre et esperer*." All human wisdom is summed up in two words: wait and hope.

She wrote impatiently, seeing the woman turning right into a corner not so far away. For a moment, Cecilia thought she had completely lost sight of her. The merchant quickly folded and placed the paper inside the pendant, even managing to tie the box with a satin bow. "We cannot take shortcuts with our customer care, mademoiselle."

"I appreciate it, but you need to hurry up," Cecilia said. "She seems to be gone now."

The salesman rushed away with the box in search of the lady, while Cecilia decided she would be better off following the wise words she had just written down. She hoped the lady, once found, would accept the gift. Then she hoped the woman would simply come back. She prudently added the thought she should expect absolutely nothing out of this event, other than her own joy in an act of kindness.

After several minutes waiting in vain, Cecilia stepped away from that area, checking the hats and bonnets on display nearby. That was when she felt a light tapping on her shoulder. Turning around, she was happy to see the young woman again.

"You didn't have to do this," the woman said quietly, holding the gift up.

"You are correct. I did not have to do it. I did it merely because I wanted to. Without further or major explanations. But if by any chance you cannot accept it, I might simply return it," Cecilia replied calmly, noticing that the woman was not prepared for what she had just heard. For a few seconds, they stared at each other with curious eyes.

"Why did you want to give me such an expensive gift? You don't even know my name."

"I don't need to know the name of a person to perform a random gesture of kindness. I just thought you really liked the necklace and I also thought it deserved to be with you, for a little bit longer experience, since you said you were glad wearing it for just few seconds."

"Do you often give gifts to strangers that you bump into the stores?"

"No, not really. I barely set my feet into stores lately. I am usually too busy wrapped up with work. It is actually my first time in a store like this. To tell you the truth, there is nothing like this market where I come from."

"And where do you come from? I can distinguish a charming accent behind your perfect French."

"Why should I give that type of personal information to an inquisitive stranger?" Cecilia sarcastically asked.

"I see. You must forgive me. I am Claudette Cerveaux. May I know your name, mademoiselle?"

"I am Cecilia Grierson. And I am from Buenos Aires, Argentina."

"Argentina," she repeated. "You come from far away. I have met Americans, but nobody yet from South America."

They remained in silence for a moment, but finally Cecilia asked if Claudette would have time to go to a restaurant for a light meal. Claudette's answer was a delightful surprise.

"Yes, it will be a pleasure. I cannot recall the last time someone has invited me to go out. The few friends I have probably gave up on me a long time ago, because I always refuse to go out with them."

"Why is that?"

"I just do not trust anyone in Paris anymore. People here are full of envy, drama and lies. They love to steal your ideas and your soul, if you are careless. But things should be fine between us. You are not from Paris. You are definitely not one of them. You must have fallen from heaven. I would call you an angel, if I could only believe in those things."

Walking towards the Eiffel Tower, Claudette recommended a saloon in the intersection of the Rue de Babylone and the Boulevard des Invalides, where they could sit outdoors.

"So, what brings you here?" Claudette asked, while searching the menu.

But before Cecilia could answer, Claudette continued, "I find it interesting that the entire world comes to Paris as if this city has the answers and solutions to the majority of humanity questions, desires and ambitions. Most of the women come in the name of love. Few come to study, even fewer to follow a career. Men simply come to be the greatest. Every chemist in town wishes to be a Pasteur, every writer wants to be a Victor Hugo, every composer wants to be a Chopin. When in reality, every person should strive to be the best of themselves, leaving their own authentic mark, creating their own original work, instead of working out a copycat strategy."

"There is nothing wrong in coming to Paris to be inspired by the greatest masters, to learn with them," Cecilia said.

"Absolutely. The problem is when you try to launch something new and you are simply crucified in return. When all you desired was an opportunity for creative independence and individuality of expression. As well as for a way of life liberated from the pressures imposed by a puritanical, hypocritic society, of course. Life here sometimes can be much more complicated than anywhere else."

"Have you lived anywhere else?" Cecilia inquired.

"I was born on a farm in northern France and, like most of the people who live in Paris, we moved here when I was seventeen, in search of better opportunity, better education, growth. They saw in me and my brother the potential for success. Sooner we became a house full of dreamers. Now, as years have passed by, I don't even know what word would better suit us."

"I totally understand what you mean," Cecilia replied. "I was also raised on a farm in the northeast of my country and just like you, I moved to the capital to get an education. Not necessarily a better one. Just an education to start with. But experience has taught me that, in order to succeed in life, especially as a woman, we must be more than mere dreamers. We must be leaders with the relentless determination to never give up. We must acquire the knowledge that, in life, certain battles will be lost, and that will not be the end of the world. We ought to learn, no matter what, which battles we must pick, in order to continue living."

"I wish I could find one single person here that thinks like you, Madame Grierson. I did not give you the chance to answer—what brought you here, again?"

"Work and study. Particularly study. It is my first week in France, actually."

"You are brave and definitely determined. There is a lot of prejudice on top of impediments in my field of work. Paris is not as liberal as you might have imagined. Women are still not allowed at the Ecole des Beaux-Arts, just to give you a mere example."

"I should not be surprised. Are you an artist?"

"A sculptress."

"That is impressive, to say the least."

"You are being kind. Sometimes I wish I could be anything else. Since I was a child, I have always played with clay and sculpture. But this is not a suitable profession for a grown-up woman. Unfortunately, I do not have any other talent. I cannot even marry a rich man, because the man I love, although not rich, is already committed to someone he says he doesn't love; nevertheless, he refuses to leave her. So, go figure that. This means I have no option other than spend my days and nights fighting to obtain a piece of decent marble from the State, fighting for the right to cast my work in bronze, begging to have my pieces exhibited in a public space, and so on. Can you tell me which fight I should pick and choose?"

Cecilia felt a pinch deep in her stomach. She knew how much hardship and harsh rejection she faced her entire life to succeed in her medical career, just because of her gender. But luckily, in her case, she was still able to practice medicine and, as a single woman, be self-sustained. She definitely was not expecting anything of that nature, not in Paris, not coming from such a beautiful young lady who seemed to be so intelligent, energetic, filled with great potential. How could life sometimes be so charming and yet so unfair? How could a country, where its motto was Liberté, Égalité, Fraternité allow schools to refuse entry to a woman whose only desire was to learn? The turn of the new century was right at hand, and still, in certain aspects, there was no universal acceptance for students wearing a skirt and a bun. Sometimes, it seemed the world remained stuck in the dark ages, Cecilia thought.

After learning that Cecilia was a physician with a great interest in patients with special needs, such as the ones suffering from blindness and deafness, Claudette pointed out that the National Institute for Blind Children was located just down that same well-maintained wide street. If, from the saloon, they continued walking north, they would reach the Hotel des Invalides, the Parisian monument whose construction was ordered by Louis XIV to shelter the disabled soldiers of his armies. Napoleon Bonaparte was buried there, in accord with the emperor's request to be laid to rest by the banks of the Seine, surrounded by the people he so dearly loved. Claudette explained all that, taking great pride in knowing so well the history of that city.

"We must order two drinks to celebrate our casual encounter, Cecilia."

"Isn't it too early for a drink?" Cecilia asked, slightly perplexed.

"Not when you are in Paris, especially for the first time, meeting extraordinary people, *mon cheri*."

Cecilia couldn't help but laugh. "I knew you were an exceptional human being the moment I first saw you."

"Likeness attracts likeness, right?" As the waitress approached them to take their orders, Claudette asked for a glass of crème de cassis in addition to two glasses of sparkling wine. "I will be mixing our own cocktails, if you do not mind," she said. "I accidentally discovered this great combination one night when I had to finish a sculpture and I was running out of the berry liqueur. I found myself forced to mix the little I had left with some wine. The result turned out to be really good. It has an uplifting taste. I hope you like it."

"I will trust your good taste. Creativity sometimes flourishes from the most unexpected circumstances."

They remained the next two hours savoring their drinks, salads, quiches, and slices of cheese, enjoying each other's company. Cecilia told Claudette about her life in Buenos Aires, how much her city looked up to Paris as a role model of modernity, classic beauty and progress. They discussed their odysseys in overcoming the mockery of their male counterparts and the bureaucracy processes that made it difficult to pursue a professional career.

"I never thought that I should have the good fortune to study in France. But now that I am here, I know I would not want to have missed the culture of Paris for anything," Cecilia said. "So far, at the Sorbonne, I am allowed to speak with my professors and fellow classmates, all males, on equal terms and respect. It makes me deeply sad to learn that the same does not happen in the artistic field. I feel guilt that I never thought about how hard the journey must be for a female artist to succeed."

"As a woman, I can attest that if you declare you have pranced off to Paris to study art, you might as well have stated you had gone irretrievably to hell, on a one-way road," Claudette protested, laughing.

"There should be other female artists who are struggling with similar issues. Any thoughts on forming an association, a small club where women with similar goals, facing the same barriers, could start a movement to increase the culture of artistic awareness and public acceptance? In a way, that's one of the reasons why I am here in Europe. To return to my country to work in collaboration with the very few others who think and act on the same principles and ideas we have, especially equal rights for women. We cannot face this journey alone, Claudette. There must be someone who can help you, encourage you, support you."

"So far, I have not found one single soul. My dearest talented friend, who shared the studio and some of the sculpture classes with me, is back in England, married, taking care of her children. Bless her heart. She knew that motherhood does not go hand-in-hand with artistic pursuits. But she values a loving marriage and being a mother more than sculpting and I believe she has no reason to regret her choices."

"I'd wish she didn't have to choose between having a family and pursuing an artistic career. But I can definitely see the challenges of having to juggle both, equally."

"Cecilia, no offense, but nobody thinks like you. Society expects a girl to be married by the age of fifteen. She should receive an education in how to read and write, how to properly address the family's bourgeois guests in several languages, how to incorporate the latest fashions into her wardrobe, how to play the piano only for the purpose of entertaining the house guests, how to set a table for a banquet. And above all, how to be submissive to her dearest husband, raising boys who will climb the ranks of the military or will be the best lawyer or doctor in town. As for their unlucky girls, they will be naturally raised to follow the footsteps of their mother. I am sorry. I just do not fit in any of that. And as you can see, I am already displaying too much of my sardonic wit."

"You are brilliant, absolutely correct in all that you say, and I admire you for your independence, intelligence and sense of humor. By the way, the drink was delightful, along with the entire meal and your company."

"I had a wonderful time; I am truly thankful for that. And for the gift you gave me." Claudette opened the jewelry box, swinging the necklace as if it was a pendulum in her hands. "I shall wear it as long as I live, as a reminder of our friendship. Would you mind hanging it on my neck for me?" She handed the jewelry to Cecilia, immediately tilting her head down, exposing her pale nape, a sharp contrast between her tied-back, dark chestnut hair and her black blouse.

Cecilia moved behind Claudette's chair, gently placing the ornament around her neck, as if Claudette was one of those porcelain dolls that you find in an antique boutique, avoiding any brusque movement that could break the delicacy of that moment, or interfere with the symbolic meaning of that gesture. "Shall we head to the Eiffel Tower?" Cecilia finally proposed.

"I would love to, but I have to return to my place. I am behind on a project I started months ago and I have an appointment with one of my models before three this afternoon." She paused, biting her lower lips, thoughtful. "Do you have any plans for tomorrow morning? You could meet me at the Church of Madeleine, Eighth Arrondissement, at ten o'clock."

"A church? I thought you did not believe in angels, heaven and all those things from above."

"I do not. I just attend the mass at La Madeleine every Sunday as a sign of protest."

"Excuse me. A sign of protest?"

"Yes. Since I learned the funeral of Frederic Chopin was delayed for almost two weeks because he had requested that Mozart's Requiem be sung. The Requiem had major parts for female voices, but obviously, the Church of Madeleine had never permitted female singers in its choir. The church finally relented, on the condition that the female singers remained behind black velvet curtains."

"Black velvet curtains? Seriously?" Cecilia was shocked.

"True story. I would not sing if I were them. Luckily, I was not born into existence to be part of that. Actually, I just had a thought that is totally the opposite. I would sing my heart out and on top of that, I would pull the damn curtain down. That would be much more effective."

"They might desire to make you look invisible, but they definitely cannot shut you down, girl." Cecilia laughed.

Claudette rose from her chair and hugged her. "I can't wait to see you tomorrow, *mon cheri*."

Cecilia thought exactly the same, but she simply replied with a smile, "I will see you tomorrow at the Madeleine."

Next day, Cecilia decided to arrive at the church half an hour early, allowing her plenty of time to admire the striking architecture of what truly resembled a Greco-Roman temple, before the horde of worshippers walked in. Standing at the portico, she eventually spotted her new friend walking graciously toward the church, dressed in an impeccable simplicity: a long, straight, frill-trimmed white gown with a high neckline and long, close sleeves. A floral-adorned hat framed her elegant face.

"You look beautiful," Cecilia said.

"You are always so kind, my friend. Shall we go in? This church does not have a bell, which I honestly appreciate. It gives me the excuse to enter at any time, never knowing if the mass has already started or not."

"I am impressed with the building. It reminds me of the cathedral in my city. They both do not look like a Catholic institution at all. If it wasn't for the high relief representing the Last Judgement on the pediment, I would not consider this a church."

The interior of the Madeleine was dimly lit, with candles flickering on several standing wrought iron racks. The single nave, with three domes over wide-arched bays, was lavishly gilded in a décor inspired by Renaissance artists. The musk smell of burning incense, combined with melting beeswax, brought an immediate feeling of comfort and relaxation to Cecilia. She suddenly had a desire to just sit down, taking a moment to silently say a thankful prayer. But Claudette kept walking towards the front.

"I always sit on the first pew on the right, and I am always the first one to leave," Claudette explained. "Somehow, I believe that truly irritates the preacher and I find that irresistibly comic."

"And what prompts you to do that?" Cecilia inquired.

"The fact that, by now, they know who I am and they know what I do for living. I am sure they are outraged by my presence here, on the first row."

"Who are they?"

"The priests, the church, the parishioners. All of them!"

Cecilia thought Claudette could only be imagining things, a conspiracy theory against her that most likely did not have any solid validation. Since when was what Claudette did for a living a crime or a sin that would outrage the church, for God's sake? But Cecilia was in no position to judge a person, much less someone she just met twenty-four hours ago. Not willing to fuel the fire, she quietly followed Claudette, taking her seat in front of the altar.

The Sunday mass proved to be a delightful service, to Cecilia's surprise. The priest, a young man with an appealing voice, finished the sermon making a parallel between humanity and the stars in the firmament. "Just like the moon reflects the sun in a starry night, we are also called to reflect the Spirit of God that indwells in us, shining his glory upon the lives of each other."

"What an appropriate speech," Cecilia whispered in Claudette's ear, recognizing the discreet fragrance of a jasmine perfume.

"Very convenient, I would say. We do have to take off our hats to the fact that he reviewed the basic principles of astronomy in the middle of a mass." Claudette chuckled. "It's time to go now."

And she simply rose from her seat and started walking towards the exit door. Cecilia had no other choice than to follow her, not without provoking a reaction of accusatory stares from those who turned to look at them.

When they reached the street, Cecilia wondered what was coming next, as she did not have a chance to plan anything for the rest of the day. As if Claudette had read her mind, she proposed a visit to the Luxembourg Gardens, stating that was her favorite place to stroll and to be inspired.

Cecilia could immediately see why her new friend loved that place. The gardens, with the impeccable lawns, tree-lined promenades, winding paths and flowerbeds, were indeed a serene paradise in the middle of a bustling city. Countless statues were scattered throughout the grounds. An impressive antique palace sparkled brightly in front of a monumental fountain.

"This is one of my favorite sculptures here," Claudette said, pointing to an unusual statue of a mythological female, nude, with a marble-cold chilling gaze. In an almost teasing gesture of putting one of her hands inside the mouth of a mask, the young woman depicted had a faint smirk.

"A French version of 'La Bocca Della Verita'?" Cecilia asked, recognizing that the inspiration for such a whimsical work of art must have come from Rome.

"'La Bouche de la Verité.' The Mouth of the Truth, by Jules Blanchard. It was presented at the Paris Salon in 1879," Claudette explained. "It does make reference to the Roman legend that one cannot remove the hand from the mouth of the truth if one has lied."

"This girl seems pretty confident," Cecilia noted, contemplating the statue.

"That is why I love her. I call her The Naked Truth. A naked girl, sliding her hand serenely in the mouth of a mask that stands in a column, where the carved mirror and laurel branches represent the attributes of the truth." She paused briefly, giving Cecilia time to digest those details. Then she continued, "Isn't it devilish? I always wonder under what accusations she was brought to the mask. Infidelity is the only word that always crosses my mind. What do you think?"

The question took Cecilia by surprise. But she managed to have a different vision of the accountability represented by the French sculpture.

"To me, the posture of the young lady towards the measure of her truthfulness is emphatically not one of fear. Here, it seems that truth is embraced, caressed. Truth seems not to be manipulated, but rather it seems to be an object of devotion and tender desire."

"Desire ... is that the reason why she is naked, with a deceiving smile?"

Cecilia flushed in front of the blunt question. "She is depicted nude maybe because that is how we are, in our raw state. The artist did not want to cover her in clothes, leaves or anything, because she does not have anything to hide. At the end of the day, that is how she is: a pure, simple, naked, daring human being."

"I really like you, *mon cheri*. Sometimes, I just wish I could be that girl. And the mouth, instead of a lie detector, could be an approachable oracle. Instead of a threatening motivator to be an agent of the truth, it should be a companion, a helper in discerning what the truth is."

"You do not want to be that girl, Claudette. She is not free; she is tied to remain in stone for the rest of her life. You can create her, a work similar to her, inspired by her, even better than her. You are a creator, you are a sculptress, not a sculpture."

"But don't they say the truth sets us free? If that is the case, the naked girl can be free in the moment she completes her task, if she dares to proceed, if she has the truth within."

"The truth ... what is the truth? I believe we will spend our entire lives in this Earth searching for it. And honestly, that is what counts. The search. It is in the search for the truth that we grow, mature, advance, make our own happiness. A never-ending task. That is life. Maybe we are just designed to not know the absolute truth."

As Cecilia took a moment to process her own words, a small blue butterfly crossed their path, insisting on flying in circles around them.

"See the butterfly?" Cecilia asked. "Do you think it knows that the moon reflects the light from the sun?"

Claudette laughed. "Unless it attended the Madeleine mass this morning, I believe it does not even know there is a moon out there."

"Exactly! That is my point. What if we are just like butterflies, flying around, living in a universe infinitely greater and more complex than our poor, limited capabilities of comprehension?"

"Then we are stuck in just living."

"Just living? That is more than enough, isn't it?" Cecilia finally held Claudette by her shoulders, as though to shake away whatever gray cloud of melancholy could be fogging her friend's mind. "Why don't we go find a place to eat? All this talking is making me hungry, and you telling me that you want to be a statue is making me angry."

***

The following weeks were marked by an intense pursuit of medical knowledge for Cecilia, her daily hours spent between lectures and observations in the major hospitals of the French capital. From the intricate surgeries being performed, the long-detailed treatments of the vast array of diseases, to the magnificent lectures, she began to obtain a valuable training and additional knowledge she so much craved. The system of instruction, both theoretical and practical, was a remarkable illustration of that genius for organization which belonged to the French. Every moment was used wisely and appropriately, no time wasted. Other than medical literature, no other reading material—not even newspapers—was allowed in the classes or hospitals, avoiding any type of distractions. But at least once a day

Cecilia would think about Claudette, looking forward to the weekend when she could take a little break from her studies and the two of them could get together in a café or in one of the many Parisian plazas.

The invitation to visit Claudette's studio came about a month after their first meeting. They usually had pre-set arrangements of places and time to meet every Saturday or Sunday, depending on both schedules and personal disposition, so Cecilia was surprised on that Friday evening when she was called from her apartment to attend a courier boy downstairs. He brought a message from Claudette.

"Mon cheri, I am wrapped in work. Unfortunately, I will not be able to meet you tomorrow at the Le Closerie as I so eagerly anticipated. But please, accept my sincere apologies. Come to visit me at my studio on Sunday, at one o'clock. We will have tea, croissants, cheese, petit fours, and of course, champagne. I would like to discuss a proposal with you. Yours, Claudette."

Cecilia was immediately curious to know what was going on inside her friend's mind, but she took a deep breath, trying to conceal any sign of anxiety. Instead, she would continue to diligently transcribe her weekly notes to her organized portfolio. In addition, she would spend the next day writing a case report on a female patient she had fully examined few weeks ago. Diagnosed with a large uterine abscess, the patient underwent a difficult but successful procedure, under the care of a large health care team led by a skillful and accomplished surgeon.

On Sunday, the walk to Claudette's studio, located at the Quai Bourbon on the Ile St. Louis, was tranquil and delightful. The pastoral, serene scenery Cecilia encountered there, in the heart of an effervescent city, was something she did not expect. Several magnificent seventeenth-century mansions seemed to be abandoned to neglect or decay, which was a shame. Later on, she learned that those residences were often portioned as rentals for less affluent dwellers, Claudette's atelier being one of them.

Nestled on the ground floor, to the left of a large gate facing the water, the atelier had its windows opened to the soothing commotion coming from the Seine. Very few pedestrians could be seen here and there, and Cecilia thought that location was probably well chosen for an artist trying to work away from curious eyes. The smell of sweet apples, heaped on some barges floating down the river, filled the atmosphere.

When she knocked at the door, she was greeted by a cheerful Claudette, her hair disappearing under a scarf tied under her chin. "You find me at my best, at my work. Excuse the dust all over me," she said, planting a quick kiss on Cecilia's cheek. "I sculpt my marble myself and even when working with plaster, I usually have both hands fully engaged on it. I do not trust my work to the zeal of a *praticien.*"

"No need for apologies, my friend. Thank you for inviting me into your sacred place."

But nothing could have prepared Cecilia for what her eyes witnessed as soon as she stepped inside the studio. A monumental sculpture, greater than life size, portrayed a mythological scene of a Greek man beheading Medusa. The work was still in progress, but anyone could appreciate the early signs of beauty, complexity and attention to details devoted to that object that surely would become a masterpiece. In the center of the vast room, another work comprised three naked figures with swirling drapes. A young woman kneeling had just released the hand of the second figure, an older, standing man who was being drawn away by the embrace of a third person, an older woman.

"Destiny. This is what this group of three represents. An allegory of aging, a man leaving behind Youth, who is on her knees, begging him to turn around and stay. The man allows himself to be led away, progressing towards maturity and eventual death, represented by the old woman," Claudette disclosed. "It was commissioned by the French government four years ago, and I am working on having it cast in bronze after being exhibited this summer at the Saloon of the Société Nationale des Beaux-Arts."

Cecilia was speechless. Somehow, she'd always known she was in front of a brilliant woman, but this was the work of a genius. She turned around, perplexed, realizing that the place was filled with sculptures of variable sizes in scale, highly unusual and quite contemporary for those with a conservative taste. Eroticism and sensuality would be common adjectives, a denominator that could easily describe the theme of Claudette's imposing work. Now that could explain her challenges in surviving as an artist. Definitely, society was not prepared yet to receive and support a female artist with such an ambitious endeavor. Not even the French, as liberal as they were, in the turn of the twentieth century, were prepared for that.

"What do you think?" Claudette asked, noticing the expression on Cecilia's face.

"My goodness, Claudette. You need to have your imperious and grandiose work exhibited in a designated museum. I do not know what else to say other than this is all splendid."

Then she sharply turned her head, startled, as she heard a soft voice from another room. "Miss Claudette, are you still coming back to me?" Suddenly, a naked young woman, draped in a see-through white shawl, appeared seemingly out of nowhere. Cecilia immediately blushed, unable to hide the changes in her emotions.

"*Oui, certainement*, Sophie," Claudette replied. "This is Dr. Cecilia Grierson, my dearest friend."

Cecilia extended her hands to the young lady, who seemed to be completely oblivious to what was going on in the main room. The girl turned around and returned to wherever she came from, sensuously swaying her hips, revealing her fleshy, perfectly rounded rear.

"Sophie is one of my best, trustworthy models, Cecilia. Isn't she adorable?"

"Yes, of course." Cecilia chuckled. "As I told you on the first day we met, you truly have a phenomenally great taste," she added, hoping that would mask the hint of nervousness in her voice. Or could that be jealousy? She quickly dismissed the thought.

"I was wondering if you would be willing to teach and refine my skills in some aspects of human anatomy," Claudette said without hesitation. "Depending on your time and willingness, we could maybe even open part of the studio to the teachings of a very few, selected artists. Painters, primarily. As a skilled female physician and obstetrician, you are very knowledgeable and aware of the variety and diversity of the human shapes, and there wouldn't be better training for us, artists, than to learn the details of the human anatomy, male and female, from a qualified doctor. What do you think?"

Cecilia was overwhelmed with so many things happening in that brief interval of time. With no desire to disappoint her friend, she answered, "I have to check my schedule and my commitment with the university first. I can definitely help you, although I honestly doubt you need my help in terms of human anatomy. The little I have seen already has proven you are a genius."

"I need constructive criticism, from someone who is qualified, someone who has utterly no intention to bring me down because of my gender or ambitions. You seem to fit perfectly," Claudette said. "Here, you do not have to give me an answer right now. Let's go to the back room, if you don't mind; Sophie is waiting. You can watch our work in progress and give me any feedback as you wish. I don't think I will ever let anyone else see me at work, so consider yourself a privileged friend, *mon cheri*."

"Privileged I surely am," Cecilia added, laughing, trying to get a little bit more comfortable. "May I take a closer look at all the artwork you have here?"

"Yes, of course. But first, let me pour you a cup of tea. We will savor some treats as soon as I am done with Sophie."

Silently and diligently, Claudette returned to her work, kneading the clay and modeling the statue's right hand, which was gently placed above the figure's fully exposed right breast. The left hand covered her pubic region.

The light breeze that rushed through the open window brought a momentary shiver to the naked model, making her pink nipples pucker into hard points. Cecilia wondered if she should close the shutters, but she was not there to interfere with the luminosity and the quietness of that moment. Sophie's gaze was so quizzical and persistent, that Cecilia was struck by the view, as if the creator, creation and model had all become one.

"We must unfreeze the sculpture," Claudette finally said. "That is the greatest lesson I've learned from my former master."

"He has succeeded in teaching you well," Cecilia said. She was wondering if her former teacher could help launch Claudette's career, bringing it to the next level, when Claudette replied.

"He succeeded in being a success thanks to my expenses, abilities and affections. I guess that is the price of learning, sometimes. One gains something, one loses something. But I do not want to talk about that."

Cecilia could not agree with the last statement said, but she was in no position to contradict Claudette either. She wondered who the former master was and what stories linked both artists, but she should respect her friend's privacy. She could sense Claudette had her ups and downs, maybe even becoming a lonely, isolated figure in the artistic field. Cecilia hoped somehow she could find a way to take some of that burden away from her. But knowing so little of each other, in such a short period of time, was a brutal reality. Cecilia would have to be patient in acquiring the confidence of this woman, if she wanted to be helpful.

She observed all the details of Claudette's atelier. Despite modeling stands supporting various sculptures in progress, the working space was surprisingly neat. Large Persian-style rugs warmed the walls, providing backdrops for the models. Paintings and copperware added a decorative touch. The studio even had a small piano, which seemed to have been treated as an extra stand for finished smaller pieces. Several busts of men were lined up on shelves, and intriguingly, the majority of them seemed to be from the same man with a much older face. A passionate sculpture of a couple embracing each other in a sensual dance brought goosebumps to Cecilia's arms. The woman's head rested tenderly on the man's right shoulder, with their bodies fluidly merging into a single shape as the man had his head turned towards the woman's face, as if to kiss her. Like every single work of art in that room, the sculpture evoked a bittersweet melancholy.

In an hour or so, Sophie left without saying much, dressed in a light jacket and a long skirt. Claudette suddenly looked tired, but her good spirits still prevailed. "Let's pop a bottle of champagne and drink," she exclaimed. "Not only by bread shall we live, right?"

"Especially in Paris, I am assuming."

Claudette poured the bubbling golden liquid in their glasses and then swallowed all of hers in a few gulps. "Do you mind if I smoke?"

"Of course not."

Claudette lit her cigarette, offering one to Cecilia, who politely declined. "So, what do you think, about all this?" Claudette asked, spinning around, her arms wide open.

"I think your work deserves to be out there, among the other greatest sculptures of all time."

"Such as?"

"Michelangelo? Bernini? Donatello?"

"They are all Italians, for your information. You landed in the wrong country, my friend."

Cecilia laughed so hard she almost choked on her drink. "Forgive me my ignorance, I am not too familiar with famous sculptors. The Italian Renaissance was the only era that came into my mind. I remember now, someone once told me he was impressed to see the sculptures displayed in the Exposition Universelle of 1889, but I cannot recall the artist's name."

"It must be an artist with no importance, if you cannot remember the name," Claudette added, a certain tone of disdain in her voice.

"You have placed my work among the classics, but I honestly think I do not fall into that category."

"You are right. Your work is very touching, very contemporary. Completely suitable for the changes that the new century is bringing."

"Nevertheless, barely anyone has taken me seriously. Can you believe that 'La Valse,' the sculpture I made of the man and woman locked in an amorous embrace, was originally not acceptable for public display, due to the indecency of the naked figures?" Claudette mentioned the word indecency by gesturing quotation marks with her hands up in the air.

"I had to eventually drape the figures, simply because it is unacceptable for a woman to be given a public commission which includes a naked man. How ridiculous is that, when the Luxembourg Gardens display hundreds of naked statues to the public? Children play hopscotch under the breasts of the Nymph at the Tuileries Gardens, but that is perfectly allowed, simply because the artist who created it happened to be born with a dick in between his legs?" Claudette was visibly agitated now, angrily pouring herself the third glass of champagne.

Cecilia could feel the pain and frustration in her friend's soul. "I will come to help you with the anatomy review. And if we have any spare time left, we should look for alternative options to make your work stand out among the others."

"I refuse to dress up as a man and change my name, as the writer George Sand once did. At least she was original in doing that, lucky her. I would be just a plagiarist, destined to drown in a world filled with dogmatism and small-mindedness."

"Of course, we have to stick to what we believe, Claudette, including your own identity. There must be a way, as you are willing to stay firm in your right of equality. It might be just a matter of time before we have a breakthrough. All great progress and advancement are preceded by chaos, intolerance, thunderstorms."

"I am just tired of all this. I have been spending my entire life, fighting, seeing no results, whatsoever. It is just so discouraging when I depend on this for living. Without my art, I might as well be dead. Can you live without practicing medicine?" she bluntly questioned.

Feeling so impotent, Cecilia rushed over and simply held Claudette in her arms. Tears were rolling from her friend's eyes. "I will see if there is any way I can help you, Claudette. I will take you to Buenos Aires with me, if I have to, in two months."

"Buenos Aires? What am I going to do in Buenos Aires? I cannot speak a word in Spanish, and if Buenos Aires so much follows the footsteps of Paris, do you really think they will accept me there? Sculpting is a very expensive art and without receiving many official commissions, it will be impossible to survive. In addition, if one cannot succeed as an artist in Paris, one is simply doomed to remain in a life filled with struggles and disappointments."

"You can teach here," Cecilia replied. "The knowledge that you have can be taught, as you said, to painters and other sculptors. That should at least take some of the financial weight off your plate. Meanwhile we can look for opportunities. Maybe London or Berlin. Even Italy. You are fluent in English, and that alone will suffice in the beginning." Cecilia wasn't sure of what exactly she was saying, but she just needed to inject any boost of hope and confidence in her friend.

So, after that Sunday, she made a commitment to visit Claudette's studio every weekend, reviewing basic concepts of anatomy of people of different ages. She grew used to the presence of naked models, men and women, walking unashamedly around the place.

Cecilia had a firm impression that her presence lifted Claudette's spirits, and although that was a temporary solution, since Cecilia would not be around for so long, she could only take and live one day at time. She was confident the exhibition of the "Destiny," in a few months, would receive the approval of the city, the public and the artists in general, since the dynamic composition simply represented a thought-provoking symbolic work about human relationship. The figures were not completely nude, but swathed in floating draperies, which accentuated the speed of the movement and took the edge off any sexual connection. All those factors should work in Claudette's favor, or so Cecilia thought and prayed for.

***

The next two months flew by, and despite her constant work, studies and teachings, Cecilia showed a renewed strength and joy in her activities. While visiting various facilities, she was especially interested in the National Institute for the Young Blind, where Louis Braille, a blind Frenchman, had attended school and taught in the early half of the century. She observed the system he had invented, consisting of a methodic combination of raised dots that could be read with the fingers, which had opened the doors of intellectual communication between the visually impaired and their fellow human beings. Cecilia was amazed at how a blind child could learn to write and read in Braille as quickly as a child with vision exposed to the common alphabet. She collected thorough notes about how the teachers not only used the Braille system to educate their pupils, but they also counted on the use of tactile and auditory senses. Toys, dolls and animals in their proportional sizes and shapes were used, along with maps in high relief. Many of the children showed great skills in manual crafting and music, which was always present.

Tirelessly, Cecilia explored the streets of Paris, walking to the four cardinal points of the city, always learning something from the sick, the blind, the deaf, the rich and the poor, even from the ones whose souls were tormented by their own demons and past history. Wherever she went, she always left a word of encouragement, a smile of gratitude, a pinch of hope that better days were ahead. She started to believe that with the great challenges she daily faced, it was her responsibility to motivate the lives of those she met along the way. If she could not change the situation, she could at least be there for them. For a hug, a smile, a comforting tap on their shoulders. Sometimes, the best remedies in life are hidden in the simplest things that are completely free to be given.

Her last week in the City of Light was marked by the nostalgic feeling that precedes any circumstances surrounded by separation and transformation. She would forever miss the short walk to the library, the clinical discussions with Dr. Pinard and Professor Bertoldini. Her escapes to the Louvre and to the Luxembourg Gardens. The green linden trees alongside the Seine. But she should be able to survive, missing all that. What she could not imagine was how her life would continue to be without Claudette nearby. She'd grown so used to that peculiar companionship, it was as if Claudette had become her sister, someone who inspired her to be a better person. Someone she would love and carry forever in her heart.

As Cecilia's original plan was to head to Switzerland before returning to Buenos Aires, she was tempted to cancel the trip to the Alps region, just to stay a few more weeks with Claudette. But as the approaching day for the art exhibition grew closer, Claudette became even more adamant in her reclusion, refusing to leave her studio, insisting that Cecilia should not change her plans. Claudette made it clear she would not bring Cecilia into her world of confusion and insecurities. Cecilia should proceed with her trip, and if destiny allowed, they would meet again, in a much more stable circumstance.

Cecilia spent the last night in Paris at Claudette's studio. To her surprise, her friend set up a beautiful dinner table. Colorful tulips were placed in vases and scented candles were scattered among the sculptures and on top of the shelves.

"I want this moment to stay forever in our minds, Cecilia."

Cecilia controlled herself, with difficulty, to avoid crying. Claudette, as always, witty, playful, with her great sense of humor, drank her sparkling wine, biting her scarlet lower lip.

"*Mon cheri*, I want you to live the best life out there, for me. I want you to kick the rear ends of those who may dare to come to block your way to greatness. And I want you to return to Buenos Aires and start teaching the beautiful anatomy of our bodies to the members of the Accademia. You must be part of the Accademia, or create one if they don't have one!"

"It will not be the same without you there—"

"I thought you would carry me with you, wherever you go, *mon cheri*."

They spent most of the night talking, drinking, laughing. Cecilia opened her heart about Jacques Copplet. Claudette, on the other hand, talked about the long affair she had with her former master. They shed tears when Claudette mentioned she suffered an abortion, years ago. They laughed, cursing the men, the lovers who brought affection, desire and pain into their lives. Claudette talked about Lady Macbeth and Richard III, her favorite heroine and hero in fiction. Cecilia talked about her favorite music, tango. They slept in the only available bed, with their petticoats on, holding each other in their arms, playing with each other's hair.

Cecilia noticed that Claudette discussed intimate details of her life without ever revealing the name of her former master, her lover. Maybe that was not that important, after all. Sometimes the story was more important than the characters.

In the early morning, Claudette woke Cecilia with a furtive kiss on her lips. Cecilia immediately sat straight up, startled, with a splitting headache afflicting her.

"Do not you worry, *mon cheri*. I will not bite again," Claudette laughed, jumping from the bed. "We need to get you ready; your train won't be waiting for you if we remain in bed. I will brew us some coffee while you get dressed."

Cecilia felt nauseated, unsure if it was the champagne from the night before, the distress of leaving Paris, the flamboyant attitude of Claudette, or the combination of all that. Her mood was down, but she made an extra effort to conceal it.

They did not talk much on their way to Gare du Lyon, where Cecilia boarded her train to Genève. At the station, they walked arm in arm, carrying on a frivolous conversation about the weather and the summer season that was approaching. They held each other as long as they could until the last train whistle blew.

"Promise me, Claudette, you will be fine, no matter what. And that we will keep in touch by letters," Cecilia finally said, apprehensively.

"Of course, I will be fine. But I do not promise anything. They say there are three things a person should never break: promises, trust and someone's heart. Nevertheless, I have seen those exactly three things being broken over and over, all the time. So, forget the promises."

Once again, Claudette made a good point and Cecilia could not find a way to immediately reply. Indeed, promises seemed like those evanescent ripples which disturb the water surface momentarily and then disappear without trace, leaving no effect. Promises do not necessarily last; they are mere words spoken to the wind, and words are like skeletons—pale frameworks made of rigid pieces of bone. In a way, she knew Claudette was more interested in the picture conjured by the powers of imagination, like living flesh, elastic muscle, circulating red blood, warm hands.

Claudette finally reached out to Cecilia, giving her a long-lasting hug. "We will see each other again, *mon cheri*. In this life, or if I make it to the next one. If there is a next one, of course." She gave a sardonic laugh, walking away without turning back, leaving behind her exclusive, indelible mark: her seductive, intense and fierce personality.

Chapter 10

"We need women who are so strong
they can be gentle, so educated they can be humble,
so fierce they can be compassionate,
so passionate they can be rational,
and so disciplined they can be free."
(Kavita Ramidas)

Buenos Aires, Winter, 1902

Cecilia abruptly decided to take a break from corresponding with Lorenzo. She could clearly see she was heading to a familiar territory of an emotional affair, the same exact path she walked twenty-five years ago. If, that time, she'd had the excuse she did not know any better—that she did not know the person she was getting involved with—this time, she would not have the same justification. She was extremely glad she had the opportunity to be in contact with Lorenzo again, through the letters they shared in the last few months. She felt very flattered, with a boost of confidence, because Lorenzo still demonstrated such an urgent interest, attention and care towards her. That should be more than enough to make her happy. Or at least that was what she tried to convince herself. In addition, there were too many things she needed to accomplish in that second semester, so it was imperative to be focused and to use her time very wisely. She would simply continue to work on achieving inner peace and happiness.

She was determined to conclude her first non-medical book, entitled *The Technical Education of the Woman*, a report to be presented to the Minister of the Public Education. In it, she described in detail the organization of several technical schools in Europe specifically designed for the training of women in areas that did not require attendance in a college. Cecilia strongly believed that the well-being of mankind in the present, as well as the fate of the human race in the future, depended more on education than on anything else, including technological advancements.

She also believed that women were the soul of society, the first ones responsible for the family's education and growth. Therefore, by offering classes in domestic economy, moral and civic education, nutrition and cooking, child care and hygiene, sewing and embroidering, art, crafts and music, technical schools should have the ultimate goal to elevate the level of instruction for women in general. This would lead to practical results, boosting independence, financial development and family support for the local communities. As much as Cecilia desired that the majority of women could have at least access to a superior formal education, as she had, the reality was that a balance between college and technical careers was essential, including domestic affairs.

Undoubtedly, a lot of women knew the basics of domestic work. But for Cecilia and other leaders in education who were embracing this cause, the science behind those tasks should go much further. Women needed to know not only how to cook a stew, but must learn how to plan nutritional meals, the costs involved in the preparation, alternative options, the seasonal ingredients available, proper management of time and hygiene, and how to efficiently and safely perform those functions, just as an example. Everywhere around the world, for centuries, domestic affairs were easily transferred from mothers to daughters at the core of their homes. But in the last half of the nineteenth century, the daily struggles to live had changed. Social and economic demands required women to enter the workforce, and as result, young girls who could not or did not aspire to follow a university career needed access to some type of technical education enabling them to live with honor and dignity.

In Argentina, according to their social position, women were allowed to do different types of work. In the countryside, the native and half-Indian women, living in huts, prepared the foods and took care of the children. Though living in scanty conditions, they kept themselves clean and were proud to adorn themselves with the most elaborate handwork and native lace. The hand-weaving of goat, llama and sheep wool, dyed with colors taken from plants, required time, patience and skill.

In the cities, women primarily worked in their households, washing, preparing meals and taking care of the children. In addition, the products of their home dairy, bakery, confectionery, weaving or embroidery were not only used by the family but often sold privately to neighbors, or at stations and small stores.

Spanish descendants usually preferred any work they could do hidden at home, as there still existed in all social classes that false pride in which they considered outside work a degradation. Unfortunately, many preferred to suffer poverty at home or receive charity, than to learn a decent occupation or to be allowed to help the men of their families in other jobs. Cecilia always had found that totally inacceptable. She had no problem with those who chose toilsome work such as common sewing, embroidery, and even washing and ironing, which was done to high perfection and appreciated by all classes of people. But the truth was that those women received very little profit, due to the competition. Cecilia strongly believed these same women could gain an easier livelihood by developing artistic features incorporated in making quality items such as dresses, corsets, gloves, bonnets, and even hair styles, for example. There was great demand for these and very good pay for work that was stylish and fashionable. This could bring those local women to the same level of talented foreigners, such as the French seamstresses and hairdressers.

As modern society was preferring the new factory type of work, it was becoming difficult to find people, especially women, with quality technical preparation in their duties as cooks, chambermaids, waitresses, to list a few. This was a major reason why the educational system should provide means to fill that void.

Taking into account individual talents, the country was also open to women who were inclined to teach, write or devote themselves to art or music. Special schools for arts and music started to flourish in Buenos Aires, in which one-third of the students were girls. They followed a course of three or four years in drawing, painting or sculpture, to perfect themselves or use their knowledge in private teaching, in schools or small academies. Music was always cultivated to a high degree, and no one ever played or sang in public except those who possessed a high level of perfection. Music conservatories with outstanding teachers already existed in the capital and produced several notable songstresses and women devoted to drama and other theatrical pursuits.

In addition, women were being seen as novelists or educational writers and were able to find papers or reviews that would publish their work with pleasure. Women were beginning to succeed in editing and publishing a great many reviews, not only in Buenos Aires but in the provinces as well, that dealt with fashionable, religious, literary and educational subjects.

Scientific studies published by women might have been the only limitation, since these had been taken up by females only in the last decade, after the commencement of co-education on equal terms with the men in their studies. The main obstacle up to the present for women in science had been in getting professorships in the faculties, in the direction or management of hospitals, laboratories and high posts on the boards, for example, where men were usually appointed by political influence and through the government. But Cecilia thought a break in these antiquated routines would soon be witnessed, and without doubt, they were heading in the right direction. A female technical inspector had been named and she was already working with great acclaim for the Board of Education. Although that maybe was a small step, it was considered a great victory.

But if Cecilia's career and social work were progressing well in that season, her emotional health was soon to experience a roller-coaster ride. As quiet and smooth as the evenings and nights had been lately, the tranquil moments were suddenly interrupted by another correspondence from Lorenzo. This time, the letter seemed to be totally disconnected from the last one. Once again, no headings, no name cited, which she quickly concluded would be the new norm.

You must know I still have everything you wrote to me when we were students. From the notes you gave me when I missed a few classes, to the book you got for my birthday, where you wished me all the happiness and success in life.

What I most adored in you? It was the fact that you loved me so explicitly and you could not find a simple way to disguise it. That actually touched my heart, I will not deny it.

For that reason, I even wrote on the header of one of your notebooks, 'If you didn't exist, I would create one.' Remember that?

And the Christmas card, of course ... Up to now, I read your Christmas card every Holiday season.

Now tell me, what do you miss the most about me? The irresistible scent of my cologne, or the penetrating depth of my gaze?

"The raging fire which urged us on was scorching us;
It would have burned us had we tried to restrain it."
(Giacomo Casanova)
L.B.

Once again, Cecilia was stunned by Lorenzo's attitude and behavior. A heat wave traveled through her entire body making her uneasy. *Did I love him so explicitly?* she asked herself, shocked, her hands trembling. She suddenly felt confused and upset. He knew how to rile her, to work on her feelings. It seemed he had the extraordinary ability to push the right buttons.

To learn that Lorenzo had saved the few little things that she gave him when they were young was almost unbelievable. To be so remembered, it seemed almost surreal. Even she had forgotten all those details, but now that he had brought them up, she remembered each occasion with vivid clarity; he was not making things up. Oh, and the Christmastime card. Everything started with that card, and she did not have the faintest idea why it was so special. She remembered she always sent Christmas greetings to her closest friends. Amalia received one card. Lorenzo received another one, that year. What was so touching in that, triggering a sequence of events that would forever mark her life, up to now? She tried so hard to remember those very small details, but her mind refused to bring her a single answer.

That evening, she did not work on her book, nor practice on her piano. Instead, she reached for her keepsake box stored in the back of her armoire. She paged through several diaries, reading and re-reading several passages where she wrote great details of her life in the year 1878, when she met Lorenzo. She could remember every nuance of that day, and experience again all the emotions of that remarkable December. Except for what she could possibly have written on his holiday card.

Chapter 11

"Yet each man kills the thing he loves
By each let this be heard,
Some do it with a bitter look,
Some with a flattering word,
The coward does it with a kiss,
The brave man with a sword."
(Oscar Wilde)

Buenos Aires, Summer, December 1878

Cecilia was totally taken by surprise on that early Saturday, after returning from the local market with some flour and powdered sugar, the missing ingredients of the *alfajores* she was planning to bake that weekend. Upon her rushed entrance through the kitchen's door, Dona Maria Eugenia handed her a small note.

"A courier just dropped this for you. He stated it is an important message from a friend of yours, Mr. Lorenzo Bianchi."

"An important message, for me? From ... Lorenzo?" Cecilia raised her eyebrows, but she did not hesitate to read the message in front of Dona Maria Eugenia. Although they never confided their intimate secrets to each other, they never really tried to hide anything from one another either.

Cecilia giggled. "It is nothing major. Apparently, my friend from Latin classes received one of my holiday greeting cards and he seems to be profoundly touched by such a kind gesture. He is requesting my presence at his house, today, at three o'clock, for an afternoon of tea. He will be sending his driver and a carriage to pick me up."

"And who does he think he is, to demand you to be at his house, being picked up by his driver, *señorita*?" Dona Maria Eugenia asked, turning her back to Cecilia, drying the dishes that were cleaned and stacked at the sink.

"He is ... my friend, as I said. He is also a senior law student at the university and he comes from a prestigious family of businessmen, lawyers, military men and even a few politicians," Cecilia nervously replied, trying to give an explanation about the unexpected invitation she had just received.

"And that justifies everything, is that right?"

"I do not understand your inquiries, *abuela*. All I know is that he is a friend from my class. I sent few Christmas cards two weeks ago to Mama and the families in Entre los Rios, to Amalia, Lorenzo and my cousins. I believe he is just being kind and extremely polite with such a reply."

"Your eyes betray your thoughts, *cara niña*. But you are already eighteen years old, mature and smart enough to know what you are doing and where you are heading. Just be careful. Guard your beautiful heart, for everything you do flows from it."

Cecilia sighed, and walking towards Dona Maria Eugenia, planted a light kiss on her rosy, plump cheeks. "Let me finish the dishes, *abuela*, so we can start the *alfajores*. I might even box a few of those treats and take some with me this afternoon. It is not polite to go to a family's house empty-handed."

They worked quietly for a while, then Cecilia added, "I was just thinking ...I can ask the driver to stop at Amalia's house, since it is on the way, if that makes you less nervous. I will invite her to come with me. I will also spend the night at her house, so you do not have to worry about me."

"It seems you have everything well planned out," Dona Maria Eugenia grumbled.

"It is just a summer afternoon with a friend and tea, *abuela*." For some reason and to her slight embarrassment, Cecilia thought there could be more than just that ahead of her. Unexplainably, she felt lighthearted and jolly, hardly able to contain her excitement during the rest of that day.

After lunch, she washed rapidly and went to her wardrobe to choose an outfit, wishing he had given her more time to possibly buy something appropriate to wear. She had only one Victorian tea-gown that was given to her as a birthday gift when she turned fifteen. She hoped it still fit. The bodice of peach silk fabric and white cotton had a rich collar of Venice lace that framed her décolletage without revealing the cleavage, and its three-quarter sleeves were gathered into wide flared cuffs, edged with more lace. The matching skirt, although a little tight now around her waist, was still flattering, with a deep ruffled flounce at the hemline. She chose a pair of porcelain Limoges earrings, white crocheted wrist-length gloves, and ivory boots. An off-white Battenburg lace fan would prove to be appropriate, not only to cool her down, but also to provide her comfort, something to hold onto, in case she needed to make a statement or disguise any nervousness. *But why would I be nervous?* she wondered. Then came the sound of the knock on her door.

"There is a gentleman at the entrance with a horse-drawn carriage, asking for you, *señorita* Cecilia Grierson," Dona Maria Eugenia approached her, fixing a strand of hair that seemed to be out of place. "You are glowing more than ever. Enjoy your afternoon, my child."

"Thank you, *abuela*."

"Don't forget the box of *alfajores*," Dona Maria Eugenia added, handing her a neat box filled with the warm, sweet treats.

Cecilia was greeted by a serious, tall, gray-haired driver in a black suit, who bowed to her immediately. "Good afternoon, Miss Grierson. I am Alfonso Cortez, the coachman for the Bianchi family. Mr. Lorenzo is waiting for you at the house."

Cecilia sensed that Dona Maria Eugenia was going to say or ask something, but before her beloved governess had a chance to say a word, Cecilia rushed to hug her and whispered, "I will spend the rest of the evening with Amalia. Please, do not worry. I will see you tomorrow morning, *abuela*."

She asked the coachman to stop at her friend's house, handing him a piece of paper with Amalia's address. Without saying a word, Alfonso Cortez simply nodded a yes, opening the door of the carriage for her to take a seat.

Cecilia did not stay long at Amalia's house, as things did not go as well as she had planned.

"Are you out of your mind? What am I supposed to do at Lorenzo's house?" Amalia asked in a tone of surprise as soon as she heard Cecilia's proposal. "Is not this the special friend you so much brag about, from your Latin class? The man that insists on sitting by your side every single class and teases you constantly? Oh, yes, that is him. Sorry, but I refuse to be a third wheel in your afternoon meeting, my dear."

"Amalia, please, stop the nonsense. It is just an invitation for some tea, for God's sake. In addition, I am sure his family will be there too. I have highly talked about you to him before, so I am positive he will be pleased to finally meet you personally. After all, he seems to be the type of man who is always delighted to be surrounded by women. Plus, Dona Maria Eugenia was not so happy that I am going by myself, so I told her you would come with me, and we would spend the night together at your house. This way she does not worry."

"She does not have to worry. I will be your best alibi. If I were you, I would not waste any more time here. Lorenzo is waiting for you. Do not let him wait for so long, nor disappoint him by bringing a crowd. Enjoy the time there, then come back here and tell me everything. Everything. I will let my parents know that you are sleeping here tonight, but we do not know the exact time you will show up. Knock three times on my window, and I will open the main door to you. Now go. Rush, rush!"

At that point, Cecilia knew she would not be able to persuade Amalia to accompany her, so she left, not before giving her a tight hug. She was thankful that she could return to spend the rest of the night with her best friend. "I will see you later, my dear."

The coachman soon took the northern pathway, heading towards the new affluent area of the city, which had started to become more populated by the wealthy families, especially after the deadly outbreaks of cholera and yellow fever of the early 1870s. The height of the terrain seemed to reduce the presence of insects which transmitted the diseases, allowing the members of the high-class elite to build mansions in several European architectural styles in this part of the town.

The journey was pleasant, despite the roughness of the cobblestone roads. A light warm breeze stroked Cecilia's face while the sun seemed to be playing hide-and-seek among a few dense clouds. The picturesque residential neighborhood slowly started to appear in front of her eyes, surrounded by green spaces enhanced with majestic *gomeros,* or rubber trees.

The carriage came to a stop on the gravel outside an elegant neo-Italian Renaissance mansion with a stone façade and high arched windows. After assisting Cecilia to alight, the coachman left, taking the vehicle away to the back of the building. Cecilia stepped to the massive, red cherry wooden front doors, contemplating the intimidating pair of golden lion door knockers. She found herself smiling as she held the cold metal ring. The door was opened at the third knock. An intoxicating scent of citrus blended with a touch of cardamom and sandalwood hit her, while an impeccable Lorenzo, dressed in a black suit, ivory shirt and royal blue silk tie, stood still at the portico. He smiled with a devastating charm.

"Three o'clock, sharp," he said. "Mr. Cortez never disappoints me." Lorenzo's first words struck Cecilia. "You look adorable," he added, extending his hand to take hers, bowing and planting a light kiss on her knuckles. She swallowed dryly, praying he would not notice how shaky she was.

"It is good to see you, after such an unexpected, last-minute invitation, Lorenzo," she finally said.

"Your beautiful, unexpected correspondence forced me to act that way," he immediately replied.

It was just a holiday greeting card, she thought. But these words did not come out of her mouth. Instead, she offered him the box of cookies. "Those are for you. *Alfajores*. Dona Maria Eugenia and I baked them this morning. I hope you like them."

"I like everything that comes from you. Although I am still waiting for the chocolate cake you have promised me."

"I do not recall ever promising you anything, much less a chocolate cake. I do not know where this idea came from."

"All I know is that you still owe me a chocolate cake," he replied, laughing.

As he locked the doors behind him, Cecilia gazed in awe at the opulence and refinement of the residence. The foyer's white walls were framed by beautifully carved wooden doors, wainscot and columns. A huge frosted glass panel, whose borders were stained in light blue, purple and earth tones, filtered the light coming from a chandelier behind it, bringing a rainbow to the hallway. At the bottom of the glass panel, winged mythological female figures faced the two entrances to the adjacent room, while a vase of lilies sat on a pedestal in front of it.

Glancing above a door to the right, Cecilia saw a mural of a Roman woman covered in a see-through shawl, displaying a mischievous smile, looking down to those below with a mixed air of curiosity and warning. Above a door to the left, there was a large oil painting of an athletic, bearded man, possibly a Roman warrior, wrapped only with a crimson cloth around his waist and in between his well-defined, muscular legs. He leaned toward a dark stone, and as he held a harp half his size to his side, his intriguing, almost angry face looked away from the instrument and from anyone entering the house. No doubt it was a stunning painting. Stunning and appealing; it was actually the first time Cecilia had the opportunity to admire the body of a semi-nude man. The thought made her blush.

"Do you like the painting?" Lorenzo's suddenly warm voice behind her ear made her catch her breath. She did not dare to say a word, much less turn her face towards him. Instead, she continued to stare at the painting, grasping firmly the fan she held in her hands.

"My father brought it from Italy on his last trip to Europe," Lorenzo explained. "My mother, a much more conservative woman, thought it was too extravagant for the main entrance, but my father simply said the house that she participated so much in creating and constructing is an extravagance in itself, so what would one single painting really add to it, right?"

Cecilia nervously chuckled, still overwhelmed by the scent of Lorenzo's cologne, his proximity, the sensual paintings on the wall, the quietness of the house. Her heart was beating so fast, for a moment she felt lightheaded, as if she might faint. She took a deep breath, trying to calm down and to look relaxed. Before she was able to say anything, Lorenzo gently touched her shoulders, moving behind her, guiding her to the living room. "Let me show you the house," he said.

The main living room was luxurious but welcoming. Velvet crimson armchairs and recliners were placed against the corners. The wooden fireplace was a work of art by itself, with Corinthian columns on each side supporting its mantel. Above it, marble sculptures of Roman emperors; on the wall, an impressive oil painting, a portrait of an aristocratic gentleman, in a gilded, elaborate frame. "My grandfather, when he was the Navy deputy secretary, years ago," Lorenzo explained. "The painting on his right, that is my father. And on the left, my mother." Cecilia could recognize the familiar trace of Lorenzo's face on his father's portrait, and even that of his grandfather. They shared the same intense, penetrating gaze, the thick, black, gently wavy hair, parted to the left. His mother seemed to be younger, an austere Italian woman with a puritanical look.

"I have no words to describe your home. It looks like a magnificent palace."

"Thank you. My parents worked very hard and diligently to build this house. It makes me deeply sad that they now have decided to move."

"What do you mean, they have decided to move? They are no longer living here?" Cecilia asked, surprised, realizing that might be the reason why the house seemed oddly quiet.

"I thought I had mentioned to you last month or so that they are moving to Mar del Plata soon. My father's business is exponentially growing in the south, and my mother has finally convinced him that they will be better off relocating."

The thought that Lorenzo could easily leave Buenos Aires to follow his parents was most likely stamped on her face, when she looked at him with eyes wide. As if he could read her mind, he turned to her and smiled back, showing a set of perfectly aligned white teeth. "But you do not need to worry. I will stay around for a while. I still have to finish my studies and I might follow up with a post-graduation career, so I don't think I will go anywhere, anytime soon."

"I am not worried about anything," she immediately replied, ashamed she was lying. "I was just wondering if you will be living in this huge mansion by yourself. Is it just you in the house right now?"

"This weekend it is just me, Alfonso Cortez and his wife, Antonieta, who is our cook. They have their own place in the back of the yard. My parents and the rest of the staff are in Mar del Plata, preparing the house they bought, before they move the furniture and their personal belongings. They will be back in a week, but they plan to be living in the new residence by the end of the summer. Meanwhile, I will be moving to an apartment near the College of Law. That will suffice my needs for lodging for the next two years, at least."

"How about this beautiful, brand-new place?"

"The vice-president has demonstrated an increasingly interest in renting it. They are still negotiating the logistics of it, but we are confident we will find the proper, suitable tenant soon."

"I am positive you will." Cecilia walked toward the imposing piano that stood adjacent to the curved stairway. "It is a beautiful Parlor Grand Steinway," she said, recognizing the impressive instrument even before opening its ebony lid, where its brand was displayed in white, contrasting letters. "Do you play, too?"

"Yes, I do play, too." He purposely emphasized the word "too." "Assuming now you can play it, I challenge you to share the seat with me soon, for a duet."

"Challenge accepted," Cecilia replied, slightly surprised at her quick answer and her own regained confidence.

"But first, I want to show you my parents' library and their numismatic collection. Then we must sit down in the dining room. Antonieta has set up a beautiful spread for us. The music will come after that, if you don't mind."

"I will follow your plan with pleasure," Cecilia replied, full of contentment to hear him saying the word "us."

The library had a vast collection of books and few marble ornaments, including the bust of Dante Alighieri, neatly displayed in a wooden bookcase which covered one entire wall, from the floor to the ceiling. A sliding oak ladder allowed Lorenzo to quickly reach one of the top shelves, where he grabbed a leather-bound book. He opened the volume carefully and gently paged through it, knowing exactly where to find the information he needed.

"One of my favorites. Shakespeare. Sonnet 18: 'Shall I compare thee to a summer's day? Thou art more lovely and more temperate. Rough winds do shake the darling buds of May, and summer's lease hath all too short a date. Sometime too hot the eye of heaven shines, and often is his gold complexion dimmed; and every fair from fair sometime declines, by chance or nature's changing course untrimmed. But thy eternal summer shall not fade nor lose possession of that fair thou ow'st, Nor shall Death brag thou wand'rest in his shade, When in eternal lines to time thou grow'st. So long as men can breathe or eyes can see, So long lives this, and this gives life to thee.'"

Lorenzo's eyes met Cecilia's, freezing her. "The poet is saying your eternal beauty will not fade, nor lose its quality, and you will never die, as you will live in my enduring poetry."

For a fraction of second that seemed to be an eternity, a thick silence remained between them, although she could hear her heart racing again. Suddenly, he snapped the book, closing it with a loud noise that startled Cecilia. He laughed, delighted. "Classic literature. It never fails." He left the book on top of the office table, changing subjects. "Follow me. Let me show you some of my father's coin collection."

There were several drawers filled with coin display boxes. "My grandfather was a generalist coin fanatic. He accumulated a broad variety of historical and geographically significant coins from Italy, France, Argentina and Chile, resulting in this vast collection that has been passed to my father, and eventually will come to me. The hobby has been slowly growing on me, although I haven't dedicated too much time to look for specific coins to buy or trade. Maybe now that I am done with the Latin classes, I will find some free time to play with it."

"I feel I am inside a king's palace, here. Everything is so impressive, so valuable. I could live inside this room with all those books, if this was my home."

"Oh... wait until you see the dining room. You might change your mind regarding the best place in this house to live in. My bedroom is pretty tempting too," he added without hesitation.

"Do you think so? As a rule of thumb, I am the type of person that barely ever changes their opinion."

"And I am the type of person expert in bending rules," Lorenzo said with a dazzling smile, his eyes again fixed on her with fierce ardor. "Cover your eyes with both of your hands. Do not cheat. I will walk you to the next room. Give me this. You don't need it." He took Cecilia's fan from her hands, tossing it on the nearest armchair.

She closed her eyes and covered them with both hands, giggling, her typical sign of mixed nervousness and happiness. He gently held her by the shoulders again, but this time, she could feel his body much closer to her. She could feel the warmth of his breath near her ears, and for a moment she felt tempted to sway away from him, scared of what would come next.

"Are you ready to walk?" he whispered.

Cecilia nodded a yes, and he carefully steered her, the sound of their footsteps on the hardwood floor echoing throughout the vast house. When they came to a halt, he let go of her shoulders. "You can open your eyes now."

They were in front of the most elegant dining room she had ever seen. Not only the walls, but even the ceiling was covered in carved wood panels. A massive gold leaf mirror above the fireplace mantel reflected the light of a magnificent twelve-armed chandelier. To the right and the left of the mirror, two shelves displayed white fine china and decorative silver plates.

The rectangular dining table, for ten people, was covered with white Richelieu embroidery cutwork lace. A large crystal vase in the center held fresh red roses, and porcelain plates, teacups, crystal glasses and silver cutlery were neatly set. Silver trays were filled with bread, biscuits, cheese, cold cuts, figs, grapes and slices of oranges. Adjacent to the end of the table, a silver cart held silver teapots, coffee pots, and kettles. The aqua-colored brocade upholstery of the chairs, with tints of cyan and turquoise, seemed to be the perfect match for a royal place.

"Lorenzo!" Cecilia exclaimed, astounded. "This is incredibly beautiful."

"Have a seat," he said, pulling out a chair for her. "We have water, English tea, milk, coffee ... but I can trade all that for a jar of sangria, if you would join me in that."

She laughed. "Sangria? Are you going to make one? At three something in the afternoon?"

"I can make the best sangria in the world, at any time."

"I need to see that," she teased him.

"Then follow me to the kitchen. You can help me dice some fruits while I find a good Spanish red wine in the cellar."

As Cecilia waited for him in the kitchen, she sighed in gratitude for that afternoon, realizing she was getting much more comfortable now. This was like a dream, like the countless stories she read and heard when she was a child, where a prince meets a plebeian, but their feelings toward one another are greater than any social disparities, greater than any possible obstacle.

Lorenzo returned briefly with a bottle of wine from Rioja, and like a precise alchemist, he mixed the beverage with water, rum, squeezed oranges and limes, sugar, diced apples, spices, and cinnamon sticks.

"Did you know that people have been drinking this since before the Middle Ages? When water was often contaminated, wine was the beverage of choice, since the alcohol killed all the bacteria. For this reason, everyone from children to elderly drank wine, and they often added fruits to give the beverage an extra kick," he explained.

"I thought it was a punch that originated in Spain," Cecilia added, trying to remember anything about the subject, at the same time wanting to hide the fact that she had never before tasted any alcoholic drink.

"Indeed, the name comes from *sangre*, which means red blood in Spanish. Would you pass me the long wooden spoon, please?"

She watched him carefully mixing the drink, the fruits spinning in the beautiful red swirl. "It smells delicious," she said.

"It tastes even better. Now we can return to the dining table and enjoy the drink." He raised his wine glass, clinking it against hers.

They sat near each other in the dining room, sipping and nibbling, savoring the fruits, cheese and snacks. Maybe it was the sangria, maybe it was the way Lorenzo was so comfortable, but Cecilia suddenly felt more laid-back. She laughed when he told her jokes; she listened, fascinated, to every single word of his stories, his voice full of joy. They talked about everything; their connection felt so intense, so right. From time to time he would pass his fingers through his hair, staring at her with a half-smile. She was feeling warm and flushed. She bit her lower lip, eventually looking away. But to her surprise, when she faced him again, his eyes were still fixed on her. At that moment, she knew she loved him more than ever.

"It is getting hot in here," he finally said, taking off his jacket and tie, loosening the collar of his shirt, after unbuttoning a few studs. He poured more sangria into their half-emptied glasses and carried them to the living room, signaling with his head to her to follow him. "Are you still up for the musical challenge?" he asked, placing their drinks on a side table, near one of the recliners.

"I am always ready for a musical challenge," she replied. "What shall we play?" she asked while reaching for the music book.

"How about Vivaldi? Is that too much for you?"

"I grew up with Vivaldi. One of my favorites."

"Excellent. We can try 'La Primavera, Le Quattro Stagioni.'"

"'The Spring, from the Four Seasons,'" she said. "One of the best-known works of Antonio Vivaldi."

"Correct."

"May I try my part first, before we play it together?"

"Be my guest."

Cecilia took her seat at the edge of the bench, straightening her back, her arms relaxed in front of her, her long curved fingers gently caressing the keyboard. When she finally started pressing the keys, the silence was broken by the sweet melody that filled the room, like the soft chirping of birds in a spring day. She lifted her head once or twice and glanced at Lorenzo, who sat completely relaxed in one of the armchairs, head leaning back against the wall, legs straight and crossed at the ankles, his drink in his hand. She was glad his eyes this time were closed. Even from that distance, she noticed he was smiling. And that made her heart skip a beat.

"I believe you are more than ready now," he complimented her when she was done, staring again as he walked towards her. She made room for him to take a seat next to her. There was something so intimate about that moment that Cecilia could not explain. She had never experienced anything like this before. His arm touched hers, triggering goosebumps on her skin. She looked up to meet his eyes, and in response, he smiled. "One, two, three," he said. From that point on, she concentrated only on the music and suddenly, they were simply one.

When they finished the piece, Cecilia was in ecstasy. If Lorenzo noticed how shaken she was, he disguised it well, as he hopped onto his feet, extending both arms to her. "We need to dance that music now."

"Dance?" She nervously giggled, surprised. "But we will not have the music!"

"I have the music in my heart and in my mind. And that is all that I need right now. You must have it inside you too. I can feel it."

It took her a few seconds to process that invitation. But when she finally consented, he firmly grasped her, bringing her body closer to him, positioning his right hand on the middle of her back. She initially positioned her left hand on his shoulder, but it did not take too long for her to realize that her arms were already holding him, as an embrace. She tilted her face down, restraining her intense desire to lean her head against his chest. With her eyes closed, she trusted he would guide her through the room as they danced together. "One, two, three," pause ... "One, two, three," pause. "Can you hear the music we just played?" he whispered above her ears.

She could only nod a yes, inhaling his masculine and sensual fragrance, floating in the air as they waltzed gracefully across the floor, humming, turning and gliding back and forth. She did not notice when he freed her hand, bringing both of his solid arms around her waist, while she wrapped both arms around his neck.

They lost track of how long they remained in each other's arms. As she kept her eyes closed, the last thought she remembered was the question, *Am I dreaming?* And she held him even tighter, craving that the moment would last longer. That was when Lorenzo lifted her face with one of his hands, reaching her lips for a tender kiss. It was the first time she had been kissed.

For a brief moment, she worried about how to respond. Would he notice how inexperienced she was in the art of love? Would he be disappointed, comparing her to any other, of the many women he had kissed? But she quickly decided to dismiss those thoughts, allowing her heart to be her guide, and simply kissed him in return. The feeling of his full lips, semi-soft, sweet and warm against hers, was like tasting dark, ripe, juicy plums. His hands were locked around her waist, as they continued to kiss, soft and slow, her body starting to melt. Then he lifted her, carrying her to a crimson velvet chaise lounge, seating her on his lap.

She held his face gently with both hands and caressed his silky hair, tracing his eyebrows with the gentle touch of her middle finger, as he remained still, eyes closed, perfectly at peace, his head tipped back. She covered him with little kisses, the tip of his nose, his eyelids, his olive, soft shaved cheeks and chin. She rested her nose against his neck, drawing in his wonderful scent. He searched for her face again, bringing her lips to his, this time parting them gently, making her open her mouth. He gently probed his tongue inside her, making her shiver. He rubbed his tongue along her upper teeth with care, and she followed him, reciprocating the same type of kiss. Their tongues danced together, a duet, in a perfect rhythm, as if they had kissed each other like that countless times.

It felt as they were one, they had always been one. It felt like heaven. He held her closer, her breasts fully pressed against his chest; both hearts were thumping. She could feel the hardness and volume of his private parts, as a heat wave traveled from her mouth to her groin. She was sweating and she could feel her body was wet. She tried to sway away from him, to catch her breath. Unable to understand what was happening, she regretted having drunk too much. This could only be the effect of the sangria, she thought.

As if Lorenzo sensed what she was going through, he released the pressure of his embrace, without letting her go, caressing her spine back and forth. She rested her head again on his chest, the rhythmic and controlled sound of his heart beating like a lullaby to her ears. "I still have to show you my bedroom, the best part of this house," he finally said.

"I have everything that I need right here, right now. I don't need to go anywhere," she replied, stroking the back of his neck.

"You ... always so romantic."

She lifted her head to face him, clearing her throat. "Is that bad?"

"No, of course not." And he pulled her towards him, giving her a long, deep kiss as if he was sipping her. He kissed her all over again, their teeth clicking from time to time.

Nobody could recall how long they remained together, cuddling, kissing, lost in each other's arms. Cecilia would freeze time, if she could. She did not realize how much she craved him until that moment. The last thing she wanted was for that afternoon to end. But the effect of the sangria was taking a toll, making both of them dizzy. "We should go to my bedroom," Lorenzo said in a low, calm voice. "We can just lie down in my bed. It is more comfortable. We don't have to do anything else, just lie down together. We have more breeze upstairs too with the windows opened."

She knew Lorenzo was a gentleman; he would not do anything against her will. But she was not sure she was in the right state of mind to know what her will was at that moment. She wanted to stay with him, more than anything. She would do whatever he wanted, she would give herself completely to him, not only because he wanted, but because she wanted. Nevertheless, she was raised as a rational woman; she knew she should keep her emotions in balance. As adults, they both should know that the actions of today always bring repercussions tomorrow.

She kissed him again, intensely, the pressure of her lips against his increasing gradually. When she paused, she forced herself to reply, "Let's stay here," wondering if by saying that, she would ruin everything with Lorenzo.

But he only nodded, in agreement, and she loved him even more for that. She would cherish that moment forever. But suddenly, a hard knock on the door made her leap from his lap.

"Lorenzo! Open the door! We know you are there."

Cecilia was puzzled as she heard voices and laughter of men outside.

"Open the door, El Bi! How many girls are you hiding inside the house with you this time?"

As the men continued to laugh, harder and louder this time, Cecilia started to feel disoriented. *This is a serious mistake—they are probably a bunch of lost drunks*, she told herself, trying to maintain her composure, fixing her hair and her dress. Her eyes searched Lorenzo's for an explanation, but he stood up and looked away without saying a word.

"Open the door, Lorenzo, or we will tell your beautiful fiancée that we found some suspicious activities in your house!" The laughter continued. Another voice yelled, "Rebecca will be furious! Don't let her call off the wedding!" More laughter.

Cecilia was visibly shaken; the air so thick, she reached for her throat, which seemed to be narrowing, making it almost impossible to breathe. She sank into the sofa, with a feeling of an impending doom. The sudden shout from Lorenzo frightened her.

"Son of a bitch, Felipe! There is nobody here. Just me. I am opening the back door. Meet me at the other side, by the patio."

Cecilia remained seated, paralyzed, unable to take any action. Her head was pounding, feeling as if it would explode any time soon, along with her chest. She heard men laughing outside, dogs barking, muffled voices fading away. She did not know how long she remained staring at the wall, at nothing. *There is nobody here. Nobody.* A small word with such an intense power, that lingered and echoed inside her mind, merciless. At that moment, she did not know what to do. She felt she did not exist.

When Lorenzo returned, he took a seat across from her, his legs and arms crossed, his eyes of steel piercing her. She looked away, holding back her tears. He was the one who broke the silence, his words cutting through the air like a double-edged sword.

"We know we both wanted to be with each other, Cecilia. We both deserved a wonderful time together. And that was all that I wanted to give to you this afternoon. A memorable afternoon. I never expected it to end like this."

She swallowed and remained staring at the wall, holding one wrist with her other hand, digging her nails into her delicate skin as hard as she could, as if that action could partially take away the pain from her shattered heart. She could not recognize the man of stone in front of her. He had transformed himself into a monster, in a blink of an eye. Her mind struggled with the questions: Why? How could she be so stupid, how could she be so blind?

"You should leave now, the same way you arrived," Lorenzo finally added.

Cecilia could barely stand up, her entire body trembling. "I will summon Mr. Cortez to take you home," he said. And walking towards her, he gave her a kiss on her cheeks, leaving her alone for the second time.

A kiss of betrayal, she thought. She wanted so badly to slap him. She wanted to kill him. If she just had the minimal strength left in her body, she would have done it. But she could hardly move, her legs heavy as if they were attached to a ball and chain. She thought she would never even reach the main door. But somehow, she did. When she finally stepped out of the house, she walked without looking back, streams of tears pouring down her face.

She walked aimlessly for hours, her arms crossed against her chest. As the sun set and darker clouds filled the sky, the dusk fell rapidly, making her lose reference of space and time. She could not think where she was going, she was merely walking away, to anywhere, to nowhere. A light rain started to fall, her tears, her fears, the pain, all turning into one. She was soaked and cold, her dress partially covered in mud by the time she reached the banks of the river, but she could care less. She desired to continue walking, towards the river, disappearing in its murky waters.

From far away, someone shouted. It seemed to be a voice of a woman, but Cecilia could not hear what was being said. She continued to walk forward. "I must only walk forward," she told herself. She was able to see the edge of the cliff when someone grabbed one of her arms, yelling at her.

"Have you lost your mind? What are you doing?"

Cecilia stared at the stranger, a woman with a heavy foreign accent. She could not understand who that person was, much less what she was doing there, in the middle of the rain—why she was saving her life. After all, she was a nobody. She just wanted to go to the river. She just wanted to die. She should die. The stranger grabbed Cecilia's hands, pulling her away, dragging her toward one of the main roads to the city, while Cecilia sobbed uncontrollably, in total despair. The woman mentioned she could spend the night with her; she knew a man that would take both of them in his place, with something warm to drink and dry clothes.

Cecilia nodded, and freeing her hands, she ran away. She did not remember how long she stayed on the streets, much less how she was able to find the way back to Amalia's house, where she collapsed, as soon as she tapped three times on her friend's window.

Chapter 12

"It was the best of times;
It was the worst of times."
(Charles Dickens)

Buenos Aires, Winter, 1902

Cecilia decided to have the next women's educational group meeting at her house, since the school break had started and there was no need for them to gather at the university's empty building. In addition, the weather had turned worse in the past few days, with the temperatures dropping considerably. The idea of a more informal session in the afternoon was met with excitement by all the ladies, especially Estella, who suggested everyone bring a dish. "Better ideas always come forth when we are surrounded by great people, great food and the warmth of a fireplace," she mentioned.

Cecilia thought of Claudette as soon as she heard that. If Claudette were here, she would have corrected them. *Better ideas always come forth when we are surrounded by great people and the greatest champagne*. Cecilia smiled to herself at the idea that they should pop a champagne bottle too. After all, it was not every day that they had this opportunity to unwind, while at the same time brainstorming their next move in enhancing women's and children's equal access to education and health.

Estella was the first to arrive, with a tray of *bocadillos*. "Look at you two," Estella said to Cecilia and Clara. "The most radiant figures I have seen all day. The hospital was filled with gloomy people this morning, except for Doctor Moretti, who stopped by to see one patient. He asked about you, Cecilia."

"Oh, is he seeing patients now? I thought he was just doing observational work, under the supervision of Doctor Santiago."

"Apparently he might have moved to the next level. He was by himself at the floor today. He looked pretty sharp, full of confidence.

How is my Clara doing?" Estella asked, as Clara had gone to check on things in the kitchen.

"She is doing really well. The other day we sat together by the fireplace, discussing one of those required literature books. She sounded so mature and bright. She also asked me to teach her to play the piano, so I am showing her the basics while I am practicing a more advanced piece. I am so glad she is here with me."

"I am really happy for both of you. It seems you two got the best of each other's company and care. By the way, would it be all right if she remains with you during the school break? Her mother sent me a letter the other day; they are still struggling with the daily stuff. I guess life in the countryside has not been as easy as they thought, unfortunately. The grass is never that much greener on the other side."

"Yes, certainly she can stay here. She might be able to help me with some clerical work. We can ask her to start today, by taking the meeting notes. What do you think? I will pay her for any additional job she performs, of course."

"I think that's a great idea. I can see her excitement in following your footsteps, Cecilia. We will be forever grateful for you taking her under your wing."

"It's the least I can do. Offering her some guidance and reinforcing the importance of a good education."

"You are one of the kindest, unselfish people I have ever met. I am so glad to see you glowing with happiness lately. I noticed you even brought a bottle of Perrier champagne. What is going on?" Estella asked.

"What is going on? We are gathering. I am happy for that. I am happy for everything that has happened in my life, bringing us to this moment, making us who we are."

They were both surprised when Clara replied, from the back of the room, bringing a new tablecloth to the dining table. "She is happy because she knows she is loved."

"Of course, she is," Estella automatically responded, not making much of the slight blush on Cecilia's face.

They were expecting six to eight colleagues to come, so when they heard the knock at the door, Estella offered to greet the new guest. To her surprise, it was the mail carrier, with a large but thin package, addressed to Dr. Cecilia Grierson.

"Who is it?" Cecilia asked.

"Just the mail carrier. He dropped this for you," Estella replied. "It is an elaborate package with the stamp fragile on it. I am wondering if it is from a secret admirer, since there is no indication who the sender is."

"You have such a fertile imagination, Estella," Cecilia replied, immediately knowing who it was from. She did her best to look natural and comfortable, taking the package from Estella's hand. Clara observed the scene quietly.

"Are you going to open it? Curiosity is already crawling on me," Estella said.

"Most likely it is something from a friend of mine. I recognize his handwriting. It might be a booklet or a picture."

"I can get scissors to cut the twine, if you would like, ma'am," Clara offered.

Cecilia gave Clara an inquisitive look, but she did not want to make the situation more awkward than necessary. She already regretted volunteering too much information, but it was too late to ignore it and to go back. "Sure. Let's see what we have here."

In a blink of an eye, Clara disappeared, returning quickly with a pair of scissors. Cecilia unwrapped the package slowly, stacking the layers of brown paper on her lap.

"It is a phonograph record!" Clara was the first to speak.

"How do you know?" Estella asked, surprised.

"Because it is," Cecilia replied with a blank face, analyzing the front and back of the cover, trying to disguise her emotions. She should have told them she would open the package later, as they should focus on their imminent meeting. It was none of their business to put their noses into her mail. At the same time, there was nothing wrong in opening a gift in front of Estella or Clara. They were like family. The less fuss she made around this, the fewer questions they would ask, the quicker they would forget it. "It is a music record from Enrico Caruso, entitled 'La Donna É Mobile.'"

"An Italian singer? Is that an opera?" Estella asked.

"Yes, it is. From 'Rigoletto,' by Giuseppe Verdi," Cecilia replied.

"Can we listen to it?" Clara begged immediately.

Cecilia, still in dismay, picked inside the cover, noticing there was more than just a record. She managed to just remove the shellac disc carefully, leaving what seemed to be a letter inside.

"Let's clean up this mess before the other guests arrive, Clara, while I turn the phonograph on. It is all perfect timing. We will have good food, good drink, good companionship, and now, good music," Cecilia added, trying to look cheerful. After placing the record on the player, the glory of the incomparable voice of that young Italian tenor filled the atmosphere, leaving the three women speechless, until the first guests showed up.

The gathering soon started, with Elvira Lopez summarizing the current situation in the beginning of the century. About four-fifths of the city's working population lived in a conventillo or other type of crowded tenement building, and raising a family of five to seven, as the average, in a room twelve by twelve feet, was a demanding and exhausting task. There were many orphaned and abandoned children, and widows made up about fifteen percent of the population. Elvira also pointed out that birth control measures were denied not only to women, but men alike. Abortion was illegal, immoral and out of the question. Therefore, it was their goal, their obligation as health care providers for women and children, to start a movement towards sex education and sexual hygiene, in the context of promoting healthy marriages and families.

Cecilia reminded them that about fourteen percent of all births were illegitimate, which left countless families economically vulnerable. Large numbers of women with children, without access to a man's wages, were forced to work for money, but their options were limited to low wage labor in small textile factories, laundry and piecework at home, while many fell into prostitution.

Old ideas merged with new scientific approaches, as the group debated the role of women in the new century. They refused to see marriage and motherhood as the only cure for all female moral and psychological problems, not accepting the range of consequences women faced if they failed at their "natural-born domestic roles." Women of all social classes were still being easily incarcerated in institutions for confinement, not only at the request of their husbands or family members, but even at the request of police, judges, or employers.

Being called to examine some of those women who fell ill, Cecilia was aware that some of them served several months simply for "bad temperament." One of them had been raped several times by her own husband. Although the case ended up in a court, the judge, after the medico-legal examination, pointed out that the sexual conduct and conditions of both husband and wife were considered "normal" and ordered the woman to return to her home, where she was expected to fulfill the marital duties. When she refused to remain under the same roof as her attacker, her own family had her placed in one of those "houses of deposit." Cecilia clearly remembered how disturbed she was when she listened to this from the patient herself. While society should strive for both partners in the marriage to be moral and loyal to the union, clearly women always paid the highest price for betraying the family ideal or for speaking up for their rights.

After a round of discussion, Cecilia thought she should bring up this topic to a few physicians at the university. Although Elvira and even Estella were slightly reluctant about spreading their point of view inside an educational place dominated by conservative males, Cecilia was adamant that they needed to partner with the very few professional men who could possibly see the tip of this iceberg. Maybe the young Dr. Giuseppe Moretti was one of them, she thought. Cecilia thanked everyone for their valuable contribution, while she popped the bottle of the champagne at the end, cheering for a future with more equilibrium. The ladies remained for an extra hour or so, this time talking, laughing, snacking and drinking.

Clara was going to spend that weekend with Estella, and Cecilia was glad; at least they had each other's company going home. They were the last to leave, bundled in their coats and scarves. It was a successful meeting, marked by pertinent questions, followed by practical proposals. Clara seemed to enjoy her new task, taking notes diligently, as she was appointed as the youngest member and secretary of the group. Cecilia was certain of the positive results they should soon reap from that gathering.

Now that the house was finally quiet, Cecilia could appreciate the sound of the firewood crackling, the fire still flickering this way and that; she watched it, hypnotized, as the hot flames continued to thrive. During the entire afternoon, she'd managed to keep her mind focused on the topics of the meeting, but now that she was alone and the night had approached, thoughts of Lorenzo engulfed her completely, the song he sent to her still resonating inside her ears. She closed her eyes and stood still for a while.

She finally decided to check what was inside the record cover, knowing it was another letter from Lorenzo. But she was wrong. This time, it was not a letter per se. It was simply a note. With a shocking message.

"You are forever in my mind. Though you weren't mine, you are my first love."

She dropped the note on the floor and suddenly, tears began to flow down her face. *Why are you doing this to me, Lorenzo? What have I done to you to deserve this? What have I done?* Now infuriated, she picked up the paper at her feet, resolute in writing him back, to throw into his face the questions that had been left unanswered for decades.

She knew she was not emotionally stable to send him anything at that moment, but if her mind was not in the right place, neither was his, she thought. How dare he—a married man, a well-known lawyer with two children—act so irresponsibly? She was glad he at least did not live nearby. Otherwise, she would have gone straight to him already, to talk to him face to face. She would yell at him, throw his gift and all his letters, his stupid poems back to him. And finally, she would end up in his arms, kissing him madly.

How this could be happening again? She was angry at herself now, tapping dry the tears that were still rolling down. The intensity of her passion and fury was immediately transferred to the letter she wrote, as she grasped her pen fiercely, gouging into the paper, while she clenched her teeth. For the impulse to write was obviously emotional, not logical nor intellectual.

Can you explain to me what you are trying to imply lately?

I must admit I am flattered by all the attention, the poems, the music, the notes, but do you think you can just continue to act this way, like nothing ever happened between us in the past?

You have called me your friend, and still, look at what you are doing. What kind of friendship is this, when you insist on hurting me, over, and over, and over with words and actions that seem to mean nothing to you? How dare you send me a note like that? Do you ever have consciousness of what you are doing?

The least you can do is say "I am sorry." I am sorry for all that I have caused, for the pain and humiliation you have suffered. Have you ever thought about that? Have you ever thought how I survived the aftermath of that evening? Do you care? Did you ever care?

You lied in front of me, you made it clear I was nobody, last time I was with you. You have no idea how much that hurts, Lorenzo. You have no idea. And no, don't you ever think that I came back to you for revenge. What would I gain by bearing a grudge or seeking revenge against the man I always loved? You have taught me that, where there is love, there is no room for hatred.

I only came back to you to see if you were able to admit how wrong you were on that day. I came back to you because you owe me an apology. C.

When she was done, she sighed in relief, still shaken. The simple act of writing made her feel in contact with him. And if that was all she could have for that moment, she would take it. She mailed the letter the next day. Other than the quick walk to the post office, she spent the entire rest of that weekend locked inside her house, listening over and over to the voice of Caruso.

Woman is fickle.
Like a feather in the wind,
She changes her voice—and her mind.
Always sweet,
Pretty face.
In tears or in laughter, she is always lying.
Always miserable
Is he who trusts her,
He who confides in her—his unwary heart!
Yet one never feels
Fully happy
Who on that bosom—does not drink love!
Woman is fickle
Like a feather in the wind,
She changes her voice—and her mind.
And her mind,
And her mind. (Giuseppe Verdi, "La Donna É Mobile")

***

The anticipated letter from Lorenzo arrived exactly three weeks later. To Cecilia's surprise, other than the first paragraph that might have evoked a small connection with her concerns and requests, the letter was written as if absolutely nothing had ever happened between them.

My dear friend,

"Do you not see how necessary a world of pains and troubles is to school an intelligence and make it a soul?"

Those are the words of the English poet John Keats. Have you read him before? You must. He is brilliant, although his poems were not always received so well by the narrow-minded critics during his lifetime. His statements are always true, and I am always amazed to find the truth in the simplest little things life bestows upon us.

How did you like the gramophone record? My brother was in Milan last April, being a guest at the Grand Hotel, the same place where this young Italian tenor named Enrico Caruso was engaged by the Gramophone Company to make his first group of acoustic recordings. Knowing how much my father and I are inclined to classic music and opera, while looking for opportunities to improve the importing business of our family, my brother convinced the group to watch a few practices, later purchasing two records for us. The company was kind enough to send us two extra copies this winter, with the request to simply spread the beauty into the new continent. So, I thought about sending one to you. We strongly believe this singer is one in a generation. There are rumors he might be heading to sign a great deal with the Metropolitan Opera in New York, next year. Once in the Americas, I believe it would be easier to convince him to head south, to perform at the Teatro Colon. Can you imagine watching him live?

How is your painting going? Are you done with Summer in Chillon? I want to see it when we meet next time. I might even have a perfect wall in my office, reserved for it, if you allow. That would make me happy, especially now, on those wintry days where the sun lacks its warmth, the icy wind does not cease, and the trees shiver with their naked branches exposed to the gray sky.

Talking about naked branches, what are you wearing now? Why don't you tell me, in detail? What perfume are you wearing? Can you describe its scent? The other day I saw, in a shopping window, a double-breasted dark green coat with a fur collar. I immediately pictured you in it. You and the green coat only. Absolutely nothing else. Maybe that came into my mind because of the sage dress you mentioned you were wearing for the ball. I have heard green is a highly fashionable color this year, and I honestly think it suits you very well.

Have you seen the international news recently? I thought you would be glad to read this: "The Commonwealth Franchise Act in Australia granted women's suffrage in federal elections for resident British subjects, making Australia the first independent country to grant women the vote at a national level, and the first country to allow them to stand for Parliament." The emergence of modern democracy is finally spreading its wings, encompassing men and women that share the same moral standards and their equal political rights. This is great news.

I will wait for your reply. For your information, you still haven't answered half of my questions from the previous letters.

Yours, L.B.

That day, Cecilia failed to stay in peace. She'd never realized how much she missed Lorenzo, and how absurd all of this seemed. Could you miss someone you never had? How could you long for something that was never yours in the first place? She tried to understand her mind; she tried to control her heart. Above all, she craved to know the true reason why she was letting herself get involved in this mess. But the more she pushed herself to a practical solution, the more she felt she was nearing an abyss of emptiness.

She did not reply to him immediately, but when she did, she was wittier and more joyful. She decided there was no point in bringing the past memories to him again. He would never admit his mistakes, much less apologize for his past misconduct. He would prove to the world that his acts were carried out with the best intentions, and at the end, everything worked out for good. No wonder he was one of the best lawyers in the country. If he was not invincible, he made the universe believe he was. She quickly concluded that, if she would not keep up with the fight, she might as well play and enjoy his game. A game he played so well by following his own rules. She knew they both were already in the rain, and when you are in the rain, it is quite impossible to keep yourself dry.

She did wonder, though, from time to time, what the relationship was between him and his wife. Did he love her? Did she love him in return? Cecilia even asked in one of her letters what Rebecca would think about all his inquiries and desires towards another woman. He dismissed it with a short paragraph: "My family knows me, and they know I love them. I would do anything for them, and that is what matters the most. The rest is out of our control. I sent yellow roses the other day. To her office. For no special reason. She told me the entire staff looked at her, envying the romantic husband she has."

Cecilia felt a lump in her throat when she read those words, but she did not allow the jealous feeling to remain there too long. For a moment, she wondered if anyone in this world truly knows another person. *Do we truly know who we are?* she pondered. *It seems we are way more complex than our own understanding.*

After this occasion, she forgot about Rebecca. If Lorenzo acted on paper as if his wife did not exist, Cecilia would just go along. Their letters continued to be regular, filled with increased sensuality, desire, poetry. There was always poetry. She loved them, and she could clearly feel he felt the same towards her letters. They also shared their affinities and differences in sciences, arts, politics, even religious matters. To her bewilderment, he confessed he was the treasurer of his parish, and as such, he attended the church every Sunday, something that was almost impossible for her to picture.

She started sharing more details of her life, her routine, what she was doing. She even confided to him, once, the clothes she was wearing. She suspected his intentions—he wanted to know her intimately, but she did her best to steer him away from the rise of an erotic passion. They had already crossed the line between a friendship and a love affair, although she would never admit they were having the latter. She doubted he would ever admit that either, as he kept mentioning, from time to time, that she was his dearest friend.

Cecilia got so used to their correspondence, to its rhythms and breaks; to the subtle devotion of their crafted words that translated into immaculate prose. His bright intelligence and his wicked sense of humor constantly challenged her, pulling her towards him. The letters sufficed her, as the air suffices the living being who breathes. Lorenzo's writing was a constant reminder that, somehow, they were always on each other's mind, just as when they were young. It surprised her how little she actually needed from him to be happy, to feel complete. She never expected much from him, other than the light touch of his presence. She did not care about his civil status, if he lived miles away or even if he had other women that he flirted with, as long as he cared for her. So, for months, her life was made of hard work, poetry, creativity, freedom and drama. Because there is always drama.

In the midst of her happiness, in the middle of this delicate and complicated relationship, there was one thing that constantly bothered her, one thing that had never changed, since the first time she met him. His self-centered personality. Lorenzo was not only a vain man, dependent on what other people thought, but a man whose motto could be, "Speak ill, but speak of me."

Even in the letters, he made it clear that he was always in control. No matter how much the two of them agreed or disagreed on any subject, at the end, he would imply she agreed because he was right; if she did not agree, obviously she was the wrong one. His words would prevail and his needs would be met, at whatever cost, as if the globe revolved around him, as if he was always entitled to be admired and praised. Cecilia chose to ignore his inflated boosts of self-importance, because trying to fight against his ego was pointless.

***

One day she decided to review a medical manuscript at the library, and was glad to see Dr. Giuseppe Moretti there. When he invited her for coffee or tea at the cafeteria, she grabbed her books and followed his distinctive bouncy strides.

"A few months ago, Estella mentioned you were at the Woman's Hospital, seeing a patient," she said as they sat down. "I was thinking about stopping at your office to check if everything is going well, and if we would have the honor to see you more often treating our patients. Luckily, we don't see many patients with true mental or neurological disorders. But that does not mean they do not exist—just that they are not to be found on our floor."

"Yes, I remember that," he replied. "You were not working on that day, a shocking surprise!"

"Actually, I was working. But from home. Not seeing patients, of course. I had a meeting with some distinguished women, health care providers and educational advocates. To tell you the truth, on that day, I even mentioned that we should share the summary of our assembly with you."

"That would be an honor. What is it about?"

Cecilia explained to him that, the more she studied, the more she was convinced there was no scientific proof that correlated gender with vulnerability to moral, psychological or pathological conditions. Women were not more susceptible to illness than men. Men were not more susceptible to immorality than women. She was afraid society was becoming the laboratory in the studies of social pathologies, but unfortunately, like any project, this study was not bias-free.

"What the scientists have chosen to measure is very selective," she said. "They've measured certain types of crimes, certain people's behavior, certain people's bodies. And their interpretation of their empirical data was subjective, but their conclusions, extrapolated as universal rules."

Cecilia understood very well the uniqueness of the different genders, their biology. But as far as she could comprehend and see on scientific papers, the biology certainly did not explain certain behaviors. Therefore, as physicians, she suggested, they should work on a model for diagnosis that would go further than the biological rules. Would the fields of psychology, anthropology, sociology, criminology and law, to list a few, help them in the proper diagnosis, the proper verdict, leading to fair treatment for men, women and children?

Giuseppe listened, all his attention on Cecilia. He scratched his head, overwhelmed with the avalanche of information and questions thrown all at once onto the table.

"Everything you said is very pertinent. But I want to warn you: you are heading to a field of eggshells. I say that because I am already on it. And there is no black and white; it is all gray. Countless shades of gray," he added with a chuckle. "That is why I started reading Freud. Although I am not one of his followers, I am very receptive to psychological explanations of socially disruptive behaviors. Not everything can be explained by biological and neurological studies, that is certain. The same way, not everything can be explained by Freud's approach either."

"But certainly, the law experts and the majority of the medical professionals, they all give a diagnosis, a final verdict and a prescription for treatment—whether this treatment might be a drug, an order for deposition, admittance into asylum or even jail—based primarily on a wrong biological diagnosis," she said.

"Is this about a specific case?" Giuseppe asked.

Cecilia thought for a few seconds before replying. "Possibly. Let's say there was this patient that once I met in one of those deposition houses. She was placed there after she found several letters in her husband's drawer, from a former high school sweetheart, a serious indication they were having an emotional affair."

"Why she was placed there? Why were you called to examine her?"

"She developed a urinary infection and refused to be fully examined by a male doctor. According to the records, she became progressively infuriated at home, with a short temper. The family said she eventually became hysterical and paranoid. The husband denied any accusation, nobody ever found anything suspicious at his house or his work, much less any letters, of course. He had been always a flirtatious and a narcissistic type of person, according to her. But he swore he never had an affair. Afraid of his and the wife's own safety and sanity, the husband admitted her, for almost a year."

"So, what was your conclusion? Did your patient just make this whole story up to frame her husband, or was she a legitimate victim of a Don Juan? Where is the truth, how and where are we going to find out, in order to give the proper diagnosis, without being biased?"

"The truth? We might never know the truth. We always need to hear both sides of the story, anyway. And at the end, the truth might not lie within either side," she replied, tucking her chin in, rubbing the back of her neck.

"The truth ... does anyone really know where we can find it?"

"Maybe in the bottom of our hearts," Cecilia said. "Perhaps calling those questions means taking the time to look into people's hearts. And that might be a difficult task."

"An impossible task. In this clinical scenario, because you are a woman, I can understand your intuitive sympathy towards your patient. In your mind, you are probably thinking the woman does not suffer from any mental issues. I can agree with that. The woman felt betrayed and she had her reasons to be infuriated, even hysterical."

Giuseppe paused to sip his second cup of tea; then he continued. "But as a man, I can see the husband could be rekindling with his sweetheart from school when they got reunited last year, after being apart for so long. He never actually forgot her. Apparently, she never forgot him either. He sent her a couple of letters, no harm. In his mind, he was not having an affair, technically speaking."

"It could be," Cecilia said. "He was just writing to his friend."

"Correct. And he stopped writing when his wife found out. He even burned all the letters. But the wife continued to be infuriated, driving everyone crazy in their house, even suspicious of her own shadow. Perhaps she threatened to kill them both and then commit suicide. Of course, she said it was a joke. Was it?"

"I don't know."

"Now, what are we going to do? We could send both to a psychologist, maybe even a psychiatrist, assuming they both would cooperate with the medical advice. Or you can grant them a divorce.

None of the options are risk-free, none of the options will necessarily lead to a happy ending."

Cecilia could not answer. "It is complicated," she finally sighed.

"It is life," Giuseppe replied. "And that means a lot of things are under our skin, but totally out of our hands. We just have to act on what we believe is the best, in certain circumstances."

Chapter 13

"To burn with desire and keep quiet about it
Is the greatest punishment we can bring on ourselves."
(Federico Garcia Lorca)

Buenos Aires, Spring, 1902

The book arrived unexpectedly, few weeks before Cecilia's birthday. The gift would be a delightful surprise, if it weren't for its title: *Dangerous Liaisons*, by Pierre Choderlos de Laclos. Cecilia's eyes flickered to the book cover in her hands, and slowly, she let her trembling fingers flip through its pages, pausing to read certain words, phrases and paragraphs that Lorenzo had underscored in black ink. His few written notes were spread in the margins, here and there, as if she was supposed to decipher a secret message inside the French novel.

She felt compelled to start reading it immediately and could hardly put the book down during the weeks that followed. Maybe because the plot seemed to represent a metaphor between Lorenzo and herself: seduction, pleasure, revenge, love. Dangerous connections. Maybe because the story was not described directly, but told exclusively through the course of a series of letters. Maybe because one of the characters shared a similar name, Cecile. And that name was highlighted throughout the book, sending shivers down her spine.

The elegant tale depicted a calculated betrayal, where two ex-lovers still keep in touch through letters. The cold-blooded French aristocrats, the Marquise de Merteuil and the Vicomte de Valmont, played the game of seduction to the point they kept scores. Their greatest pleasure was to cause the loss of virtue and shatter the hearts of those intimately close to them, especially those capable of experiencing true emotions. The story could be easily taken as an assault, especially to Cecilia and to any conservative woman of high moral standards, if it wasn't for the beauty of its prose, the subtleties of the language and the ability to draw the reader into the story. The main protagonists seemed to be so hardened to the ordinary feelings that perhaps the only sentiment that could destroy them was real love.

In part one, Cecile de Volanges, a naïve young woman, is betrothed at an early age to a man she had never met, the Count of Gercount, a former lover of the Marquise de Merteuil. When Cecile develops a girlish crush on her music tutor, the impoverished Chevalier Danceny, she does not know how to respond to his letters or his attention.

To make matters worse, following a plot planned by the Marquise de Merteuil, the Vicomte de Valmont deflowers Cecile. The young girl, although confused and filled with guilt at first, gives into the affair with Valmont, despite still being emotionally attached to Danceny. Cecile lets Valmont advance, as she welcomes a lesson taught by the Marquise—a young woman should take advantage of all the lovers she can acquire, especially in a society so repressive and contemptuous of women. The result is a "master-apprentice" relationship, where Cecile is courted by Danceny by day, while each night, her now insatiable curiosity is appeased by the pleasures from Valmont. Not falling short, the Marquise also starts an affair with Danceny.

Valmont and the Marquise act as though they are above the conventional laws and morals. They are independently wealthy, intelligent, finely dressed and with refined manners. The Marquise is portrayed as sadistic and depraved, which of course is not displayed to the people who surround her. Her true character is revealed only in the intimate letters she shares with Valmont, her former lover. Meanwhile, Valmont, an unscrupulous libertine with the trained eye of a predator, has singled out the emotional weakness of another woman, the virtuous Madame de Tourvel. The ex-lovers have a bet where, if Valmont succeeds in seducing Madam de Tourvel, the Marquise will travel to him and spent the night with him, for one more time.

Valmont eventually manages to win the heart of Madame Tourvel, but at a high cost—this time, he falls in love with his prey. In a burst of jealousy, the Marquise mocks, threatening to trash his reputation as the greatest lover in Paris. She also refuses to honor the end of their agreement, since Valmont has no written proof that his relation with Madame de Tourvel has been consummated. War between the two ex-lovers is declared, and in a turn of events, Valmont abruptly and cruelly dismisses Madame de Tourvel with the laconic excuse: "It is beyond my control."

Reading the book, Cecilia could not help but question why Lorenzo had sent it to her. She was dubious about his true intentions; instinctively, she knew she should not trust him. In her notebook, she wrote down all the sentences and paragraphs that he deliberately emphasized. Just as the novel was about what people say to each other, what was Lorenzo trying to say to her? She wondered if what was left unsaid, not highlighted, could actually be even more important than what was said. She remained staring at the pages of her notebook, where countless words gave rise to a wide range of interpretation:

My dear friend.

A carriage has just stopped at the door.

Come back, my dear ... Come back. I have need of you.

You can only thank me and obey.

You see that love does not blind me.

To conquer is our destiny, we must follow it.

Perhaps at the end of the course, we shall meet again.

This language astounds you, does it not?

What is it you suggest to me? To seduce a young girl who has seen nothing, delivered defenseless into my hands?

You do not know how solitude adds ardor to desire.

It is very necessary that I should have this woman.

He sings duets with her.

Nothing amuses me so much as a lover's despair.

Only a piece of muslin covers her breast; and my furtive but penetrating gaze has already seized its enchanting form.

She was obliged to trust herself to me.

I held this modest woman in my arms; I pressed her breast against my own; and in this short interval, I felt her heart beat faster. Her heart throbbed with love, not with fear.

I dare not to put my name on this letter.

The shame caused by love is like the pain, you only experience it once. You can pretend later, but you do not feel it anymore. Yet the pleasure remains, and that is something.

I shall possess this woman. I shall steal her heart.

Cecile.

Cecile.

Cecile.

A cold chill went through Cecilia's body, as she read those lines over and over again.

She was able to reply to Lorenzo only after she was done with the book. She was glad she took the time to allow her emotions to settle down, instead of questioning him in the heat of the initial moments. She was definitely calmer and her thoughts seemed clearer by the time she regained the confidence to write to him again.

My dear,

Thank you for sending me another gift. Books are forever the best thing one can give to a friend. I must confess not only the title awakened in me a curiosity to know what the story was all about, but also the words emphasized by you made me wonder what was the message you were trying to convey.

As much as I enjoy a game of suspense, I will ask you boldly, expecting from you a bold answer. Why did you send me a book like that? Why did you underscore so many words and paragraphs with dual meanings?

Did you like the book? I couldn't help but trace a parallel between you and the Vicomte himself. I am still wondering if you are pleased and proud of his personality.

I was also wondering if your wife has read the novel, and if so, what were her thoughts about it. Who could she be in the book? The Marquise herself? Is she the one plotting with you to destroy an innocent heart?

Who am I? Cecile, maybe? Madame de Tourvel? Or am I a chameleon, taking turns in each chapter—in each letter I am actually one of the characters? If it is up to me, I would say you are deeply in love with me. You have always been, and just never had the courage to admit it. It would ruin your reputation as a Don Juan. It would ruin you. And better have somebody else ruined than yourself. But that is just what I think, based on what I have received from you. It doesn't necessarily mean it is the truth. The Universal truth. It has so many facets, like a mirror fallen onto the ground, shattered into countless pieces. Whoever finds a piece of that mirror will only find a piece of the truth; because that fragment only reflects the image of the place and the person that holds it. What is your reflection on that piece of a mirror? Is the Machiavellian Vicomte Valmont, the man you also see?

I was so impressed with the novel that I brought the topic to a colleague and friend of mine, a neurologist from the university, with ties to the psychology and psychiatry departments. What he briefly explained to me is that the type of people portrayed by the Vicomte and the Marquise fall into the category of those with personality disorders, including, but not limited to, narcissists. Many of those people present as perfect citizens to society; several are even considered models of success. It is only those who live with them in a more intimate capacity that are subject to the atrocities of their cruel behavior. Just like the novel describes, many people who know the dangerous liaisons in a friendship do not know what they were capable of, until they became romantically involved with them. The needs of narcissists are based on sex, power and control. Their greatest delight is in duping others, causing them pain.

My doctor friend mentioned that, more interestingly, those people might not be even aware of who or what they are. Their behavior might not be necessarily a choice they made. Nevertheless, science has not yet proved there could be a chemical imbalance or even a genetic predisposition in those cases. He said those types of patients are the hardest ones to treat, mainly because they are the most convincing liars. In his opinion, this particular group of people most likely do not have the capacity to change in adulthood, as their neurological brain might be simply wired differently.

His advice was plain: If you are aware you are dealing with this type of person, no matter how bad you feel for them now, it is guaranteed you will feel a whole lot worse as time passes. You cannot change who they are, no matter how much you want to help them, unless they recognize their own personality problems and look for care. For most of the cases, you must accept them like that, or get out of their way. A lot of times, getting out of their way might be the best solution. Not necessarily the easiest, but the best.

So, as you can see, the book was a great asset to the expansion of my knowledge and mainly to help me accept each person for who they are. And with that knowledge, it is up to me to make the right decision, to choose the best path, not only to remain afloat, but to walk with my head up.

I will finish this letter with the words of William James: "Acceptance of what has happened is the first step to overcome the consequences of any misfortune."

With love, C.

***

Cecilia would have liked to do nothing on that Friday evening, but sometimes, fate gets subtly permeated into one's life, changing the course of actions, leading to unforeseen scenarios. She had a demanding day, with many more patients than usual, and she was not feeling so well. Her throat was tickling and her nose was becoming more and more stuffed, as hours passed by. All she could think about was going home, taking a hot bath and slipping under the white cotton sheets of her bed, pulling them up to her chin.

Perhaps, first, she would find a letter from Lorenzo at her desk, to cheer her up. She had not heard from him for more than a month now, and apprehension had started to creep into her. His absence stabbed her. She should not have been so harsh with him last time, she thought. She had no right to act as a "want-to-be" analyst, judging him from a book he sent, a gift he had given to her. She should write him back, maybe even apologize for her attitude. Maybe he was hurt. And she never had the intention to hurt him. Never. Even when he might have deserved it. She should write to him that weekend.

But Cecilia could not go immediately home after work. Estella had stopped quickly at the lunch break with a worrisome request for an after-hours meeting. She suggested tea and sweets at the elegant café, Las Violetas, which Cecilia could not decline. Although Estella had returned to work in the same hospital, their shifts were different, making it almost impossible to have quality time with one another. Despite feeling exhausted and maybe even sick, an evening with Estella would be beneficial.

Las Violetas, with its French stained-glass windows, ornate woodwork and Italian marble columns, teemed with customers by the time Cecilia arrived. She heard animated chatter by businessmen who just left work and groups of friends who were enjoying the beginning of a weekend. Even a few lovey-dovey couples seemed to have pleasure in being more expressive in this environment, where the warm aroma of roasted coffee and honey filled the air. Estella waved at her from a small round table for two by the nearest entrance window.

"I forgot how fancy this café is. I should have gone home and changed, but I would be way late," Cecilia apologized, noticing that Estella looked showered and refreshed.

"Oh, I do not care for how elaborate this place is. I am here for their pastry and the coffee. And your guidance, of course. I need your advice about something that I encountered two days ago. But first, what shall we order?"

"I am going stick to an aromatic tea. Chamomile, please. And a *medialuna* with strawberry jam."

"Sounds good. *Café con leche* and *profiteroles* for me."

A white-jacketed waiter took their orders, after pouring water with lemon into their glasses and offering them linen napkins that were neatly placed on their laps.

"So, tell me, what happened two days ago?"

"Well, I was called at Clara's school."

"Clara? What happened to her? She was fine the entire week and this morning when I left the house."

"No, I don't think anything happened to her yet, but I do not know what she is up to." Estella paused.

"What do you mean? She is an excellent student who has been keeping a good grade record. She is very attentive and responsible; introverted, but kind. Why did the school contact you?"

"The principal told me that one of her teachers—Mrs. Roselia—has noticed lately how Clara has been daydreaming, more than what is considered usual for a teenage girl. But what disturbed the teacher most was the book she caught Clara trying to hide under her desk, this past Tuesday, in the middle of a geography class. Mrs. Roselia first thought the book was a mystery that the girl maybe found at the library. But when she thumbed through it, the poor woman was embarrassed to death by the few underlined words she saw. She knew the book did not belong to the school and she could not fathom who had the audacity to give such material to a young lady."

"Good Lord, what book could Clara be carrying to school that was so outrageous? Luther's canon?" Cecilia asked, a mix of sarcasm and curiosity in her voice.

Estella signaled with her finger for a pause, while she reached for her purse. Meanwhile, the waiter returned, bringing a silver tray with their beverages and pastries. Once he left, Estella dropped a single cube of white sugar into her coffee, and while slowly stirring it, she leaned towards Cecilia, almost whispering.

"I brought it with me. Clara does not know anything about this. She does not even know the school has notified me. I asked Mrs. Roselia to let me see the book, and she requested me to get rid of it; they would not tolerate that type of material in the school. They will forgive the incident this time only, considering Clara's outstanding performance and for the sake of her family. But she will not be given a second chance."

Estella furtively lifted the book from her lap to the tabletop, as if hiding a valuable object from the people that surrounded them. Cecilia, immediately distraught, choked and spilled half of the steaming hot tea on the table, as her eyes were fixed on the familiar cover: *Dangerous Liaisons* by Pierre Choderlos de Laclos.

Flushed with embarrassment, she excused herself from Estella and the waiter who came promptly to help, offering to move them to a different table.

"I am so sorry. I'm afraid I need to go to the ladies' room." Barely able to contain her emotions, she rose from her chair, stumbling slightly.

For a moment she was not only hurt, but furious. The only thing Cecilia could think was that Lorenzo had the guts to start corresponding with Clara, sending the girl the same book he had sent to her. Clearly, that was not Cecilia's copy, since she had placed her book back inside the keepsake box, the night before. Everything else inside the box was there and apparently in order, since the first day she received something from Lorenzo.

After few moments in the bathroom, with her back leaning against the locked door, Cecilia suddenly remembered when Lorenzo had asked who was the young girl with an undisguised charm in the picture at the ball, in the newspaper article. Immediately, every little thing started to make sense: Clara's interest in the piano. The discussion of classic books. The green coat. Clara was even wearing a green coat a few weeks ago; according to the girl, an early gift her mother had sent to her. "Oh my God," she murmured before she reached the sink, throwing up.

She would have stayed in the restroom longer if it wasn't for Estella, knocking at the door. "Cecilia, are you still there? Are you all right?"

"Yes. I am fine," she lied. "I was not feeling well this morning and somehow my stomach now seems to be upset." She opened the door.

"You don't look good, my friend. There is not a drop of blood in your face. Let me take you home."

They walked awkwardly in silence for a little while, the uneasiness crawling under Cecilia's nerves. She wondered how Lorenzo could be such a traitor. How could he play so dirty?

"Do you know how and when Clara got that book?" she finally asked, feeling a little more at ease with the fresh breeze that started to blow that evening.

"No, I have no idea. I read just a few parts, here and there, where she has underscored sentences."

"I don't think Clara has underscored the sentences or words," Cecilia replied, finding the courage to clarify things to her friend. "I believe Clara has no guilt in this, but the opposite. It might be my fault, now that I had a little bit of time to think over it."

"What are you talking about?" Estella asked, perplexed.

"Remember this past fall, before the tango night at the Victoria, when you brought part of a newspaper to the hospital?"

"Yes, of course I remember. I left the pages with you."

"Well. One of the articles was about two lawyers in Buenos Aires."

"Yes. I noticed how your mood changed when you saw that. What has that to do with Clara and her book?"

"I have been in contact with one of the lawyers since that day, by letters. Lorenzo Bianchi. I believe he is the one who sent a copy of the book to Clara. I say that because he sent me one copy too. With several underlined words."

"What? Why did he do that to you? And why Clara?"

"I might as well start from the beginning. It is a long story." Cecilia's voice cracked. "I met Lorenzo when I was finishing my studies to become a schoolteacher, at the Latin classes that I took at the university. I was only eighteen years old. Same age as Clara ... Lorenzo had one more year to graduate from law school. We became close friends during the time we had classes together, and it didn't take long for me to be completely in love with him."

"A former boyfriend?"

"No. He wasn't my boyfriend at all. He was just my friend. I loved him, but I never thought he would like to date someone like me. I honestly never thought he even suspected my feelings for him."

"Someone like you? Beautiful and smart? Friendly and caring?"

Cecilia forced a smile. "Maybe a little bit intelligent, somehow friendly and, yes, caring. But I definitely never saw me as a pretty girl, especially for Lorenzo's standards. And now I am even questioning how smart I was, or I should say, how smart I am, considering all the mess that I might be responsible for."

"No matter what you have to tell me, Cecilia, the qualities you carry within are intrinsic to you, even when you do not see them. One cannot simply erase who a person is, just because he or she got involved in one messy situation."

"Well ... after the conclusion of the school year, one day Lorenzo invited me to spend the afternoon at his house. And that was the last time I saw him, twenty-five years ago. We spent hours together, lost in each other's arms, sharing endless kisses and hugs. We talked, we laughed, we had a few drinks of sangria. We played the piano; we even danced. It was the most perfect day I have ever dreamed. Until some of his friends showed up at his door screaming: 'How many girls do you have inside the house this time, Lorenzo? Open the door, unless you want us to report some suspicious activities to your fiancée—'"

"What? Was he engaged?"

"He was. And I had the misfortune to discover that, right after the moment he invited me to spend the night there. Maybe I should be thankful for those guys who showed up at this house; God only knows what could have happened to me, alone with him."

"Did he say anything? Did he say that he loved you, that he was sorry? Maybe it was one of those arranged marriages, you know, when the parents get involved and promise their only heir to be married to an aristocratic, dull rich girl." Estella made an ugly face, then started to laugh. Cecilia couldn't help but join in.

"Only you, Estella, to make me laugh in the midst of this sorrow and despair. No, he never apologized, much less said he loved me. That is my problem, my mistake. I contacted him when I saw your newspaper, with the deepest desire and expectation that maybe now, twenty-five years later, he would say that he was sorry. Deep inside, maybe I expected him to demonstrate that, somehow, he once loved me. But he never did that. He never even admitted he did something wrong back then. The letters started with something very brief, friendly and casual. But suddenly, they have been evolving into a connection that is now beyond my control. We write to each other constantly, we exchange poems, he writes as if ... he loves me. As if we love each other. Or so I hope. I am so ashamed, Estella."

Cecilia was glad they were actually in front of her house by this time, as tears were flowing mercilessly down her face. "Do you want to come in?"

"Of course. I cannot leave you crying and in this stress. You must calm down. Everything will be all right at the end, I promise. How about I brew you a new cup of tea? No more choking and no more spills this time, please!" Estella laughed, trying to lift Cecilia's spirits.

And that evening, Cecilia once again opened her heart to Estella. She showed her friend the wooden keepsake box and all the letters Lorenzo had written to her. The note when he sent her the phonograph record. Her notebook, with all the sentences highlighted from the novel.

She explained to Estella that she had sent him the article about the tango night, where their picture was on display. Clara's beauty certainly caught his attention, because he had asked who the young girl was. And in her ingenuity, Cecilia had opened the door to the devil. She told him briefly who Clara was, and where she lived during the week.

"It would be an incredible, compelling love story, I would say, if we did not take into account that he is married, with two grown-up kids," Estella said. "And now ... he is also flirting with another young woman? A *ménage á trois* is not enough for him?"

"I feel so lost and so stupid for falling again into his trap. I do not understand how he can be so cruel. Maybe I am just blind, not able to see him for who he is."

"You are not stupid, much less blind. Any woman in your shoes can only be lost and confused. Look at those letters! Look at the gifts he has sent to you! Who wouldn't love those? Who wouldn't be lost? You loved him, with all your heart, and that is not your fault. I can see you still love him, and most likely you will love him for the rest of your life. And I am totally fine with that. You should be fine too. Love is the reason why we are here. It is always worth giving it, living it, receiving it. But from the moment you realize your own life might be at stake, that is when we must slow down, step on the brake and ask ourselves: what is in this for me?"

"I am so embarrassed to be involved in this. I am so sorry for not protecting our dearest Clara. She is just a girl, on the verge of discovering the whole new world ahead of her. And because of me, someone is playing with her feelings, her emotions. That is all wrong!"

"Cecilia, listen to me. Never, not even remotely, blame yourself for something that did not entirely depend on you. It seems you have been blaming yourself since the night he wronged you. Feeling ashamed is only going to make things worse; nothing good will come out of it. Why are you doing this to yourself? Isn't it enough that you have carried this burden for a quarter of a century, all by yourself?"

Cecilia sighed, feeling too weary to elaborate any answer or an explanation.

"You told me in the beginning that you started this connection with him months ago in the expectation that he would apologize to you. Well, you clearly requested that, and he simply chose to ignore you. To me, that is a sign he is a coward," Estella said. "Or something is wrong in his head. That could explain half of his behavior. But you, my dear, you are a woman with a solid foundation; not only one of the bravest, but also the most selfless woman I have ever met. You are always caring for others. It is about time to take care of yourself. Forgive yourself for all those years that you assumed it was your fault. That was a lie. We need to heal ourselves in order to progress in life. Painful emotions burden us, but we must face them. And that requires courage. But courage, my friend, we know you have plenty."

"Everything is so painful now," Cecilia added, wondering if Estella could truly understand what she was going through.

"I know it is. But I still remember something you told me when I suffered my miscarriage, years ago. You told me that it is not the event that causes our continual suffering, but rather the beliefs we created to cope and make sense of out of that event where we suffer the most. Do you remember that?"

"I am afraid I do not remember half of what I say." Cecilia smiled. "You always had a much better memory than me."

"Sometimes, we believe we are worthless, not good enough, not pretty enough, not smart enough; damaged, blinded in some way, but these voices in our head are pure lies. You have believed almost your entire life you were a failure with Lorenzo, but I hope you can see now that is simply not true."

"I need to write to him one more time, then we will talk to Clara, if you can give me that chance," Cecilia requested.

"Feel free to do whatever your heart and mind guide you, my dear. Just remember to act upon your principles of an authentic life. A life rooted in your values, morals, love and compassion. I will not bring any of this to Clara, until you let me know what we should do next. Sometimes, doing nothing is the best plan of action."

When Estella left, the night was filled with emptiness. Cecilia went straight to bed. Longing for light, she waited in the darkness, tossing and turning, until the first rays of the sun announced a new day; exhaustion finally took over her body, allowing her mind and spirit to briefly shut down in a short nap.

The central post office was open until one o'clock in the afternoon on Saturdays, allowing a feverish Cecilia to run over there before lunch. She was determined to put an end to that madness, by sending Lorenzo a telegram:

How long did you think you would flirt with Clara without being caught? You should be disgusted by your low behavior. The girl is young enough to be your daughter. If you are a man with the minimal sense and wisdom, please, leave us both alone. C.

Chapter 14

"What is done from love
Is always beyond good and evil."
(Frederick Nietzsche)

Buenos Aires, December 1902

The end of the year was at hand, and that meant the school classes would be finishing soon. Even the artists at the Calle LaValle suspended their activities at the month of December. The week that followed the incident at Las Violetas went relatively smoothly, despite the fact that everybody was very busy, in a rush to have the last tasks completed before the holiday season. Cecilia put all her efforts in grading her students correctly, preparing the seniors for their graduation at the School of Nurses. This was also the time that she reviewed not only their accomplishments, but also her own. The hospital always required a big staff meeting where the directors and department heads were present, to analyze their clinical and laboratorial performances and quality control. Cecilia was pleased with the good year they had, and she was ready to introduce some proposals for the following semester.

The evening she found another envelope from Lorenzo on her desk at home, it was the first time she felt hesitant in opening it. She was trying hard to move beyond what was her routine in the last six months. This past week, she had actually been at peace, focused on her work. She should just ignore the letter, because no matter what the content was, surely it would only bring distress and additional pain. But curiosity is one of the first and basic raw feelings that is bestowed upon us, from the moment we are born. One can never easily turn it off; the mind, whirling with thoughts, just keeps running back to it, over and over again. Especially for those with a vigorous intellect, for those who want to see what is there, what is next. Cecilia took a deep breath before reading its content.

My Dear,

I almost got worried when I received your telegram. I thought something extremely serious had happened to you. I sighed in relief when I realized it was nothing catastrophic. Thanks to heaven.

I just did not understand a word you stated. For a moment, I wondered if you meant to send the important message to someone else. You always seem to be a very fair woman, so I was quite perplexed by your senseless accusations. Who is Clara, by the way? Would you be jealous if I was about to seduce her? Of course, you were. That was my impression from the telegram. If I could have heard your voice at that moment, I am sure you would be screaming.

I haven't had a chance to reply to your last letter because you know how December is. A month of chaos. Accounts need to be closed, cases must come to a conclusion, piles of files must be categorized and archived properly. On top of that, my father's health is declining lately. I had to spend a few days at his place, assuring my mother and their staff that everything is under control.

So, did you read all the book in one sitting? I had a feeling you would. I did. I actually read it during my last trip to Europe. And I enjoyed it. It was a perfect pastime during those long days at the sea. Rebecca read it too, of course. It is our tradition to read a book together in the winter. But she did not like this one. Apparently, it was too much drama for her fragile heart.

I must tell you, I found your comments and comparison of the book characters to me or you a little bit pretentious. Do you really think the classic novel is a portrait of our current situation? I can only assure you— that thought never crossed my mind. Although I must admit: I underlined the parts that reminded me of you. I almost laughed when I learned you discussed the book with your beloved friend, the newest Freud of South America. I bet he made a very good first impression on you, being a "doctor of the mind." I was even more amazed at how the two of you can come to conclusions about other people you don't know anything about, diagnosing them quickly based on poor assumptions. That was a little bit pathetic, but I honestly did not care, nor take any offense. Being a lawyer, I am faced with all sorts of accusations day and night. But back to the book, I am glad it was a valuable gift, that it opened your eyes and increased your knowledge; and for that, we all must be thankful for my kind act.

By the way, you asked me why I sent you the book. I did it because you challenged me with a note, to send you not only one, but two tokens of my feelings for you. I thought a few things were odd when I received that. First, the envelope was sent without your traditional crimson wax seal; second, it was a bold move: "Do you love me? Yes or No for Truth. If you only Dare, send me two signs that you Care." Third and at last, it is the only correspondence, that your handwriting seemed a little bit flawed, the only script finished with two of your initials, C.G.

But as a man who loves a challenge, I gladly accepted playing your little game. Since music and books are two of your passions, I sent you first the phonograph record. Then one day my eyes got caught on a pile of books in my home library, volumes that needed to be placed in their correct spots on the shelves. All the books were about law and justice, except for that novel, Dangerous Liaisons. That was when I thought about your truth-or-dare silly game again. Since I had already completed part of the task, I told myself I might as well finish it, with a bang. And apparently, I did.

Do you have any plans for the holiday season? I will spend Christmas Eve at my parents' house, but I have to be in Buenos Aires on December 27, for a meeting in the beginning of the following week. I have already made a reservation for the two of us, at Café Tortoni, for lunch on that day. It is a Saturday; you should not be working, so I thought eleven o'clock would be appropriate.

Looking forward and counting the days to see you. Yours, L.B.

Cecilia could not believe her eyes. She read the letter several times, to make sure she was not missing something. Of course, she was missing something. Actually, she felt she was missing everything. What did he mean by saying, "Who is Clara?" What trick would he be pulling from his sleeve this time?

Clara was setting the table for supper when Cecilia poked her head into the dining room, announcing that she would not stay for dinner. "I have a few things to take care of this evening, Clara. I will be back late, so make sure you lock the doors. Do not wait for me."

"Yes, ma'am. Are you leaving now? I hope you don't get caught in a storm out there." Clara's eyes did not disguise the urge to add another question, and she finally added, "Is everything all right?"

For a split second, Cecilia thought about asking the girl about the book. "Yes. Everything is fine." Turning around, she walked out of the house, embracing her large purse, reaching the wet cobblestone streets.

It had rained earlier that evening, and streams of dirty water were still pouring quietly in the gutters, flecked with cigarette butts and dead leaves. Lightning crossed the humming dark sky, competing with the traces of light from the iron streetlamps. Cecilia sped up in the direction of Estella's house, hoping her friend would be at home, praying she would not be caught outdoors in another possible outburst of rain.

Pedro was the one who greeted her, surprised to see her.

"Doctor Cecilia! What brings you here at this hour? The weather doesn't seem to be too cooperative today for you to be outside and alone."

"Yes, you are absolutely correct. Maybe I should have waited until the weekend to talk to Estella, but you know how we women are. When we are determined to have something discussed, solved or concluded, we want it now, or even better, yesterday." Cecilia chuckled. "Is she available? I hope I am not interrupting dinner. She is not expecting me, and of course, I can talk to her on another occasion."

"She's in the bedroom, probably finished with her toilette. I will tell her that you are here. Please, have a seat. And forgive us, the house is a mess."

It took just a few minutes for Cecilia to hear the steps of Estella rushing toward her.

"Cecilia! What a surprise! What does bring you here in this stormy weather? You should have brought Clara with you, at least."

Cecilia was not sure if Pedro knew about the girl's school incident, and she thought it would be more prudent to release the minimum amount of information in front of him.

"Everything is fine. Clara was actually setting the table for us, when I suddenly had the urge to simply come straight to you. Remember the night I wasn't feeling so well at Las Violetas? We were supposed to talk more about the young woman we both saw recently, but with me being sick, I did not have a chance to show you a few things I have gathered about her. Do you think this is a good time to go over it?"

"Yes, of course, it is." Turning to face her husband, Estella continued, "Pedro, why don't you excuse us for a moment? The newspaper I got you this morning is on your nightstand. The sports section has something about a new soccer club that has been formed in the city. I thought you would like to know more about that."

"She is politely kicking me out, Doctor Cecilia. I will let you ladies talk in peace. Have a great evening."

"Thank you, Pedro. Same to you."

Estella brought Cecilia to the kitchen, offering her a seat while she placed a kettle on the stove for tea.

"Estella, I need you to look at this letter I just received from Lorenzo. He is acting like he has no idea who Clara is. To make things worse, now he is telling me that he sent the gifts because I challenged him on a truth-and-dare type of game. It seems he has no idea what my telegram was all about, and now I have no idea what he is talking about either."

"Did you send him a telegram?"

"Oh, yes, I forgot to tell you. The following day after the incident at Las Violetas, I went straight to the post office. In the telegram, I asked him how long he was thinking about flirting with Clara without being caught. I added it was such a disgusting behavior, considering the girl is the age to be his daughter, and I demanded that he leave us both alone."

"So, this is the letter he replied to you?"

"Yes. Please, take a look."

Estella read it, and with a stern look on her face, her following question had an affirmative tone. "Could it be that Clara wrote him first? Clara Gomes. Her initials, C.G."

Cecilia's heart suddenly began racing, the palms of her hands sticky with sweat. A feeling of betrayal started to rise inside her, a sheer terror striking her mind. Cecilia Grierson and Clara Gomes. They both shared the same initials. What a strange coincidence that she never realized before.

"Why would she do that? How would she know about him? Unless ..."

"Unless she has opened your letters before you got into them. She is the only person who gets those letters before you arrive at home, correct?"

"Yes." Cecilia paused, trying to follow Estella's thoughts. "But the letters do not look tampered with. The envelopes are sealed every single time. How about the book she had? Hasn't Lorenzo sent her a copy, with underlined words, just like mine?"

"I don't know if the book is just like yours. Let me get it, so you can see it for yourself."

While Estella left to get the novel that was Clara's, Cecilia stared at the stove. Steam was now fiercely spouting out of the boiler, the grumbling of water whooshing for freedom. For a moment, she felt her blood was boiling in her veins, but in this case, there was no escape valve for the turmoil she hid inside. She turned off the fire, watching the hot vapors disappear in the air.

"Here it is." Estella handed Cecilia the book.

The cover was identical to the one Cecilia had. But to her surprise, on the flyleaf of the book, she recognized Clara's handwriting, in charcoal pencil. Clara's name was written in a girlish form, followed by the drawing of two overlapping hearts. Somehow, Cecilia could definitely see the letter L drawn on top of the first heart, while the second, a leaning and smaller heart, resembled the letter B. As Cecilia paged through the book, familiar phrases were underlined, also in charcoal pencil. The name Cecile not once was highlighted.

"Clara clearly wrote her name and his initials on the flyleaf. And the underscored words were done with the same charcoal pencil she used in the beginning. The book Lorenzo sent me is marked in black ink, and the phrases are highlighted throughout the entire volume, up to the last pages. If Clara is doing this on her own, she might not have had the chance to read the entire book yet—and that's why the marks are not seen in the second half of the novel."

"That could be possible. But how and where did she get this copy?" Estella inquired.

"That remains a mystery. We must confront her and demand an explanation for all this. We have already guessed and we were quick to judge Lorenzo. That could be our mistake."

"Regardless of her participation and fault in this affair, Lorenzo is not an innocent," Estella said, shaking her head. "It is clear he would not be ashamed if he was teasing with another young girl, on top of flirting with you. He is very audacious and arrogant in every single paragraph. It is rather presumptuous of him to assume you will meet him in few weeks. Has he forgotten that he is married? Who does he think he is?"

Cecilia swallowed, gritting her teeth. Apparently, even she had ignored the fact that Lorenzo was married. In addition, despite all those years, she still did not have a clear idea of who he truly was. Honestly, what did she really know about this man? Not much; she knew very little. Other than what he had revealed in his letters, and the few moments she shared with him while they were both students, she could not say much about Lorenzo at all. She might have created him in her mind, twenty-five years ago, based on the desires of her own young heart; based on what she wanted him to be, not on who he truly was.

"Can we talk to Clara as soon as possible? Her classes will be finishing in a week, and before she leaves for the holiday break, I just need to put an end on this."

"Tomorrow after work, maybe?"

"Tomorrow sounds good. Meet us at my house at seven in the evening, for dinner. Thank you, Estella. I will skip the tea. Let me rush back home while the sky is still holding back the showers."

The walk home was lonely and somber, as emotions tore Cecilia from all directions. She did not want to be angry, but she was. Angry at Clara, angry at Lorenzo, angry at herself. None of this made any sense; none of this should be happening, if it wasn't for her loving Lorenzo so much. She did not want to love him, but since when is love a feeling we can pick and choose? Her eyes swelled with tears, which she did not bother to wipe away.

Back at home, the dimmed light in Clara's room was still on. Cecilia wondered if the girl was awake. She wondered if Clara was lying in bed, naked or dressed only in the green coat. She wondered if Clara was touching her own body, thinking about Lorenzo while creating endless romantic fantasies, discovering the pleasures and the power of her young body. Cecilia leaned her head against Clara's door, pressing her ear against the solid wood; not a sound was heard, and she felt ashamed of her own deplorable behavior.

She locked herself in the bathroom, filling the bathtub with hot water and a few drops of lemon oil. She craved to drown her sorrows, but she knew the night would be long and restless. For that reason, she remained there, quiet, playing absent-mindedly with the soap on her sponge, hearing the rain that started to pour outside, until her entire body was frigid and numb.

Not able to face Clara early in the morning, Cecilia left the house as soon as the first rays of the sun appeared in the sky, taking with her the last letter from Lorenzo. She was glad the rain had stopped, and despite her exhaustion, she had faith that the day in the hospital would fill her heart and mind with joy. Looking back over her life, she admitted that most of her happiest times had occurred when she was actively engaged in helping others.

Whenever she gave the gift of uplifting someone, she always experienced a feeling of gratitude, which in turn made her optimistic, feeling better about her life overall. As she approached the hospital, she clearly remembered the first day of her clinicals. Surrounded by men, a speck of fear had touched her soul, until she forced her own thoughts to quiet, telling herself: "Each day we have a choice that moves us more towards love or more towards fear. When we make the choice of love by helping others, our hearts are filled with gratitude. And when our hearts are filled with something positive, there is no room for something negative, like fear, to lodge."

Deep inside, she believed she was ready for whatever the day would bring. Including the possible revelation she would obtain from Clara that evening.

Cecilia returned home with a bag filled with vegetables and a chicken to make a stew. She found Clara studying in the living room, books spread all over the place. The girl was embarrassed by the disorganization, surprised at the same time, for Cecilia was never home before five o'clock. Cecilia couldn't help but feel love and affection for this young lady who so much reminded of herself at a young age.

"Mrs. Cecilia, you are early today! I am so sorry for this mess!"

"It is all right, Clara. It is a good mess when we are surrounded by good books. What are you studying now?"

"History. Trying to memorize all those dates and facts is a burden."

"It could be. Try to look for the logical sequence of events that happened. Try to find a way to make it relatable, how past events impact our world, our community, our lives. Instead of just memorizing names and dates, think about the story that goes with them. Remember, there is always a story in history."

Clara suddenly rushed to her, holding her tight in a hug. The unexpected gesture momentarily paralyzed Cecilia, until she regained the strength to hold the girl back.

"You are the best, Mrs. Cecilia. I guess it is time to clean up all this and start preparing our evening meal."

"Your aunt is joining us at seven. I will make some *cazuela*, so if you can help me with the ingredients, I will prepare the chicken and get the stock going in the terra-cotta pot."

When Estella arrived, the simple meal, seasoned with garlic and smoked paprika, combined with the earthy flavor of vegetables, was bubbling and ready to be tasted. Estella and Cecilia spoke about frivolous things, and when they ran out of topics, an awkward silence hovered above the dining table. Cecilia kept her eyes on her bowl of stew, while Estella finally brought up the reason why they were meeting on that day.

"So, Clara, Mrs. Cecilia and I have something to discuss with you." Estella cleared her throat and sipped her glass of water.

Cecilia flushed, as she noticed how Clara's face suddenly became pale.

Estella reached for her purse, placing the book that belonged to Clara on top of the table. "I was called by the school few weeks ago. Your teacher was very disturbed when she found this book with you. Where and when did you get this? Or should I ask how did you get this?"

Clara lowered her head, her eyes downcast, not daring to look at Cecilia or Estella. "I saw it at the Avila bookshop and I bought it," she finally said.

"Do not lie to me, much less to Doctor Cecilia, Clara." Estella's voice was firm, making Cecilia intervene.

"Clara, please, we are not upset with you. But we believe there might be a huge misunderstanding and you might be involved with someone or something that is not suitable for you. It is very important that you tell us the truth, before someone gets hurt," Cecilia explained, with a trembling voice.

"I am not lying. I bought the book at Avila."

Cecilia could see tears rolling down the girl's face, which tore her apart. Clara suddenly seemed so vulnerable. They should have planned this better, maybe started the conversation at the end of the dinner, not in the middle, not like this. But no matter how much they had thought about making things easier, approaching this would not be a simple task. At same time, they were all adults, even Clara. And Cecilia, being the oldest and the one most affected in this story, felt obliged to take the lead with a resolute determination to put an end to this confusion.

"Why did you buy the book? Why did you write your name and the hearts that mimic the initials L and B on the flyleaf? Do they stand for Lorenzo Bianchi?" Cecilia inquired.

Clara started sobbing, making Cecilia get up from her chair. "Let me find a handkerchief."

"Clara, please, calm down and put yourself together!" Estella's demanding voice startled the girl. "You should have thought about the consequences of this before starting this drama."

When Cecilia returned, Clara summoned the strength to reveal what happened. But first, she begged them both for forgiveness.

"The first time I saw the envelope addressed to Dr. Cecilia Grierson, it was sealed with the justice emblem, which made me panic. Since the passing of my uncle—I must say, my stepfather—there were rumors about how I could be involved in his death, because I was the only one in the house at the time of the accident. I was falsely accused of causing his death, even by my own family. So, when I saw the justice symbol, I immediately thought the case was opened again, that the judge was looking for me. I thought he was contacting Doctor Cecilia to inform her about my arrest."

"Your arrest? What are you talking about, Clara?" Cecilia asked, completely puzzled.

"Her uncle Juan took custody of Clara's family, when he married his deceased brother's widow, my sister, years ago," Estella explained. "I was never in agreement with their union, but that was the way my sister felt best to obtain a livelihood. Unfortunately, when Clara was fourteen, there was a freaky accident. Juan felt from a ladder. Her paternal grandmother, never too fond of our family, raised questions and pointed to her own granddaughter as a main suspect. Of course, the forensic investigation closed the case and determined the death was truly an accident, and we never brought this subject up again. But as we can see, the damage was already done to the girl."

Turning to Clara, Estella asked, "So, what did you with that letter?"

Sobbing again, the girl replied, "I opened it. I didn't mean any harm, I swear it! I just thought the letter was about me—I thought they were looking for me."

"It's all right, Clara. Thankfully, you are safe here, nobody is ever coming for you. I am so sorry for all this confusion and the pain it has brought upon us all," Cecilia finally said. If yesterday she was angry at Clara, today her heart was filled with compassion.

"Still, that did not give you the right to open all the letters that were addressed to Doctor Cecilia! Do you know that tampering with letters is considered a crime? You could go to jail because of that!" Estella was now screaming, making the girl cry even more.

"I did not open any other letters, Aunt Estella. I could never do that. But after I read the first letter, I was just curious to know who Mr. Lorenzo Bianchi was. I thought he and Doctor Cecilia were ... past sweethearts."

Blowing her nose, now completely red, and drying her eyes, Clara continued. "So, when a second envelope arrived, I was even more curious to know its contents. But I did not open it, I swear it. Instead, I looked for it, the next day. I searched for it, all over the house. And when I was about to give up, that was when I found the wooden keepsake box at the back of Doctor Cecilia's armoire. I am so sorry, please forgive me. I know what I did was wrong. I shouldn't have touched something that doesn't belong to me."

"Did you write to him?" Cecilia bluntly asked, tense.

"Only once. I wanted to know if he loved you. So, I forged a note. I tried to mimic your handwriting. A stupid game of Truth or Dare. I noticed he signed his letters with his initials, and as afraid as I was to sign your name, I just finished it with your initials too, C.G."

"And the book?" Estella asked.

"After he sent the record, the second package for sure was the second response for my note. So, when I found the book inside the keepsake, I knew it was his next gift. I copied some phrases he underscored in the book, and every day I would read a little bit of the book. Until one day I had the idea I could buy myself a copy, if I found one at the bookstore."

"So, he never wrote you a letter or sent you a book? He never mentioned to you anything about a green coat? I saw you in one the other day." Despite the shock and embarrassment, Cecilia still had a few questions that needed answers.

"Of course not. He doesn't know who I am. After he wrote that he imagined Doctor Cecilia in a green coat, I asked my mother to make me one and send it to me, which she did, for my birthday. I know, it was all silly. I am deeply sorry."

"Why did you continue to pry into Cecilia's personal life? Why did you ask your mother for the coat?"

Clara looked away, trying to hide her naked emotions. "Because Lorenzo loved Mrs. Cecilia and I ... I wanted to feel that love. And as I read his letter... I ended up falling in love with him."

Chapter 15

"Enjoy the little things
For one day you may look back
And realize they were the big things."
(Robert Brault)

Buenos Aires, Summer, December 1902

Cecilia's mind gradually shifted to the present, after all that happened among her, Lorenzo and Clara. As awkward as the days were, following the dinner with Estella and Clara, Cecilia decided there was no need to punish the girl or even herself, besides the pain and embarrassment they had already experienced. Estella even suggested moving Clara away, but after a day or two dwelling on the thoughts, Cecilia knew life should simply proceed forward. It would probably be beneficial for the girl to spend at least that summer break with her family, away from the city, and hopefully, away from any form of communication with the past. Cecilia hoped nature in the countryside would be the best remedy for a young heart filled with confusion and guilt.

The guilt of the past. For Cecilia, she had tried to move past memories, tried to erase them, but now she came to a simple conclusion: that was not the point. The point was to embrace those memories, understand them, forgiving herself—and whoever else needed forgiveness along the way. Only after that you are truly free to move on. After all, the past is part of you. Like creator and creature, like an artist and art. The past molds you, while it transforms you; it frames you. But it should never enslave you.

For the first time in almost a year, Cecilia realized that the dreams which had haunted her so often had actually stopped. She now could see them more as a symbolic representation of her heartbreak, an inner turmoil of a constant subconscious pain from believing she was a failure. Unconsciously, part of that eighteen-year-old girl that was still alive inside of her believed she was a nobody, and for that reason, Cecilia had spent almost her entire life trying to prove herself the opposite—she was somebody.

When she thought about all that, her eyes immediately filled with tears. But this time, she was not ashamed of crying. *You are allowed to cry*, she told herself. *You were hurt. And when we are hurt, our natural, physiologic response is to let the tears roll down. Without ever admitting this before, it seemed you were always looking for an apology. As if the world owed you an explanation, totally forgetting that you needed to give that acknowledgement to yourself first. A self-apology for believing in something totally wrong, for all these years.*

On that day, she wrote a lengthy letter to Lorenzo. But she would not mail that one. She would deliberately deliver it to him, face to face, on December 27th.

***

In a last-minute decision, as a prelude to a new beginning, Cecilia decided to have a holiday celebration at her house, a night for a small gathering: old acquaintances from Casa LaValle and professionals from the university, including Dr. Moretti, Dr. Gutierrez, Estella, Pedro, Dr. Elvira Lopez. Even Eloisa D'Herbil and Gabino Ezeiza were invited. And to Cecilia's delight, they all confirmed their presence.

For the occasion, she decorated the house with golden and silver bells, and the fresh scent of red roses and green eucalyptus branches, arranged in porcelain vases, mixed with white hydrangeas, filled the air. A nativity scene was displayed on top of the piano; the clay version of a gentle Mary and a stoic Joseph, leaning towards the baby Jesus, evoked the universal message of peace and love on Earth, in the years to come.

Even the walls of the living room received a special treat, being dressed with new framed paintings by Cecilia herself. In one, a profile image of Michelangelo's statue of David faced a giant; another painting featured a ceramic jar with flowers, surrounded by ripe figs. Finally, the panoramic landscape, "The View from Chillon."

The small but elegant dining table was adorned with golden candelabras and red candles, whose flames flickered in a warm breeze from the open windows. Roasted turkey and vegetables, stuffed tomatoes, rice pudding, mince pies and loaves of *panettone*, the traditional Italian Christmas bread, baked with fruits and almonds, completed the setup, served on gold-rimmed fine china. Bottles of sidra, wine and champagne stood among the dishes. Cecilia was proud of all her effort put into the preparation of a night of thanksgiving and happiness.

Estella and Pedro arrived at the same time as Gabino Ezeiza, his wife and their five children, who quickly asked permission to play hide-and-seek outside. Cecilia noticed it did not take too long for one of the little ones to return, crying bitterly, fretting she had lost a ring she had brought with her. But when the mother looked at her in dismay, the child recaptured her composure, and stepping aside, she closed her eyes and prayed. One of the brothers who walked in took the scene as a joke, and laughing, he provoked her, "What is the good praying about a ring? Will praying bring it back to you?"

That was when the mother stepped in. "Perhaps not," she said. "But praying can do this to one who has faith: it gives the strength to the person who is quite willing to move forward with or without whatever that is, if that is God's will. And being able to move forward without a ring, is this not as good as if she had it?" The mother paused, but the children did not say a word. "Now you both go play." And immediately they ran out of sight, as if nothing had ever happened. Cecilia watched from a distance, amazed by what she had just witnessed.

As the guests arrived, conversations buzzed on several topics. While Giuseppe Moretti and Dr. Gutierrez esteemed the benefits reaped by the industrial revolution, Martin and Dr. Elvira Lopez raised doubts if a wealthier country could possibly worsen inequality. As much as the global trade was a positive factor by enriching some people, clearly it was also leaving countless others behind, triggering unrest and political backlash.

"Quality of life can be considerably improved by elevating applied arts to the level of fine arts to all," Eloisa D'Herbil commented soon after her arrival. "We have in our hands the opportunity to make this new century the best of our times, don't you all think?"

"The voice of wisdom," Antonio Mancini replied. "A year ago, for example, a writer was finally internationally awarded for his literary work. A special recognition of his poetic language, his idealism, artistic perfection and a rare combination of the qualities of intellect and heart."

"The Nobel Prize for a linguistic artist who confers a great benefit on mankind, along with those outstanding human beings in the fields of medicine, physics, chemistry and peace," Estella reminded them.

"But if I am not wrong, the winner, a French poet, was heavily criticized, since many believed that Tolstoy should have been the one honored," Gabino added.

"Stubborn and arrogant Tolstoy?" Martin laughed. "Most likely he would not accept such a prize; with the good excuse he does not want to be institutionalized."

"There will be always someone who is self-entitled an anarchist," Cecilia replied. "But regardless, the baroness is correct. We must take advantage of this period we are in, a moment of prolific creativity, where even anarchists can express their feelings, not only through any form of arts, but mainly through the way of living, in the constant pursuit of happiness and fairness for all," she thoughtfully added, walking towards Eloisa, welcoming her with a warm hug. "It is a pleasure having you here, in my modest house," Cecilia added.

After the dinner, the baroness and Gabino Ezeiza alternated their time between the musical instruments—the former on the piano, the latter with the Spanish guitar he brought in, each one contributing to a wide range of sounds that were uplifting and harmonious. Eloisa finished the night with a delightful tanguito, a piece she had recently composed, named "Que si, que no."

(He)
Yes, no
No, yes
Only, only,
Only, only
I love you,
I love you, I love you.

(She)
Yes, no
No, yes
My sighs,
Sighs, sighs
Are for you

(He)
No, yes
Yes, no.

I also sigh,
Sigh, sigh.
I sigh.

(She)
Yes, no,
It will be.
How much I sing to you,
I sing to you, I sing to you,
For truth.

Que si, Que no
(El)
Que si, que no
Que no, que si
Que solo, solo
Te quiero a ti
(Ella)
Que no, que si
Que si, que no
Que asi te quiero,
Te quiero, te quiero
Te quiero yo.
(El)
Que si, que no
Que no, que si
Que mis suspiros,
Suspiros, suspiros,
Son para ti.
(Ella)
Que no, que si
Que si, que no
Tambien suspiro
Suspiro, suspiro,
Suspiro yo.
(El)
Que si, que no
Que si sera
Cuanto te canto,
Te canto, te canto
Para verdad.

When Christmas Eve finally came—quietly and blissfully—Cecilia inexplicably experienced a release from sadness, injustice and guilt. The silence of that night suddenly gave her the hope of a glorious morning, a possibility to start afresh. A freshness that had more power and glory than rejection, oppression, fear and resentment.

Cecilia couldn't help thinking of the Almighty as a master artist with an extraordinary sense of humor, one who has in his hand a long brush, always creating abundant life on a plain canvas, making something beautiful out of every situation, out of every human being. And that thought alone not only made her smile, but also brought her an immense sense of peace. So, willing to capture that placid moment for posterity, she decided to write something to herself. She wouldn't call it a letter, but instead, an unpretentious note. A Christmas token.

Keep your heart in peace; let nothing in this world disturb it. Because all things eventually come to an end. All things, but love. Therefore, in all circumstances, no matter how hard they are, we should rejoice. Rejoice, rather than be cast down. May we never lose the greatest good and the greatest vision, which is the peace and tranquility of our souls. Always keep in mind that the root of peace lives within the habit of resignation. And by resignation one must not interpret it as an act of abdication, but a courageous act of acceptance combined with a step of faith that leads us to the ultimate freedom. Faith that we will continue to thrive, regardless of occasional losses. Just like a child, who is hushed in his mother's bosom, faith should quiet us by resignation. It is faith that makes us quite willing to do without whatever we so much prized before, with a content heart that is at rest, with the certainty that, at the end, everything will work for our own benefit.

Chapter 16

"Love is a fire that burns unseen,
A wound that aches yet isn't felt,
An always discontent contentment,
A pain that rages without hurting."
(Luis Vaz de Camoes)

"If I speak in the tongue of men or angels,
But do not have love,
I am only a resounding gong or a clanging cymbal
Resounding in the wind."
(Letter of the Apostle Paul to the Corinthians,
Chapter 13, verse 1)

Buenos Aires, Summer, December 1902

On the anticipated Saturday to meet Lorenzo, Cecilia woke up early. She tried to look and behave as if their casual meeting was nothing exceptional. But deep inside, mixed feelings were making her nervous. What should she wear? What were they going to talk about? Would he notice an awkwardness displayed in her face? She opened her armoire, somehow disappointed; not sure what to choose, she threw several pieces of clothing on her bed.

She tried a variety of combinations, and when she was about to lose her temper with her own childish attitude, she decided on a simple, dark purple sheer cotton and organdy dress, the only fashion treat purchased when she was in Paris. Its square neckline and short sleeves, combined with the two natural textiles, complemented Cecilia's softness and suited her elegant structure. The classy dress made her think about Claudette. She wondered if her friend would approve any of this.

Most likely not, she thought. She would probably have added, "In this world, there are those who are mad; then there are those who are mad but insist on going one step further. You are a perfect match for the second category." Cecilia chuckled at that reflection. At the same time, who was able to guess the unpredictable and sassy Claudette?

She wondered how and where her friend could be at that moment. Cecilia had written to her several times, but sadly, she only heard from her once. It took a while for Cecilia to finally understand that she could never force herself into someone's life, no matter how much she loved them. So, eventually, she stopped the letters. But she never forgot or stopped loving her Parisian friend.

She arrived promptly at eleven o'clock at the majestic Café Tortoni, located on the wide and recently inaugurated Avenida De Mayo. For some reason, she thought she would find Lorenzo waiting for her at the entrance, but instead, she was greeted at the door by a polite maître d'. She mentioned she was meeting a friend, Mr. Lorenzo Bianchi, but the gentleman cleared his throat and without hesitation, corrected her, "Yes. Dr. Lorenzo Bianchi. He has made a reservation with us. Please, follow me to his customary table."

Cecilia gave an exasperated sigh before walking to a smooth, round, green marble-topped table, located at the far back left of the café, almost hidden by a large column and a burgundy colored curtain that led to another room. Out of sight of most of the other customers and away from the entrance, Lorenzo most likely had met several other people in this café, she thought. The idea that he could also have easily met other women in this same spot made her stomach swirl. She was glad the waiter came in time to offer her a glass of cold water.

Reaching for a handkerchief inside her purse, she gently wiped her brow and cheeks. She could see her reflection in a nearby wall mirror; despite the heat, she looked glamorous and lovely. She hated the humidity of this season, but that would be her best excuse; she would never admit she was sweating because of the nervousness of a fevered anticipation. She was thankful for the beauty of that cozy sanctuary; its atmosphere of wealth and security momentarily took her mind off this awkward wait.

The elegant café originally had been opened at the corner of Rivadalvia and Emerald Street in 1858 by a mysterious French immigrant known simply as Touan, who took the café's name from one on the Boulevard des Italiens in Paris. Cecilia only knew about these details because the café eventually moved to its current location in 1880, taking the place of a Scottish temple that she had visited before. Inspired by the fin de siècle Parisian coffeehouses, Café Tortoni was a popular meeting place for the elite in the beginning of the twentieth century. Embellished with art nouveau decoration, intricate moldings and dark carved oak panels, its massive Corinthian columns contrasted perfectly against the chandeliers, the Tiffany glass ceiling and several Tiffany lamps. The venue was charming and glamorous; on the walls, gilded mirrors shared the space with local and European paintings, awakening the guests' desire for comforting food, good company and long conversations.

Cecilia was about to get up to ask the maître for an available newspaper, as a pastime, when she saw him—tanned, tall, elegantly dressed in a black suit and white shirt, striding in her direction with his unique confidence and his mischievous, beautiful smile.

"You are late!" she defiantly said, rising from her seat.

"It is good to see you too, Cecilia," Lorenzo said, his charming smile still on his face, his fragrance even better than what she could ever remember. "Waiting may be harder sometimes, but in doing so, we can appreciate more and rejoice in the fulfillment of the desires of our hearts."

"Five more minutes and I would be gone."

"I doubt it. Leaving me is never that easy. I can see that in your face."

"I am afraid your self-assurance might have caused some damage to your mental faculty, sir. In addition, I believe you might need a pair of spectacles, for seeing things that are not quite there." Cecilia smirked, feeling already totally at ease at his presence. Incredibly, the entire moment suddenly felt like twenty-five years ago—a young man, a young woman, at least at heart. Two friends. Teasing with each other, being comfortable in front of each other. The first few minutes of this encounter already confirmed what Cecilia once feared: the love she had for him hadn't changed. And in fact, it confirmed that her feelings towards him would never be different.

Lorenzo's intense dark brown eyes lingered on her a few seconds longer, but she remained still, holding his gaze, unable to read his facial expression, unable to discover what his look meant. He was still a puzzle she could never figure out. "Shall we have a seat and restart this conversation?" he finally suggested.

"That sounds terrific."

The waiter, a handsome young gentleman, delivered them the menu with perfect solemnity, as if he was serving Alfonso XIII, the King of Spain. It seemed he knew Lorenzo well enough to bow with a shy smile, but at the same time, politely and discreetly asking him, "What would you like to drink today, Dr. Lorenzo?" Turning to Cecilia, he kept his respectful smile, but his question was shorter. "How about you, madam?"

Lorenzo ordered a glass of Hesperidina as an aperitif, while Cecilia opted for her customary aromatic tea.

"You should try one of these," Lorenzo said, smirking, pointing to his enigmatic orange brew mixed with mint and tonic water.

"It is too early for alcohol, for me, at least."

"Maybe. I remember last time I offered you something to drink, much less strong, you almost lost your mind."

"I honestly do not remember ever losing my mind to anything or anybody. But if that remotely was the case, do not forget that things change in twenty-plus years."

"Some things change, I would say," he corrected, staring at her again. "Some things do not." He paused to slowly sip his drink, enjoying the moment. "Like this drink, for example. For thirty-eight years, it has constantly maintained its bittersweet flavor, without a single alteration. Did you know this was the first product patented in Argentina?"

"No, I did not."

"It was. And I found the history behind it fascinating, because the inventor was actually an American immigrant who worked not too far from here, at La Estrella."

"It is the pharmacy where I usually send most of my patients to obtain their medications and compounds."

"See? We have more things in common than we could ever imagine," he said. "My favorite drink and your best remedies come from the same place. And back to the drink, because of its claimed therapeutic effects, it was actually distributed to the soldiers during the Triple Alliance War, to revitalize the wounded. Maybe you should consider adding it to your arsenal of medical treatments too."

"Really? Impressive. Does it do anything good to you?"

"It must. As you have noticed, I am still looking good, in one piece."

"I see it. No wound left behind?"

"No wound left behind," Lorenzo confirmed, teasing.

"Well, so cheers to the Hesperidina!" she replied, laughing.

"To the Hesperidina. To no wounds left behind. And to us!"

They raised their drinks with Cecilia shaking her head, which did not go unnoticed.

"What is the 'no' motion all about?"

"You ..."

"What about me?"

"You are so unpredictable; sometimes it is even funny. It is the most I can say about you, for now."

"I will take that as a compliment, for now. After all, we cannot take everything too seriously. Do not be so Cartesian."

"I am not Cartesian," Cecilia protested. "You haven't seen me for a quarter of a century, and when you appear, the first thing you do is to accuse me of something I am not."

"I am not accusing you of anything, nor was that the first thing I did. I just see you still think and act very systematically, the same way when I first met you. You are always questioning everything, always starting from a point where you search for a truth that cannot be doubted. But we should not forget that the truth is not always black and white; it is not always written, not always on top of the bookshelves, nor in their bottom or even the middle. Sometimes, the truth is wrapped in the shadows of our delusions; sometimes it might be in the boxes forgotten in a dark basement. In very rare occasions, it might be even hidden in a toast, between a glass of Hesperidina and a cup of tea."

Cecilia couldn't help but reply with a tight-lipped smile across her face, "I believe sometimes the truth might be hidden in someone's heart. But the problem is, we cannot see someone's heart. We can only perceive what might be in it, by observing someone's actions. And even at that, there might be some damned good actors out there, making fools out of their entire audience, by their realistic, exceptional performances."

"So, if that is the case, what is the point of insisting on knowing the truth hidden in someone's heart? And let's be fair, then. For every good actor, there must be a good actress out there too. The balance of nature. The simple law of equilibrium described from the classic Greeks to Darwin."

"You are right," she said. "Look around us. People live for the moment. How many of those people out there are simply honoring each other's illusions?"

Lorenzo shrugged, not giving an answer, initially. "The world is surrounded by illusions, don't you think? Like it or not, this is simply a fact."

"Perhaps it is because we are too afraid of taking off our masks. It would force us to tell the truth; it would force us to reveal our true inner selves." Making herself look away from his eyes, she sipped her tea.

"Have you ever thought maybe we are not meant to be unmasked?"

"Maybe. Perhaps that is something intrinsic to our building blocks, something inherited from one generation to the next."

"Possibly. A mechanism of self-defense, a mechanism of survival."

Cecilia was going to add to this, but her thoughts got interrupted when their waiter returned to take the order for their meals.

Lorenzo took the lead, suggesting an array of selected cheeses for two, with imported green olives, nuts and crackers. For the main course, the lomito ahumado, a sandwich made with smoked tenderloin and sautéed mushrooms, was recommended, along with a tenderloin steak au gratin with cheese and tomato.

"So, how was your Christmas?" Lorenzo inquired.

"Christmas itself was quiet, but peaceful. I had a small celebration at my house and invited a few friends. We had a wonderful gathering. Even the baroness Eloisa D'Herbil came, to my surprise and delight."

"I haven't seen her in a long time. Did you tell her about me?"

"No. After all, the world does not revolve around you, Lorenzo."

"Yes, I know. Copernicus, Galileo and Sir Newton have proved and discussed that topic to exhaustion." He gave a sardonic smile. "But I was just wondering if you had mentioned to her that you both have me, in common."

"I don't know about her, but I do not have you."

"You know exactly what I meant. Is she still beautiful and charming?" Lorenzo defiantly asked, staring at Cecilia, waiting for her to show the slightest change in behavior, any minimal sign of distress.

"Indeed, she is not only beautiful and charming, but brilliant and smart."

"Ahh. All the qualities I appreciate in a woman."

"All the qualities I appreciate in any human being, regardless of their gender. How about your Christmas? Is your father feeling better?"

"Yes, thank you for asking. I thought he looked better this entire week. Maybe there is something about the holiday season that sparks in all of us a desire to live, love and laugh. My father, my son and I took a few days to go hunting. We took it easy and slow, as my father's arthritis is taking its toll, but it was wonderful. A quiet time outdoors, just the three of us, the wind, the sun and the smell of the earth."

Cecilia could picture that clearly in her head, just like her vivid childhood memories in the pampas. The images from the transcendentalist Henry Thoreau's book, *Walden—or Life in the Woods*, a reflection upon simple living in natural surroundings, spiritual discovery and self-reliance, flooded her mind.

"By immersing ourselves in nature, we can always gain a more objective understanding of society, through personal introspection. The majority of us are so used to and dependent on the commodities of the modern life in the cities that we forget and take for granted how easy it can be to acquire the four necessities of life," she said.

"The four necessities of life. Food, shelter, fuel and love," he replied.

Cecilia held her hand to her mouth and laughed. "I would say love is the fuel of life. So, according to Thoreau, if I am not wrong, clothing would be the fourth essential requirement."

"Who needs clothing when we have shelter, food, fuel and love?" Lorenzo greeted this supposition with his own great and genuine burst of laughter.

"Talking about nature and Christmas, I have something for you." Cecilia reached underneath the table, bringing up an eleven-by-fourteen-inch package wrapped in brown paper with a red satin ribbon and bow. "Belated Merry Christmas."

Lorenzo, caught by surprise, contemplated the package with fascination, his eyes brighter and wider. "What are you up to this time?"

Cecilia looked sternly at him. "Open it!"

"I will. But first, I have something for you too. Way smaller in size than what you gifted me, but hopefully with a great value." Reaching for an inner pocket on the side of his jacket, Lorenzo placed a small rectangular box in front of her. "I am sorry. It is not an elaborate package like yours. I could reuse the red satin ribbon from the gift you gave me, if you would like it." He laughed at his own joke.

"You don't have to. It is the thought that counts. Thank you, anyway."

She opened her box, gasping at the exposure of an exquisite Victorian folded fan, in sheer black silk chiffon fabric, with a hand-painted white monjita bird and hand-stitched sequins. Its upper part featured a delicate Chantilly lace, with scalloped trim edgings. The black wooden sticks were stamped with an elegant gold design. She had not seen this coming, and a glorious feeling immediately filled her heart. She remembered she lost her fan in his house last time they were together. Or stating it correctly, he deliberately took the fan from her hands, tossing it into one of the armchairs of his parents' library. She never had the chance to retrieve it, and even if she had, after that dreadful evening, it would be certainly ruined and lost. It was definitely nice of him, such a thoughtful gesture. That meant a world to her.

"Do you like it?" he asked.

"It is gorgeous. I love it."

"I am glad to hear that. I hope you do not lose it."

She raised her eyes to meet his. "I won't," she finally said.

Once again, she caught him admiring her; the way he looked at her was thrilling. She wondered what would be like to kiss those full lips again, to run her tongue across those white pearly teeth one more time. She looked away for a moment, immediately dismissing those thoughts. Pointing to the gift she gave him, her voice was like a command. "It is your turn now."

"It is so well wrapped I am tempted to leave it alone and just open it in my hotel room."

"No! You cannot do that," she protested.

"Of course, I can. Nobody tells me what I can do or cannot do, remember?"

She sighed in a sign of frustration and rolled her eyes up. "Yes, of course I remember that. But it would be nice of you to open it now. Just so you can tell me personally how you like it."

"I told you before I love everything that comes from you. I don't know why you have a problem in believing it."

This time she flushed, hating herself for that. On the other hand, Lorenzo laughed as if thrilled at not only knowing, but especially for pressing, the right buttons.

"Come on, open it, or I will take it back!"

"You can never take back something you freely gave to me." His firm voice brought goosebumps to Cecilia; somehow, those words felt like an irrevocable law set in stone.

"Fine. It is not a big deal."

"Oh, so now you are going to play tough? Do not play as if you do not care, when inside, you are dying for the opposite. I just hope we can wrap it back up. In case this is a portrait of a nude muse, it would not be advisable to walk outside displaying such a personal item."

"I can guarantee this is a not a portrait of a nude muse. Why would I give you a portrait of a nude muse to start with?"

"Because you know I would love it."

"You would love it if I gave you a plain rock, so I wouldn't have to go that far. Too much trouble."

"You are too sophisticated to give me a plain rock. Besides, too much trouble is a relative term. But let's see what I've got, before our food is here."

Lorenzo carefully and slowly unwrapped his package, as if undressing his bride on their nuptial night. As if his pleasure was not necessarily in discovering the gift, but in seeing Cecilia's expectations grow exponentially high, as he took his time. Finally, when he opened his box, a thin gift tissue revealed a framed canvas; specks of green, yellow and blue showed through the delicate paper. He took the painting out of the box, and holding it with both hands, arms extended, he contemplated the artwork, speechless for a period that seemed an eternity.

"So ..." Cecilia finally said when she could not take the silence anymore.

"The view from the Chateau de Chillon. One of the most fascinating and romantic medieval castles in the world. I still cannot believe you were actually there. Not a lot of people have visited that place, especially from the Americas."

"It is a hidden jewel, undoubtedly."

"Only found by those who are innate explorers, those curious and inquisitive travelers who crave for much more than a simple, ordinary touristic trap."

"Only found by those who are in constant search for peace and tranquility," she added.

"Did you find what you were looking for, over there?"

"Today I can say I found part of it. Because the search for peace and tranquility is a constant endeavor, just like the search for the truth. Maybe I did not realize those findings while I was there. But while painting the canvas, and when I finished it, I was able to experience all the beauty, the calm, the serenity of that place. I can close my eyes, and my mind will take me there. To a faraway land, to a solid fort, built with massive ancient stones, in the middle of nowhere, surrounded by mountains of white peaks, by a lake whose rippling waters perfectly reflect the immense blue sky. A safe place where you can be one with nature, where the clarity and the freshness of the light nurtures you, restores you, heals you."

"A place where we can simply be. Any time," Lorenzo concluded. "It is a splendid painting. I still cannot believe you are giving it to me. I feel honored. See how far you went to give me a perfect gift?"

"It wasn't planned," she immediately replied.

"How can you be so sure? It could be written in the stars."

"Well ... I am not necessarily inclined to believe in predestination, and I did not think you believe in such things either."

"Necessarily inclined to believe it or not, that still does not change what can be a possibility."

The waiter returned, and before they started sharing and sampling their meals, Cecilia helped Lorenzo wrap the painting again. Such a small, innocent minor task, but strangely, it immediately made her realize that they still formed a good pair. Despite all their differences, despite all that life had thrown at them, it seemed they still had so much in common; there was some chemistry, some connection, something that bonded them somehow together. She wondered if the name of that something was actually love.

They spent the next three hours chatting, tasting the dishes, sipping their drinks and reordering them frequently. They stimulated each other's imagination and intellect in endless discussions. They talked about silly things; they talked about more serious things. They admired each other's knowledge and free spirits. Lorenzo's face evoked an eloquent contentment, and his most passionate beliefs were exposed without reservations. He exhibited a dry wit and never for a moment did he let his gift for mockery down. But she suspected behind that exterior, there must be a generous heart, capable of great tenderness, capable of love. She noticed that, yes, he had physically changed a little—he kept his hair shorter, a few grays showing near the sideburns, and perhaps a few pounds were added to his torso. Nevertheless, he carried his years with grace, for his beauty might have changed, but certainly had not dimmed.

Cecilia was glad she was able to see him now in a totally different light, a totally different perspective, from what she had from the past, from what she had in her mind. Without judgement, without resentment, she was able to live that exact moment for what it truly was, without suppositions, assumptions, fears or remorse. It felt like, suddenly, the world came to a halt and that was all they both had: that moment, where words, laughter, love and friendship all unified together, like the perfect ingredients of a life's elixir.

"You are a strong and courageous woman, Cecilia." Lorenzo's phrase sounded out of context, catching her off guard. As much as she was aware of her own qualities, she never really thought she was exceptional or above anyone else. Hearing his words, she blushed, and with her eyes down, she couldn't help but think about Claudette. For sure, her friend was stronger and way more courageous. Or so she truly believed.

"Why are you saying that? I honestly do not consider myself that strong nor courageous." She paused, reflecting on his comment. "Maybe courage is something like music, like a painting. Or like any knowledge that we aim to acquire and excel in. Once we set our minds and our hearts to succeed, what we set our eyes and goals upon, with determination, it will grow. As long as we have vision, discipline, faith in our own capabilities, faith that the universe will always collaborate to our advancement. We are all courageous, Lorenzo. Every day we are faced with challenges that require us to step in faith, to the unknown."

"Like us here."

She chuckled. "Yes. Like us here." She took a deep breath before reaching for her purse, removing from it a rectangular pearl-white envelope. "Before I forget or change my mind," she said, holding the letter tight in her hand, as if she was not ready to let it go.

He grabbed the envelope out of her hand. He contemplated her handwriting; only his full name carefully written on the front.

"A final letter, perhaps?"

A lump came into Cecilia's throat, making her swallow it dry. Avoiding his eyes, she replied, "Perhaps."

"This suddenly now sounds like a farewell. Am I right?'

"Who knows?" And she meant it. For who could ever imagine she would meet him again? Who could think she would be there, he would be there, on that exact day, on that exact spot, talking and laughing, enjoying life as if that was the most precious moment they ever had? That was all they had: a moment.

And she knew she would freeze that moment in time, if she could; she would extract it carefully, with the precision of a surgeon holding a scalpel, making a delicate excision. If only that was a picture of a movie; she would frame the piece; she would paint it. Or maybe even better, she would prepare it diligently, to be analyzed under a microscope, so she would know, in greater depth, the intimate details about it. If she only could do that.

But she knew better now; for her, she was allowed only to enjoy every single part of it, because when that moment would come to an end, the only thing plausible was to carry it in her heart and in her memories. Like a sweet fragrance of the flowers that bloom in the spring, like the smell of the wet grass from the pampas, like the warmth of the sunlight in the mountains, or the song of a bird outside a window.

"I have a meeting at the Museum of Fine Arts at three," Cecilia broke the temporary silence, somber-faced to the sound of her own words.

"I wish I had more time with you."

I wish I had all the time with you—it was definitely wonderful while it lasted, she thought, praying he could not read her mind. But aloud, she said, "Time ... wouldn't it be nice if time was malleable, if it could be bent?"

Lorenzo laughed. The genuine type of laugh that made her heart melt. "We need a full other encounter to talk about this: bending time. What a preposterous idea! Oh, all the things we would do differently, if we could only bend time ..." He stared at her one more time, before opening his jacket, carefully placing the envelope in an inner, hidden pocket.

To prevent her eyes filling with tears, Cecilia blinked them continuously. For that, she also forced her mind to go somewhere else. The museum was calling her and she knew this was the end of a chapter and the beginning of a new one. Their time to say goodbye had arrived, and she summoned the strength to stand up and leave.

"I must go now, or I will be late," she said.

"And God forbid you ever be late," he joked. "What kind of meeting do you have at the museum, by the way?"

"A year ago, by curiosity and as a suggestion of a French sculptress, a friend of mine, I was checking with the museum if they offered classes for painters and sculptors on human anatomy. To my surprise, they did not. But they were kind and interested enough to get my contact information, in case they needed someone to help them in the future. Well, last week, I received a letter from the museum director—an invitation for a collaboration as an anatomy instructor."

"How interesting and bold you are." Lorenzo smiled, surveying her from head to toe. "Unstoppable Cecilia."

She laughed, flushed. "Possibly."

As they both stood, he extended his arm to her, but as soon as he held her hand, he did not hesitate in pulling her closer to him. "Let me give you at least a hug."

Cecilia did not resist either. They held each other quickly, but intensely, as if they did not want to let go of each other.

"It was really good seeing you," he whispered near her ear, making her shiver.

"The same," she replied, giving him a furtive kiss on his cheek, leaving immediately after, without looking back.

She walked all the way to the museum with certain confidence, somehow lighter, although the bittersweet feeling of a farewell lingered in the air. On the streets and all around, the world continued to move, unaware of her presence: couples walking hand in hand; a mother pushing a stroller with a sleepy baby boy inside; a teenaged girl in a blue dress carrying a small terrier dog.

Flashes of life passed through Cecilia's mind—the baby growing to be a military member, fighting in a futile war he had never fathomed, a battle he did not create; the couples, some growing older together, some growing apart; some staying healthy, some suddenly dying from another epidemic outbreak. The girl, giving up a potential career as a writer, in order to marry her sweetheart. That is life, with its polarity permeating everything. That is life, where the only thing you have total control of is your thinking, how you react to something suddenly thrown at you. Looking back now, Cecilia realized that maybe nobody has ever the power to completely change what life throws at them; the only thing that can be changed is how they view the situation. Each situation.

Out of the blue, the terrier dog escaped and ran to Cecilia, bringing her attention to the current moment. The owner, a girl probably only sixteen, rushed in her direction, apologizing for the inconvenience.

"That's all right," Cecilia said. "It is a beautiful dog. What is his name?" She leaned down, taking the dog into her arms.

"It is a she. Her name is Esperanza. But we call her Ranza."

"What a delightful name. And what a fortunate owner she has."

"Thank you, ma'am. I rescued her from the street on a rainy evening; she was a lost puppy. My mother did not think she was going to make it. But I could not abandon her, much less let her die. So, I prayed and prayed, hand-feeding her until she was up and running."

"You gave a home and life to Ranza," Cecilia said with a smile.

"I think actually she gave hope to me. But I must go now, ma'am, or my mother will kill us both for my delay."

"Sure. Continue to thrive. Both of you!" Cecilia's advice felt more like a prayer, a request to the universe to continuously bless those who never lose sight of hope.

She continued on her way, thinking how much she not only had grown in wisdom, but acquired the gift of true freedom. That was being able to look in someone's eyes who had hurt her before, and thinking: there is no payback; there is only love in return. Intuitively, she was confident that there will be a time when men will not suppress the women in their society, nor suppress themselves by denying their own feelings, their own vulnerability.

There will be a time when men and women will pick up from where they were left off, and when they become wise enough, they will learn their lesson, she believed. Humanity will not continue to go back to the way things were before, because only a fool does not learn from experiences. But people shall witness the opposite: they will accept the facts and they will move forward with their new norm. There will be a time when humanity will be set free. Free from cages of fears, free from unquestionable submission and mockery. There will always be time to cry, but there will be countless moments to laugh. A time to sing loud on the streets, a time to be quietly curfewed indoors. A time to curl down, a time to stand tall, in life's constant search to obtain the perfect balance between fate and free will.

Cecilia climbed the marble steps of the National Museum of Fine Arts, with a slight trepidation about what lay ahead. But that did not last too long; as soon as she reached the main hall, her attention was drawn to a new exhibition recently set up, entitled "The Solace of Nature." Among beautiful and impressive oil painting landscapes from local and international artists, it was a small canvas of an erythrina, with bright carmine flowers against its lush canopy and crooked dark brown trunk, that caught Cecilia's eyes.

The single tree stood alone in the middle of a vast, windswept golden-green grassland across from it. Above the tree, a dark blue sky spotted with dense gray clouds was a prelude of an imminent thunderstorm. The painting was a trustworthy representation of the vivid life in the wilderness: the strength of a rooted plant, the plenitude of a solitary experience, the constant changes of the elements, the resilience of the natural world, with its hostile natural forces, that can easily be transported to daily human experiences. Cecilia found deep comfort in that painting, in the beauty constantly upwelling from the mystery called life.

For the first time in a long while, she felt truly grateful for being part of that exact moment, for the opportunity to experience all that she had experienced. Thinking of courage, physical and spiritual resilience, she repeatedly asserted a belief in her own moral fortitude and strength of character. Of course, we can all be guilty of subjectivity and somehow bias of heart or mind when telling stories, inflating our own capacities, painting bygone troubles a little bit more daunting, perhaps to augment our triumphs, maybe just to impress a given audience. But deep inside, we know who we are. We know our stories, our battles, our struggles, our victories.

And she had to be proud of that selfless victory. She was now finally convinced that love survives deception and inevitable heartaches. She had this assurance that love overcomes tears, fears, loneliness. In the midst of grief, the cycle of life always offers us renewed hope and joy. And as the path of life is a winding one, you must always embrace that ride, knowing that sometimes, you might simply return to where you started. On the other hand, you could also end in a different, unexpected place. Who really knows?

Regardless of where one lands, deep inside she knew there would always be something great, completely complex and utterly unexpected, that would transform people's souls. For the first time, Cecilia discerned that love is what truly makes us stand tall and move forward. And that was enough to bring a genuine smile to her glowing face.

EPILOGUE

Dearest L.B.

They say, for generations, love has been a favored topic of philosophers, poets, writers and even scientists, without anyone ever coming close to one conclusion, a proper definition. There has been so much debate whether love is a choice, whether it is permanent or fleeting; something biologically programmed or culturally indoctrinated. They say love is one of the most intense emotions that we experience as humans, ranging from interpersonal, unconditional and unlimited affection for a person, to pleasure. They say love can bring one to madness. In the name of love, we see the rise and fall of families and empires. In the name of love, we so often witness wars, leading to chaos and ruin, changing forever the course of our planet. At the same time, they say love is the fuel that leads us to positive changes, bringing hope to people, something that we so instinctively and constantly crave.

To me, love is something that has taught me more about life than anything else, more than any other books, any other classes. It is love that has taught me a little bit how this world works. It is love that has shown me how beautiful and how horrific each person in this world can be. It is love that has shown us, me and you, that we can be both the cause and the cure for so many of our own afflictions.

I have always wondered how such a simple four-letter word, a simple concept, can bring within so much peace, and at the same time, so much turmoil? So much beauty, and at same time, so much monstrosity?

Maybe the answer is simpler than what we ever imagined. Maybe the answer lies within the fact that love is perfect. The only thing in the entire universe that is completely perfect. And being perfect, love must carry, within, everything—the good, the bad; the beauty, the ugliness, the peace and the war. Love is dynamic. It can grow, evolving in strength and depth, but it can also dim and fade away.

To understand love and what it bestows upon us, undoubtedly, is one of the most important lessons a human being can learn in a lifetime. Because love is the only single thing the entire human species searches, craves for. We need love, like the air we breathe. Love is the fuel behind all of our actions, what guides us to stay or to move, to remain the same, or to change. Love is the only thing that carries in itself the capability to transform us into different people. Hopefully, better people.

And when we think about our lives, I can see we are able to love so many things ... We can love objects, experiences, memories. But no other love can compare to the love for another human being. And it is hard to explain, maybe because our lives are just so busy; the noise and constant humming of the city, its lights, its frenetic pace, all outshine what we call love.

To understand love, maybe we must silence all the voices, maybe we must bring forth only our reverence. Because love is an emotion, but it is not only an emotion; love is an action, but not only actions. Love is a change. And being the change, it changes us. We love our family, our friends, because they change us, constantly. Because they show us a better version of the reality. A better version of us. They not only add something into our lives, but they transform us, they change our perspectives—our way of thinking about the true meaning of being here, living.

And as the world has four seasons, we are blessed with the four loves. The Storge, the empathy bond, the natural love and affection of a parent for a child; the Philios, the friendly love between siblings, the friendship between people who share common values, interests and activities; the Eros, the romantic love, the most coveted of all types, and for that reason, one of the most powerful and dangerous; and finally, the Agape, the selfless love that exists regardless of the circumstances, the greatest of the four loves.

It is very difficult to define love because it is an experience that the majority of us cannot fully comprehend. Perhaps because we already start with a wrong pre-concept about it. We experience love with our own set of beliefs and expectations, assuming we know a lot about it, instead of listening to it, observing it, just like an apprentice faces his or her first lessons by the diligent observation of the master. So, blindly, the majority of us simply fall in love. Literally. We fall. Into a trap. Blindly. And that is when we ruin everything. Because when you start anything, from the initial assumption that you already know everything, then there will be nothing else for you to learn. And love is definitely an experience that we learn. We are not born knowing how to love.

We fall in love believing that the feeling we are experiencing will last forever. But when the relationship has not even started, when everything apparently fails, you drop down to your knees, you raise your voice to the heavens, asking, "How is it possible?" You were so sure you loved that person, and if that was love, it should last forever, and if it indeed would last forever but that person "is now gone," what would become of you? That is when you start to think that "maybe love does not last forever..."

But when I look back, through the years since I have first experienced love, I am forced to rethink what I used to believe. The truth is: it is completely possible to love someone forever. Nevertheless, it will not necessarily be the way you thought it would be. Maybe, in part, this confusion is our own fault. Because unfortunately, when we fall in love, we allow our intense emotions to define love in its totality; we allow it to take over the rational side of our minds, forgetting that the mind has always a way of protecting the heart, but the opposite is not true ... only God knows what can protect our minds. And when that happens, we simply ruin everything. We ruin the love that was there.

But that love, although ruined, remains. Love simply remains.

Do you know why? Because if someone you love is capable of changing your life in such an extension, if this same someone has helped transform the person you have become, if this same someone has added a special touch of paint in the canvas of your life, and you admire and appreciate the result you see in the mirror every morning, you do not have any other option but to love this someone in return.

Obviously, there will be people that you are not necessarily fond of, who maybe have transformed you the most. I could list a few of those, and I can assure, I do not love them. But if you loved this someone before, this someone who changed you in such a dramatic way, you will simply love this person back. Forever. It does not matter if you like the process or not, if you want to stop the process or not. It does not matter if you try to find a thousand reasons to hate this person. It does not matter if your life path and the path of the other person have turned completely to opposite directions. It does not even matter if you have found and love another person. You will continue to love that someone.

And that does not mean that your life will come to a halt, a stagnation pond where only algae grow. No. It will not be a living hell. It does not mean that you will not be extremely happy, joyful. No. It simply means this person will never be completely out of your life. That is all. You will never completely forget that person. That is all. But you will continue to thrive. So, do not even bother fighting with your mind to get rid of that someone. Because that person changed you in such a way that allowing him or her to go, completely, would be an impossible task. You would lose part of yourself, making you a handicapped person, a cripple.

And if someone would say, "This is so sad," all we have to do is honestly quiet ourselves, quiet the voices that chatter inside our minds. Then we will be able to contemplate this beautiful truth, as almost a mystical experience. To imagine that one human being can affect another, in this profound, intimate way, is something incredible, near divine. This alone teaches me much more about life, and human nature, than anything else I could ever imagine. And when I think about this, I cannot help but let one or two tears roll down my face, from time to time. But I am fine with a few tears now. Because without tears, we cannot appreciate the real value of a single smile.

At the end, I can see everyone will always have a love story to tell, something that he or she will never be able to completely share with anyone else. They will try to put it in words, they will try to put it in verses; they will try to explain it, they will try to understand what happened, but they will all fail. At the end, I hope they will just be happy, grateful, for the opportunity they had to live it. To experience it. Just like I did.

The other night, cleaning up boxes and papers, I found this letter, written by my grandfather, part of the diary he kept as a passenger of the Symmetry ship during his voyage from Scotland to South America. It was dated May 22, 1825. He was not a writer, nor a poet. But I found it ... fascinating. His words felt like a reminder that we, like constant settlers, must leave behind old prejudices in order to form proper and better ideas. Nostalgia should not be linked with regrets but rather with the enthusiasm on our part to immerse ourselves in this new existence and to embrace the foreignness that always lies ahead of us.

"Must we bid you adieu? We will bear you in our Breasts. We will look to the South. We will court your forms in distant climes. Our present children will prattle your names, and our future offspring shall learn your songs. When we have passed the sun, when we have found

what we may call a new heaven and a new earth, we will hold you in remembrance, and a third part of the Earth's circumference shall not separate you from us, even when there (if we ever get there) our friendship shall operate; our mutual correspondence will demonstrate that our reciprocal love is immortal."

AUTHOR'S NOTE

This novel is the result of a year of research and writing, based on the life of Dr. Cecilia Grierson, the first female physician in Argentina and the founder of the School of Nurses in Latin America.

The path that led Cecilia Grierson to study medicine, with all the difficulties she had to face, must be seen in terms of the slow, but important, reforms and changes in the law that gave women greater access to education not only in Argentina, but throughout Latin America. The harassment she endured as a medical student and afterward led her to adopt a militant posture to change the real living conditions of women. With her prolific academic activity, combined with her selfless vocation, patience and courage, her story of perseverance and fight for equal rights is a living proof that history encompasses many unknown heroines, capable of greatness.

The restless work of Cecilia Grierson went far beyond what was briefly described in this book. As an example, she founded the Society for Domestic Economy in 1902. This organization, later renamed the Technical School for Home Management, was the first of its kind in the country, and in 1907, she instituted the Domestic Science course at the Buenos Aires Girls' Secondary School.

Following her 1909 report on improving conditions in Europe regarding education, living standards and the availability of vocational schools, the National Educational Council approved a curriculum for vocational schools in Argentina. Cecilia Grierson published *Educación técnica de la mujer* (*Women's Technical Education*), introducing the study of day care in these schools.

In addition, Cecilia held teaching positions in the School of Fine Arts and the National Secondary School for Girls, where she taught from its inception in 1907. Grierson was publicly honored in 1914 on the occasion of the silver jubilee of her graduation, an homage repeated in 1916, when she formally retired.

She lived in scenic Los Cocos, Cordoba Province, practicing family medicine on a largely *pro bono* basis and teaching. She inaugurated a school in the rural town, as well as a residence for teachers and artists. She was allowed credit for only a few years of service upon her retirement and received but a modest pension; she lamented most, however, that she was never offered the Chair position of her alma mater's School of Medicine.

Cecilia Grierson never married. The noted academic and activist died in Buenos Aires in 1934, at age 74, and she was buried in the British Cemetery.

As a historical fiction, it was my goal to render authenticity to chronological, geographical and historical details of the several characters, based on the references cited below. Nevertheless, the story line is fiction. With that in mind, I took the liberty to create scenes, actions, characters and their perspectives, as genuine and close as possible to what I believed they lived and as suited my fictional representation.

ADDITIONAL READING

Taboada, A. *Vida y Obra de Cecilia Grierson, La Primera Medica Argentina*. Triada S.C Editores, 1983.

Fiedczuck, A. *Cecilia Grierson: Una lucha sin tiempo*. EAE, Germany, 2019.

Stewart, I.A.D. *From Caledonia to the Pampas. Two accounts by early Scottish emigrants to the Argentine.* Tuckwell Press, 2000.

Grierson, C. *Educacion Tecnica de la Mujer*. Classic Reprints.

Commala, M. *Buenos Aires, Pasado y Presente*. Edifel Libros, 2018.

Carreto, A. *Vida Cotidiana en Buenos Aires*, volume 2. Ariel, 2013.

Gardner, J. *Buenos Aires. The biography of a city*. St. Martin's Press, 2015.

Ruggiero, K. *Modernity in the flesh. Medicine, Law and Society in turn-of-the-century Argentina*. Stanford University Press, Stanford, California, 2004.

Rodrigues, J. *Civilizing Argentina. Science, Medicine and the Modern State*. Chapel Hill, 2006.

Margal, G; Manso, G. *La Historia Argentina Contada por Mujeres*. Volume 3. De la Batalla de Pavon al Inicio del Siglo XX (1861-1900). Ediciones B, 2018.

Dujovne, B. *In Strangers' Arms: The Magic of Tango*. McFarland, 2011.

Cahill, S. *The Streets of Paris: A Guide to the City of Light Following in the Footsteps of Famous Parisians Throughout History.* St. Martin's Press, 2017.

Ayral-Clause, O. *Camille Claudel. A life*. Harry N. Abrams, 2002.

Historias de la Ciudad. Una revista de Buenos Aires. Ano XIV, numero 64, Agosto, 2013.

ACKNOWLEDGEMENTS

I am grateful that there have been so many great minds and hearts who helped, encouraged and inspired me for the creation of this book. The journey has been nothing shorter than a constant excitement.

A special thanks to the Creator and Master of the Universe, for every good and perfect gift – including skill and talent — comes from above.

Many thanks to editor Emily Carmain, for polishing and shaping the novel to its brilliant format. And to author and colleague Dr. Darryl Field, for sharing such valuable personal information and insights on how to start the journey of writing and publishing your first book.

My deepest thanks go to the artist group of St. John's Episcopal Cathedral in Jacksonville, Florida, especially the talented artists Mrs. Jean Dodd and Father Lou Towson. Their knowledge and love for art, in addition to their patience in teaching the basics of oil and acrylic painting, were fundamental during the entire year I worked on this book. Special thanks to artist and friend Dr. Remedios Santos. Without you – Mitzi, I would not have met the artist group at the Cathedral, and this book would be utterly boring without all the art that I learned to appreciate and enjoy with you all in the past years.

Thanks to my wonderful friend Claudia Borges and the amazing group of women in Jacksonville, members of my Book Club. Thanks to author Patricia Daily-Lipe and artist Francesca Miolla-Tabor, members of the Jacksonville Branch of the National League of American Pen Women. Your support and encouragement were a constant gift; your cheers kept me going.

Thanks to many, many friends in Brazil and Argentina. I could not list all their names here, but you know who you are. You are my friends from childhood, from the Sunday Bible schools, from the University of Brasilia, from my English and Spanish classes. I am sure you will find a phrase or two in the book related to what we shared in common – a beautiful life. I am so thankful to have you near or far, but always in my heart.

No author can write anything without the unconditional love and steadfast belief of their family. Toan and Andrew, my dearest boys. Thank you for bearing with the longest nights I stayed up late. Your love is the reason for everything.

Thank you to my talented, chameleon brother, Waldson G. de Farias. He can draw, paint, play guitar; he can work with wood and carpentry; he can travel around the globe with a backpack; he can even design the best book cover and website I could ever dream, besides his job as a military firefighter. You are the best!

Thank you to Aldenor G. de Farias and Alba G. de Farias. Dad, Mom, you taught me how to read by the age of four, and the love for books only grew stronger in me as time passed. You are both a tower of inspiration and resilience, and your lives are the purest example of selfless love.

Thanks to my little brother Williams G. de Farias, and the Nguyen family, for your love and constant support.

Last, but not least, thanks to the many artists – musicians, songwriters, poets, whose works of art are always my companions. Sting, Phill Collins, Peter Gabriel, Tears for Fears, Yuna, Carlos Gardel, Marisa Monte, Ivan Lins, Renato Russo, Leila Pinheiro, Mario Quintana, Carlos Drummond, Tom Jobin, to name a few. Their beautiful music and poetry are eternal.

ABOUT THE AUTHOR

There is a saying in her native country, Brazil, that "every dentist has a little bit of artistry and craziness inside." The first part must be true, at least, when speaking of Debora G. De Farias. Graduated in Dentistry from the University of Brasilia, followed by a Master's Degree in Health Sciences, she also obtained her equivalent D.D.S degree from the University of Florida, when she moved to the United States in 2001. Debora is passionate about her health career, literature and arts. An avid reader since the age of four, she grew up surrounded by books, fascinated especially by the true stories of those unknown heroes and heroines that are part of our history. This is one of the main reasons she began the writing journey with her first historical novel, *Standing Tall.*

Debora lives in Jacksonville, Florida, with her husband, Toan Nguyen, and their son, Andrew. When not writing, reading, or promoting beautiful smiles, Debora can be found painting. Her art reflects her interest in travel and culture, the realistic depictions of the transformative effects of light and color.